PRAISE FOR

"In her latest thriller, Frey writes with authority, weaving together themes of family secrets, domestic violence, and childhood trauma. The characters are complex and believable and the plot expertly crafted. A highly compelling page-turner!"

—Wendy Walker, bestselling author of *What Remains*

"You had me at neighborhood murder club! In a fast-paced, exciting read where every neighbor is a murder suspect, Rea Frey has once again woven together an enticing tale of suspense. One bit of advice: don't trust anyone."

—Georgina Cross, author of *One Night, Nanny Needed*, and Amazon bestseller *The Stepdaughter*

"Chilling from the first page to the final line, *Don't Forget Me* is a fast-paced, riveting read with layers of family secrets, each one darker than the last. I tore through this book, desperate to see whether my theories were correct—only to be blown away by an ending I never could have guessed."

—Megan Collins, author of *The Family Plot* and *Thicker Than Water*

"In a deviously clever story, Frey brings a top-notch thriller alive with insane tension and a shocker story. You won't soon forget this stellar read."

—J. T. Ellison, *New York Times* bestselling author of *It's One of Us*

"Poignant, emotional, and yet marvelously malevolent, *Don't Forget Me* is written with Frey's traditional gorgeous prose while simultaneously being suffused with dread. The final outcome is deeply shocking and terrifying. Certain to keep readers turning the pages!"

—Christina McDonald, *USA Today* bestselling author

WHEN SHE'S GONE

WHEN SHE'S GONE

A THRILLER

REA FREY

THOMAS & MERCER

Text copyright © 2025 by Rea Frey

Published by Thomas & Mercer, Seattle

www.apub.com

Amazon, the Amazon logo, and Thomas & Mercer are trademarks of Amazon.com, Inc., or its affiliates.

ISBN-13: 9781662522901 (paperback)
ISBN-13: 9781662522895 (digital)

Cover design by Damon Freeman
Cover image: © Anastasiya Deriy, © Fotyma, © kosmofish, © Kwangmoozaa, © S ch / Shutterstock

Printed in the United States of America

for all the girls
who love to flip

1

Now

"Lu, slow down!"

I jog to keep pace with my four-year-old as she barrels through the throngs of Boone's Creek locals loitering on the sidewalk. The yearly Halloween parade is a standing tradition, though this is the first year I've allowed her to attend.

Her homemade witch costume, complete with a sparkling black tutu, bounces while she weaves, heavy footed, in and out of monsters and Marvel heroes. Her witch hat tips dangerously to the left. She swings her pumpkin bucket freely, and it whacks into a clown's leg. I mumble an apology and scoot past the frightening costume.

In my jeans and hoodie, I feel wildly unfestive, but I hate Halloween, and most people who have any idea of my personal history are aware of this fact. It's a miracle I'm even out tonight. Normally, I'd be tucked away in my cabin with chili and a cold beer, placating Lu with dumb movies and waiting for tomorrow to come. But between Lu's excitement and my friend Faith's insistence that I get out once in a while before I turn into a literal pumpkin, here I am.

I scan the crowd for Faith, but she's not here yet. A few locals recognize me and offer shy waves. It's still strange, after all this time, how some people view me. It's always divided into two camps: those who follow gymnastics and those who are true-crime buffs. There's never an in-between.

I wave back but keep my eyes on the prize: Lulu. Finally, I grip her black leotard and tug her to a gentle halt. "Lu," I say almost breathlessly. "You have to stay next to me, okay? I don't want us to get separated."

She scratches her nose, then reaches down to straighten her striped green-and-black stockings. "But I'm a big girl now."

"That's not the point." I adjust her hat and scan the crowd, looking for safe faces. There's Adele, from Lulu's art therapy class. Dave from the library. Janina from music. I also look for Joe but don't see him yet.

As if reading my mind, Lulu bounces up and down on her tiptoes, though there's no way she can see over the towering costumes around her. "Where's Uncle Joe?"

"He'll be here." I take in the decorated lampposts, thick with cobwebs. Inflated pumpkins and skeletons with orange LED eyes blot out the town square, masking every storefront. A giant banner sags over the entrance to Main Street. It seems the entire town's turned up tonight.

I try to keep myself calm. It's just a night like any other. It will come and go, and then we can get on with things. Instead of counting all the reasons I despise Halloween, I focus on what's right here: The crisp air. The gorgeous pines, clogged with fake fog, that seem to watch me from behind their ghostly white curtains. When a bat flies overhead, dread scurries up my spine like a spider.

"Mama?"

Lulu's tiny palm plays with the frayed, gaping fabric of my jeans. She absently rubs her sticky fingers over the knotted half-moon scar right below my kneecap. Her hair is tangled under her hat, her dark eyes excited for what's ahead. Her favorite stuffed animal, Bun-Bun, dangles from her plastic pumpkin.

"What, baby?"

She drops her hand, blinks up at me. "When do we get candy?"

I smile. "Soon enough." After the town parade, the shop owners will open their storefronts so kids can run up and down the block, begging for treats. Because everyone in Boone's Creek lives mostly on larger plots of land, spread out—or in cabins, a little removed from town, like us—this is what you do if you want to trick-or-treat by foot.

A firm hand on my shoulder makes me jump, and I berate myself for it. I turn and lean into a side hug from Joe, whose attention has already turned to Lu.

"Well, well, what do we have here?" he asks, carefully crouching down to inspect her outfit. "Are you a mouse?"

Lulu places her hands on her tiny waist and cocks a hip, clearly outraged. "No, silly. Guess again!" She taps her black boot.

"Hmm." Joe strokes his chin, which is currently covered by a sparse, patchy beard. Beneath that beard a jagged scar runs from his lower lip to the tip of his right ear. Eighty-one stitches, once upon a time, followed by two reconstructive facial surgeries. His dark-brown eyes are drawn and bloodshot, and I wonder if he's had as much trouble sleeping lately as I have. "A spider?"

"Uncle Joe, I'm a witch! Duh!" She points to her hat.

"Oh, a witch! Of course, of course." He inspects her outfit again. "But where's your hideous green nose? Or your hairy wart?"

She makes a face. "I hate warts *so* much."

Her lisp nearly breaks my heart as her *s*'s ram into each other. Though I'm not concerned, Janina from music class says we might want to start speech therapy soon.

"Me too," Joe confirms. He stands and shakes out his bad leg, yet another reminder of his motorcycle accident. He crosses his arms as he looks me over. "And you're supposed to be?"

"The witch's mother," I say, rolling my eyes. I gesture to his outfit. "It seems we were on the same wavelength tonight."

He laughs as he glances down at his work boots, jeans, and plaid flannel. "I'm going for lumberjack vibes. You can't tell?"

"What's your excuse every other day?" That gets a laugh. I shiver and face the crowd, practically willing the parade to start. I check my phone to see if Faith's texted, but she hasn't. Lu blabs to Joe about her classes this week. Though I would just as happily hoard Lulu all to myself, she's at that age where she wants to be among people, and as she's too young for school, a handful of classes will have to do. True to form, she makes friends wherever she goes, though Joe is definitely her favorite, Faith a close second.

And though Joe is not her real uncle, he might as well be. He's the only semblance of family she's got, and I appreciate him for it. As thoughts of my real family trickle in, I easily cut them off. There's no point in going to an even darker place, especially tonight.

Luckily, the parade starts, and I clap along with everyone else as creatures of all shapes and sizes march up and down Main Street with spooky music and effects. Some are on stilts. Others wear terrifying masks. Joe scoops Lulu onto his shoulders so she can have a clear line of sight. He hobbles a moment, then rights himself, and I refrain from thrusting out an arm to help. I keep glancing up at Lu to make sure she's not scared, but she's eating it up like pie. She doesn't have a problem with Halloween like I do, and I'm glad I haven't tarnished this night for her. Halloween should be fun for kids. It was fun for me once too.

Once the parade is done, Lulu slips from his shoulders and begins to stalk off toward the first shop.

"Lulu!" I follow closely behind. This walking-off thing is new, and I don't like it. I never want to scare her, but she needs to know the world isn't always a peaceful place. Even in a town like ours. Especially in a town like ours.

Lulu strikes up a conversation with every shop owner we pass, and because of it, she gets extra heaps of candy and conspiratorial winks.

Joe whistles as he limps along beside us. "Well, she's cleaning up."

"Yep." I'm thankful Joe's here tonight. He knows enough about my past to understand I hate this day and everything it represents. But I know he's wrestling his own demons too. Around this time, five years ago, is when his wife left him after his accident. She said it changed him too much, and she just couldn't bear to stay. Especially after he went on disability. Though I've never met her, I hate her for leaving him to rot.

I don't think he's ever shaken himself out of that depression, though I know hanging around Lulu helps. Lord knows she needs a stable man in her life.

While Lulu is chatting up the bookstore owner, Joe places a warm hand on my arm. "How are you really, Cora? I know this is a hard day." I swallow. "I'm managing." Before I can extend the same question to him, Adele interrupts.

"Cora. *There* you are." She pulls me aside. "I was hoping I'd see you here. I wanted to talk to you about Lulu's last session." She folds her arms over her glittery costume, which, for the life of me, I can't figure out.

Adele never shares much information about her and Lulu's sessions. Immediately, my heart skips a beat. "Everything okay?"

"It's fine. It's just . . ." She glances off to the side and then back to me, her German accent fading into a beat of silence. "I asked Lu to draw a family picture yesterday, and it was just the *oddest* thing." Adele pauses an uncomfortably long beat, and I wonder if I'm supposed to guess. I tamp down my impatience, however, and wait. She drops her voice to a whisper. "It was you and her at your cabin, but instead of the trees, there were all these shadowy figures just watching you two. Lurking. They had red, beady eyes and looked really scary."

My skin pricks. People watching? From the trees? I consider it, then stuff it down, this giant fear that's haunted me for decades. Perhaps Lulu *has* picked up on my paranoia. Then again, maybe she was just drawing our security cameras? Sometimes you can see the red lights blinking from the woods. I shrug, trying to make light of the dark places to which my mind tends to crawl. "Well, she's a kid. She's got a big imagination."

Adele's forehead wrinkles as she tries to absorb my apparent brush-off. "I just want to make sure everything's okay at home, you know, since it's . . ."

She doesn't finish that sentence because she doesn't have to. Everyone treats me with kid gloves around this time of year. It's fine. "I'll talk to her, okay?" I say, plastering on my best parent-of-the-year smile.

"Oh, would you, Cora? That would be *fabulous*." Adele lets out a breath and teeters off in her gaudy platform shoes.

"Everything okay?" Joe asks, closing the gap once again.

"Yeah, fine." I turn back to the bookstore to grab Lu, but she's not there. "Joe, where's Lulu?"

His eyes grow serious as he snaps to attention and tracks back to the store. There's a clump of children talking to Dave, but none of them are Lu. *No.*

"Lulu!" Alarm tightens its grip as I rotate in a circle.

"Cora, she was right here. I'm sure she just went on to the next store." Joe's sensibility, while generally calming, is having the opposite effect.

"Lulu!" I call her name again, panic rising, but my voice is swallowed by the machine-gun pop of fireworks. The spray of multicolored lights explodes in a fiery burst above us, then rains down in oversize plumes of smoke. It easily captures the whole town's attention. But not mine. I am moving as fast as I can from shop to shop, backtracking, running from end to end. Joe can't run, but he's keeping up as best as he can. An ex-cop, his instincts are sharp, sharper than mine. If he's not panicked, then maybe I shouldn't be either.

Except I know better.

My heart whips so viciously in my chest, I feel like I might throw up. Fear spreads like wildfire, swallowing me whole. I grip a brick wall as people in scary costumes lumber in and out of sight. Anyone could have grabbed her. Anyone could have taken her, and Lulu is so damn trusting, she wouldn't have even thought twice. Suddenly, Joe lopes into view, his arms spread wide. And that's when I see it. There, on the edge of the sidewalk, face down, lies Bun-Bun. Lulu never goes anywhere without her favorite stuffed animal.

Joe spots it at the same time. He reaches down and plucks the animal from the dirty pavement and brushes it off tenderly, the first lines of panic etched on his face.

Maybe Lu just wandered off, but maybe she didn't.

Maybe this is something else.

2

Before I can let my mind drift into what this could possibly mean, how my past might be catching up to me after all, Joe slices his way through the tightly packed throngs of strangers and friends, asking if they've seen Lu.

While some people know us, some only know *of* us, as I tend to keep to myself after living my life in the limelight for so long.

It's like I'm underwater as I watch him do all the talking. He's the one asking the questions, shooting off descriptions. Shouldn't that be me? My bad knee buckles as I trip to the edge of the sidewalk. Black spots dance in front of my eyes. I'm having a panic attack. I haven't had one since I was a teenager. I grasp at anyone and no one, but it feels like I'm going to die.

Where is Lulu?

I can't be still right now. I tell my body to move and finally manage to get back to my feet, lurch away from the sidewalk, and stumble toward Joe. He turns to me midsentence as he describes what Lulu's wearing, and stops cold when he sees me.

"My God, Cora. Are you okay?"

Just like that, the air whooshes from my lungs. I remember how to breathe. I remember where I am. I remember that Lulu was literally just here, which means she couldn't have gone far. I grip his flannel shirt, which is rough in my hands. "We have to find her, Joe. Please."

"We're going to. I promise." His eyes scour the space. "I'm sure some cops from the local precinct are here somewhere. If she doesn't show up, we'll go to them. Maybe she just wandered off." His eyes drift to the thick, dense forest off Main. Beyond this small slice of town, there are miles of woods. Every year, hikers go missing. But not children. Never children.

The thought of Lulu, alone with her pumpkin bucket full of candy, drifting into the forest, sounds like some haunted twist on a classic fairy tale. It's enough to make me whimper. My girl. My sweet girl. She has to be around here somewhere.

In minutes, Joe has gathered Dave, Janina, and Adele, mainly because they are the only real adults in her life besides Joe and Faith. Where is Faith? I listen as he spouts off commands. *We'll divide and conquer. No need to panic. We will find her.* Lulu trusts them. But do I? As I blink and gasp for breath, I realize her teachers are little more than strangers. I pay them money to teach Lulu, but what do I really *know* about them? Are they good people? Can they be trusted? Shaking my head, I will myself to stay calm. This will all turn out okay. Lulu has to be here.

A flicker of hope pierces the terror. Maybe she just wandered off, like she did last week in the market, where I found her on aisle twelve, fist deep in a bag of chips. I picture some version of that now, her tiny frame hunched on a stoop, mining candy because she knows I'll allow her only a handful. The more I think about it, the more I'm convinced this is what happened. Lu sneaked off to a corner to stuff her face with sweets. It should make me feel marginally better, but it doesn't.

I scan the streets again, looking for clues. Maybe a trail of wrappers will lead me right to her. My eyes slip back to the woods, and I shiver. But then I think of Bun-Bun, and that's where the fantasy stops. Lulu would notice she'd dropped him. She would come back for him.

The panic is back, a vicious attack in my chest. Though Lulu wasn't planned—a surprise after a meaningless one-night stand—she is literally the best thing that's ever happened to me. I know it. Everyone knows it. Everyone who's ever met Lulu knows it. She *dazzles* people.

I close my eyes, thinking back to just this morning when she took a nap under her favorite blanket, her thumb hooked in her mouth like a lollipop. She's still so small, so innocent, even though she thinks she's such a big girl.

"Cora!" Joe snaps his fingers and brings me back to the present. "Are you listening? We're going west." He hitches his chin toward the street, and I take off in a speed walk, leaving him in the dust. I know we should stick together, but I have to find her. "Lulu!" I scream her name again, and a few people stop and give me the side-eye. I don't slow to ask anyone if they've seen a little girl. There's no time. If I were Lu, where would I go?

The end of Main Street is abrupt. The offshoots are barren, scattered with small family businesses on random patches of gravel lots. Lu would never walk these streets alone, and certainly not at night. None of the stores are open, but I peer into their windows anyway. Could she have gotten inside one of them? Could she be in there now, hiding beneath clothing racks, like she sometimes does in department stores?

"Lu." Her name is a mere whisper on my lips, and I can feel myself coming undone. All the memories I've buried, everything I've tried to forget, are pushing at me faster now, like a train gaining speed.

"Cora, slow down." Joe winces and rubs his leg as he catches me. He doesn't have to say it. I can see it written all over his face. This is getting serious. "I think we should go to the police," he says.

I nod, only once, before I burst into tears.

3

Joe gives me space and shifts uncomfortably on his bad leg.

In the few years I've known him, he's never once seen me cry, but then again, Lu has never gone missing. He tries to calm me down, tells me it's been only a couple of minutes and she couldn't have gone far.

"I'm going to go tell the others to keep an eye out, and then we'll call the police, okay?" His eyes are tortured as he says it. I know Lu means just as much to him as she does to me. Without her, he's really not got much. The thought is sobering, as I realize I don't either. Lu is my entire world now.

But I don't want to wait. I think of our sleepy police force, how long it might take them to get here. Maybe it's faster if I just go to the station. I smear my tears away, watching as Joe backtracks and gathers Dave, Janina, and Adele to fill them in. My eyes stalk the rest of the crowd still milling about under the fireworks. I'm not religious, but I pray that at any moment, Lulu is going to appear with her jaunty little walk, a lollipop wedged in her cheek. I'll reprimand her about walking off. She'll make an excuse as to where she went. We'll go home. I'll tuck her into bed with Bun-Bun and kiss her soft cheeks and tell her a story.

More than anything, this is what I crave.

Joe ambles back, and I tell him what I'm thinking—that he can call the police, but we can still go to the station. He motions toward the parking lot. Part of me doesn't feel safe to go anywhere, but I know that every second counts. As if sensing exactly what I'm thinking, he speaks up. "Why don't I stay here, and you go to the police? That way if she shows up, she sees a friendly face. Just keep me posted, okay?"

I nod but don't move. I feel numb.

"Here. Let me get you to your truck at least."

I'm grateful I don't have to ask, because it feels like my legs have stopped working. They're nothing but rubber beneath me. Cars are knotted together on Ruby Hill, vehicles hogging space wherever they could find it. When I get to my pickup truck, Joe stops me with an arm in front of my chest, as if guarding me from something.

"Cora." He stabs a finger toward my windshield, where a bloodred card is tucked carefully beneath a windshield wiper. I wave him off, impatient to get to the precinct.

"Probably a flyer."

He gestures around to the other cars. No red cards. My stomach flips. I approach it fast and slow all at once, as if my brain and body are at war with each other. I pluck it free and flip it over, uncertain of what I'm going to find.

"Oh my God." The words slip from my lips as I show the card to Joe.

WE HAVE YOUR DAUGHTER
DO NOT CALL THE POLICE

My vision blurs and my breath halts in my lungs. How can anyone *have* my daughter? She was just here. My stomach aches, and I drop to my knees, dry heaving against the parched earth. This is all happening, just as I always feared it might. The card flutters to the cold earth.

Who did this?

From my hands and knees, I pan the hill, as if the culprit is watching, but I can't think of anything except Lulu. A guttural cry escapes my throat while I think logically about what it is I'm supposed to do next. I fumble for my phone, but Joe stops me.

"Cora, what are you doing?"

I scramble to my feet and ignore the ache in my knee. "I'm calling the police."

He hesitates. I know, as a former cop, he's seen all sorts of things, but I'm not sure he's ever worked a kidnapping.

"Let's think this through a minute." His words are too easy for the situation, but his fingers tremble as he brings them up to claw at his beard. "If they're watching you, Cora . . . you don't want them to hurt Lu." His voice breaks.

I ignore his advice and frantically dial 911. This is my *child*. Fuck these people and their threats. The phone stutters and clicks in my hand, and I stare at it, practically willing it to connect.

"911, what's your emergency?"

"Hi. My daughter has been kidnapped. They left a note. Lulu Eloise Valentine. She's four years old, last seen wearing a black leotard, green-and-black-striped tights, and a black tutu. We're on Main Street for the parade. Please hurry."

There's the clicking of keys but nothing else.

"Hello? Can you hear me?" I take a few steps toward the top of the hill for better reception.

"Cora," a woman says after a few moments, her voice robotic. "Didn't we tell you not to call the police?"

I freeze, every hair on my skin stiffening to attention. I stare at my phone again and then turn around, searching for human eyes among the cars and trees. The masks down below could easily conceal a kidnapper. It could be anyone here.

"What is this?" I whisper.

"You need to follow our instructions if you want to get your daughter back," she responds neutrally. "Do as you're told, or things will get much worse for both of you." The woman disconnects the call, and I feel like I've been gut punched.

"What is it?" Joe takes a tentative step toward me.

I examine my phone. How could they have hacked 911? *They didn't*, I quickly realize. Somehow, they've hacked my cell. I will myself to think back to when I've left my phone unattended recently, how anyone would have been able to get to it. I make a mental list of every stranger I've talked to in town or any run-ins with people in the last few weeks, but my brain scrambles, wanting to pivot back to the task at hand: Find Lu. Find her right now.

"They hacked my phone," I explain. "It was a woman. They have Lu." My eyes fill with tears again. "Joe, what am I supposed to do?" Dread pumps through my veins. I need to move, to drive, to scour every inch of this town until I find Lu. I glance at the card again, each word an icy slap.

WE HAVE YOUR DAUGHTER
DO NOT CALL THE POLICE

Why now? Why like this? Why on *this* Halloween? And then it hits me. My sordid history. The significance of today and everything that came after.

Whoever did this doesn't want my daughter.

What they're really after is me.

4

Then

I shift nervously from foot to foot in a lame attempt to stay warm.

We've been waiting outside Atlanta's scariest haunted house, Smorgasbord, for half an hour. My entire body is numb from the cold. I tap my nose with icy fingers, but I can barely feel it.

Jessie, our gymnastics captain, smacks her gum loudly at the front of our pack, hands stuffed into her faded jean jacket. She's wearing an acid-washed jean skirt with fishnet tights, an Ace bandage wrapped protectively around her injured knee. Her bangs are crisp and high, her lip gloss sports flecks of glitter, and every girl on our gymnastics team wants to be just like her. Except for her injury, which has most likely knocked her out of any possibility of attending the Olympic trials in Boston next week.

I chew nervously on my bottom lip as I stare at her bandage. We all know one injury means the difference between success or an early retirement.

I can't think about that now. After trials, we'll get a brief rest for the holidays, and then everything revs up for the 1996 Summer Olympic Games. The pressure of representing my country in my own hometown feels too big, like the weight of the world is riding on my shoulders . . . and at the same time, it's all I've ever imagined. I've been working since

I was three years old for this *one* thing, and now that it's right here, I'm afraid I'm going to mess it all up.

All the other girls chat and giggle excitedly ahead of me, but I stay quiet. For some reason, I never quite seem to fit in, even though we travel and compete together. When I perform well, they seem to like me, but other than that, I feel invisible. Outcast. *Ostracized.*

"Cora, what are you doing? Come *on!*" As if to prove that I'm not invisible, Madeline yanks my sleeve as the line finally chugs forward. I've been too lost in thought to notice.

The truth is I hate haunted houses, and I'm scared to death to go inside, but I don't dare tell them that. When I was younger, I liked Halloween, but now that I've outgrown trick-or-treating, I pretend the holiday doesn't exist. But I said yes to this invitation, mostly because everyone else on the team is here. Most of the girls are a few years older than me, and I want to appear cool, like them. If they want to get chased by psychopaths with chain saws, then so do I. If they want to be jammed inside dark halls with strangers, screaming for their lives, then I'm up for it. I have to be.

I will my heart to stop thumping so hard and dig my fingernails into my palms. Ahead of us, a pack of boys from the gym roughhouse and poke fun at each other. I recognize some of them, but not all. Jakayla's brother, Luke, waves at us, and I wave back. He's not a gymnast, but he's always around the gym. Jessie notices that I wave and scoffs.

"Jakayla, could your brother be more of a skeeze? Why is he, like, always around?"

"I heard he was totally stalking Katie Hobbs last year," Madeline snickers. "He had all these weird pictures of her in his locker."

"Ew, gross. Is your brother a *stalker*, Jakayla?" Jessie pops tiny bubbles in her gum and looks from Luke back to Jakayla.

Jakayla opens her mouth to defend her brother. Though I never talk to him, he seems nice enough. He brings us water when we need it and refills the chalk bin. Jessie waits for a reply, but luckily Nicole changes the subject and nudges Laura.

"Did you see Ryan's here? Are you going to make your big move tonight?" She makes kissy-faces, and Laura tells her to knock it off. Some of the girls have crushes on the boys from the gym, but I'm always too focused on my routines to develop one of my own. Jakayla throws Nicole a thankful glance, and the conversation is forgotten.

While we wait, I roll out my neck and bounce on my toes. My muscles are sore from the earlier competition. I placed second all-around and first on both floor and vault. I'm still reeling over the fact that I was the only girl from our team to place. After a great showing at Karolyi Ranch this past summer, my coach is hopeful that I have a real shot at making the Olympic team. I don't brag like some of the other girls, but deep down, I'm hopeful too. Of course I am.

In all the years we've known each other, none of my teammates have been over to my house, but my entire room is a shrine to the 1992 Olympic gymnastics team, and I've been working since then to make the '96 Olympics my reality. My parents have been wildly supportive, basically revolving their entire lives around my training schedule. Plus, the fact that my dad is one of the US gymnastics team doctors makes a lot of the girls assume I have an automatic shoo-in. I don't see it that way. I still have to earn my spot just like everyone else.

I exhale a visible breath as we inch nearer the door. I check out the massive brick building we are about to enter, which was previously a warehouse of some sort. Suddenly, the metal door at the top of the stairs bursts open, and a man in a horrible clown mask appears in the frigid air with a chain saw raised overhead. It revs menacingly as he begins to run down the line, the metal teeth grinding dangerously close to our faces. I press my hands to my ears and whimper like a baby, but the chain saw is much too loud to hear me. My entire body shakes uncontrollably as my breath snakes in and out of my mouth, and I realize I really, *really* do not want to be here.

Once he's gone, Jessie, Madeline, Laura, Jakayla, and Nicole burst into nervous laughter.

"Oh snap," Nicole says, locking eyes with me. Of all the girls, she's my favorite, and I have high hopes that we can be real friends someday.

I press my hand to my heart. "Do we really want to do this?"

All the girls look anxiously at me, then back to Jessie, who hooks her thumbs into her pockets and blows a massive bubble with her bright-pink gum. It pops, and she begins smacking it loudly again. "What? Like *that* was scary? Trust me, we're in for a wild ride tonight, girls." She lifts her eyebrows, which have specks of glitter in them too. Her blue eye shadow makes her eyes look even smaller. She turns and limps forward slightly as the line moves again.

I count only four people in front of us. The boys from the gym have already vanished inside. I think of the positive affirmations I say to myself before every competition, but those don't work now. Something is telling me not to go in.

Don't be a baby, I tell myself now. *It's just some dumb haunted house. You'll be fine.*

"Ooh, we're next," Laura says. She rubs her hands together. She was smart enough to bring mittens.

I bounce on my toes again in an effort to generate warmth and also shake out my nerves. I'm surprised my parents even let me come tonight, but they were thrilled when the girls asked me to join. They worry about me training most days, getting my homework done, and then repeating the same process all over again.

My ankles have been bothering me lately, too, though I don't dare tell them that. If I tell my dad, he has to report it to my coach, and I don't want anything to lessen my chances, especially after what happened to Jessie. Now, everyone's eyes are on her, to see what might happen next. Pushing all thoughts of injuries from my head, I remind myself that after my victory today, I deserve some fun.

I glance toward the parking lot. My parents are going to pick me up after, and I'm already imagining how nice it will be to crawl into bed, surrounded by my favorite stuffed animals, though I would never admit to the girls that, at fourteen, I still sleep with them. And a night-light. To calm myself, I dig my left hand into my pocket and find my favorite worry doll. I poke her sharp body and hold her tight. Years ago, my dad bought me a little basket of worry dolls. Mostly, I keep them under my pillow, but over the last year, I've brought one or two to big competitions or places where I feel nervous, like tonight. The girls would probably think it's babyish, but I don't care. It helps me stay calm.

Jakayla helps Jessie hobble up the steps as the pack in front of us vanishes into the haunted house. A whirl of fake fog escapes the door, and I shiver again. We all huddle near the entrance, wondering what awaits us.

"You excited?" Nicole asks me now. She's the shortest of the bunch but is the best on bars.

"For this?" I ask. "Not really." I shrug.

"No, silly. For trials." She smiles, her two front teeth crossed over each other like an X. "I think you really have a shot."

"Thanks." I scratch my frozen nose and smile. "I think you do too."

She sighs, suddenly looking much older than sixteen. "As if. I didn't place. I'm going to have to impress Béla if I even have the slightest chance."

Of course she's right. Béla and Márta Károlyi own the gymnastics circuit. Nothing happens without their consent. While I initially worried I was too young to even try out, another girl, Dominique Moceanu, recently burst onto the gymnastics scene, and she's the same age as me. She placed first today, which tells me I have some stiff competition next week. Before I can say anything to placate Nicole, the door explodes open, and a guy with a clipboard motions us inside.

"Enter at your own risk," he says.

The girls all let out staccato screams as they dash inside ahead of me.

I waver on the precipice between light and dark, safety and uncertainty, before I gingerly shuffle into the strange, smoky shadows. The air inside is thick and white, and it takes me a moment to get my bearings. High-pitched screams drown out a cacophony of deep, ghostly moans blasting from a speaker in the corner. A strobe light flickers menacingly above me.

"Guys?"

I have the feeling that I'm already alone, that my team has left me—forgotten me, even—but up ahead, the rhinestones on Jessie's jean jacket pop and twinkle in the half light.

You can do this, I tell myself again. *It's just make-believe.*

The door slams shut behind me, pitching me into complete darkness. I can't even see my hands as I lift them in front of my face. The strobe light winks on and off again, finally orienting me.

I reach for Nicole, who appears like a ghost from the shadows and offers her hand. She squeezes my fingers, and I squeeze back.

We move deeper into the unknown.

5

NOW

Joe doesn't immediately answer. He can tell I'm processing.

"Look, we have two options here," he finally says. "We can go to the police anyway, or we can wait until these psychos give you more instruction." He scratches his jaw again, narrowly avoiding his scar. "What do you think this is about? Money?"

I'm shaking too badly to comprehend what he's suggesting. There's been enough written about me to know that I definitely have had financial success, though that was years ago. Could this be a straightforward ransom situation? It doesn't feel straightforward. It's Halloween. Given my history, it feels personal. Deeper. More sinister.

My past comes ricocheting back to me all at once. Darkness. The woods. Broken bones. Screams I will never forget. A whole life spent looking over my shoulder, wondering if they'll come back.

Now maybe they have. Maybe this is all tied to my past. Joe's question hangs between us, but I can't answer it. I pace back and forth, shaking out the buzzing in my hands. I can feel my lungs closing up again. I can feel myself getting small. "Joe . . ." My voice fades as I fall to my knees, my hands gripping the cold, dry earth.

"Cora." Joe rushes to my side and carefully lowers himself beside me. "Hey. We're going to find her," he says now. "They're not going to get away with this."

"You don't know that!" I scream, pushing him away. Knocked off balance, he tumbles back and catches himself on an elbow, his bad leg stiff and straight. I'm too panicked to apologize. "What am I supposed to do, Joe? Help. Please help me." My eyes search his face as I sit back on my heels.

He rights himself and sighs. "Like I said, you need to decide if you want to go to the police."

Of course I want to go to the police. But that bloodred card stops me. And that woman warned me on the call. Am I willing to defy their orders again? Our precinct isn't known for solving major crimes. The worst thing that happens around here is an occasional hiker who's lost their way, or vehicle vandalism. I don't think, in the whole history of Boone's Creek, that a little girl has ever been taken. Maybe I'd rather take my chances with Joe. He'll know what to do next. To prove my point, he gestures to my phone.

"We need to grab you a burner. Yours has been compromised."

I can't focus on what he's saying. Instead, my head fills with images of Lu. Torturous scenarios flick through my mind, one after the next, and I scramble to my feet, wanting to shut my brain off.

"Let's swing by my place for the phone," he says, steadying me with a firm grip. "Make a plan."

I almost snap at how calm he's being, but I know it's just from being a cop. It's not because he doesn't care. I move to the top of the hill again and stare down at the crowd below. Adele, Dave, and Janina are nowhere in sight. What if one of them found her?

That small surge of hope dies on the vine. I remind myself that she's been taken. No one will find her here. No one might find her anywhere.

"Oh my God, Joe. I can't believe this is happening." *Again.* My body feels like it's going to spill back onto the ground, but he pulls me against him. I focus on how he smells: like cedar and woodsmoke.

I grind my teeth, count to ten, try all my old tricks that don't work. Instead of calming down, I feel claustrophobic and break free.

"Let me drive you."

"No." I shake my head and climb into my truck, trembling but numb.

"Cora, I don't think you should drive."

I tug my door shut in response. "I'll meet you at your house. You might need your car. Let's go."

He gauges me once before nodding and slapping the hood. "I'll be right behind you."

My fingers squeeze the steering wheel until my knuckles turn white. I stare at my phone again and am tempted to redial 911 and make demands to that woman. But what can I really do? Threaten her? With what? How do I know that wasn't just some AI-generated voice?

As I start the car and reverse down a bumpy patch of grass, a sickening thought lands like a boulder in my gut: What if they've already hurt her? What if she doesn't make it back to me?

I slam my foot on the pedal and speed down a desolate side street on the way to Joe's. I keep my eyes peeled for clues. Lu's hat, blown off in the wind. Her tutu. I glance at Bun-Bun, wilted on the passenger seat.

As the miles whip by, I focus on the breath moving in and out of my lungs. I try not to think of how similar this is to what happened *then*. How both events could be related. How, after all these years, they could still be out there, plotting for this very moment. Waiting all this time to finish what they started.

I let out a terrified scream in the cab of my truck and stab the window down to gulp in the icy air. All this time, and I thought I was better. All this time, and I'm right back to where I started. A victim. Left to rot. Left to die.

In an absolute daze, I pull up to Joe's door and shove the truck into park. The engine purrs, and the cold air stills around me. He's not here yet. I stare at the simple cabin, a relic that's been in his ex-wife's family for more than fifty years. When she left him, she left it, too, though he gets squirrely when I ask what he's going to do when she decides to sell it and he has nowhere to live. It's homey inside, like mine, which is why Lu likes it too.

Lu.

Just her name makes me want to jump out of my skin. She should be here, spilling her bucket of candy and sorting through it to decide which pieces she can keep. Outside, I fidget with my keys, stalk the yard, and stare into the inky sky. Tears blur my vision until the stars come into view, white diamonds in a sea of black. Instantly, I think about how much Lu would love to pull out the telescope and stargaze tonight. A cry escapes my throat again as Joe's car crunches over spare twigs and rocks. He jerks to a stop and motions for me to follow.

I stand there, paralyzed, until he physically guides me toward the cabin. As I walk up his wooden steps, I try to imagine this is any other day. I'm bringing him groceries because his leg is too bad. He's helping me with the app on my security system. I'm chopping extra wood. He's showing Lu how to wield an axe. We're drinking beer as she hacks into a baby log, wood chips flying everywhere. I can hear the pitch of her voice, see her standing right here, climbing into his rocking chair, begging for her toes to touch the ground. Then climbing onto Joe's lap for a story. Watching the sunset. Catching fireflies in mason jars. Running wild.

Her whole life unspools around me, as if it's escaping me. As if I've *imagined* it. I lean against his porch rail and close my eyes. These memories are a coping mechanism from when I was a child. Focus on what's normal to drown out what's bad. But nothing can drown this out.

"Cora, come on."

His voice urges me to cross the threshold, to step inside. I command my feet to walk, for my heart to stop breaking, but it refuses to listen. Inside, he flips on a lamp and tosses his keys on the coffee table. I follow him into the kitchen and shift uneasily from foot to foot. I keep my eyes peeled. Are there people watching through the windows? Could someone be out there? Chills stud my flesh like a fever. Joe slumps forward on his island, defeated, both elbows banging sharply against the well-loved surface.

"We need to come up with a list of suspects," he says. The words pull me back to the gravity of the moment, but he doesn't even flinch.

Suspects? Just that word shoves me back to a place I've tried so hard to forget. My daughter is gone. Someone took her. They left a note. This isn't some terrible Halloween prank. This is *real.*

He yanks open a kitchen drawer and rummages around, then tosses me a burner phone. "Use this to text me. Yours is definitely bugged." His mouth works on only one side, giving him a boyish, lopsided look. I focus on his mouth, I focus on the weight of the tiny phone in my palm, I focus on his kitchen sink behind him, which offers a slow, painful drip from the leak he can never seem to fix. There's a beat of silence as I mentally sort through everyone Lu knows.

"What about her teachers from tonight?" he finally asks when I don't offer anyone up. "Could they be involved somehow?"

I recoil. "No," I say, more confidently than I feel. But hadn't I had the same thought at the parade? But *why* would they take her? There's no motive. I hesitate as I think of what Adele said earlier tonight. How concerned she always seems about Lu, as if I'm not ever doing a good enough job as her parent.

Joe's phone buzzes, and my heart leaps. Maybe someone found her! Even as I think about it, the thought slips from my mind. She didn't wander off. She was taken. We are swimming in different waters now.

He pockets it without responding and turns his attention back to me.

"I really think we should go to the police," I say.

"If that's what you want to do, we'll do it, Cora, but . . ." He trails off.

"What?"

"If you spook whoever this is, they could take off with her, or worse. We need more information before we pounce."

The word *worse* hangs between us, unbidden. I swallow. "So now what?"

24

"I think we should head to your house."

"Why?" I spit out. "To just twiddle my thumbs and wait? This is bullshit!" I slap my hand on the island, and the sharp sting of the wood beneath my palm brings me back to myself. My voice bellows around his empty home. I suck it all in. The pain. The scratch in my throat. The uncomfortable silence.

The memory of *then*, seared into my flesh like a scar.

"I'm such an idiot," I whisper now, clawing at my neck, my hair. "What the hell was I ever thinking, moving Lulu back here?" The irony is not lost on me now—how I've spent my whole life running from home, and then, to prove to myself that I was all better, that I was okay, that I had moved on, I placed us right back in the danger zone. And now look.

"I did this." I stab my chest. "This is my fault."

"Cora, stop. It's nobody's fault. It's . . ." His voice breaks.

I place a hand flat on my chest as stars dance in front of my eyes. "Oh my God." I move my arms, twirling them toward myself. "She's going to die, and it's all my fault."

"Hey, stop it." His voice is sharp as he motions toward the couch. "Let's sit and calm down."

But I don't want to sit. I don't want to breathe, don't want to calm down, don't want to wait for the news that my darling daughter is dead. Instead of the couch, I rush outside and spill onto the porch. I'm too fast for Joe. The cold shocks my limbs and floods me with a new surge of adrenaline. I sip in air, my lungs burning from the effort.

I tip forward, fists on my knees, and force the air in through my nose and out through my mouth. When I pitch back upright, I'm dizzy and tilt to the right.

"Cora, I think you need to come back inside," Joe says from behind me. "Let me get you some water."

"No." I jerk away and move toward my truck. "I need to get home. I need to find her. I need . . ." I don't know what I need.

"You can't drive like this, Cora. I mean it. Come back inside. Let's calm down."

My eyes are desperate to latch on to something concrete. They land on the dense rows of forest. I imagine sets of eyes leering from between the branches, stalking me. Again, I consider what Adele told me earlier about Lu's drawing. Could she have been right? Has someone been watching us?

"I need to go," I whisper as I climb into my truck and reverse down his bumpy drive. I hear him yelling my name, a sharp bark that dies in the wind.

I keep the windows down and force myself to breathe on the short drive back. Tears splatter my cheeks. This is all my fault. *I* did this. I brought this on myself . . . and Lu.

I should have completely disappeared when I had the chance. Changed my name. Changed my life, instead of waltzing back to my hometown like it owed me something. All these years I've put on such a brave face. I handled the spotlight, then faded into anonymity with grace. But it's all a lie. I'm still a mess. I'm still a victim, no matter how much I pretend not to be.

I shudder at that word. *Victim.* I've raised Lulu to be strong, to be trusting but cautious, to keep an eye out but not carry the weight of the world on her shoulders. Not yet anyway. Now, no matter what happens, if she survives the night, she will be a victim too. She'll be just like me, in more ways than one.

I turn onto the main road and gun it toward my side of the woods. I can't fathom what's going to happen to her, what she's going through right this very second. I smash the gas pedal, speeding down roads as familiar to me as the back of my hand.

When I approach my driveway, I look for clues—hidden cameras in branches or anything out of place—but it's late and too dark to suss anything out.

I park and take another shaky breath, wondering what I will find when I head back inside.

6

THEN

Everything is hazy.

I've never been in a haunted house before, and now I know why. I don't like loud noises, and I definitely don't like being scared. I push in behind Nicole, her tiny body a semicomfort as the little knot of my gymnastics team hurries down the shadowy hallway, giggling and egging each other on. We zigzag back and forth, fake black walls forming a maze around us. My breath is tight in my chest, and I'm worried I'm going to have a panic attack. I've had only one, a year ago, right before a regional competition, and I truly thought I was dying before a doctor explained it was just anxiety.

My father laughed that away; apparently, I'm too young to be anxious, though I feel anxious all the time. I feel anxious that I'm not good enough at gymnastics; I feel anxious that my body is changing; I feel anxious that I don't have any real friends; I feel anxious that I want to be an Olympian but that I might let everyone down, especially my dad; I feel anxious that I've never had a boyfriend or even come close; I feel anxious that I'm missing out on normal life with school and friends and parties, but I also can't imagine having a regular teenage life either. I'm anxious that I'm not doing any of it good enough . . . that *I'm* not good enough.

The screams bring me back to reality, though my heart slams much too fast in my chest. The diet pills do that to me sometimes. My father gave me an extra one before competition today, because we find it gives me more energy. He says it's our little secret weapon.

It's hard to tell what's happening around us until the maze spits us out on a large concrete floor. I wait for my eyes to adjust again and take in what's around me. There are doors to the left and right, and I'm guessing, as we walk down the endless corridor, people are going to try to terrify us. I link arms with Nicole and try to steady my nerves as best as I can.

As we near the first door, I discover there are staged scenes in each room, kind of like a movie set. The first one looks like a hospital, where a victim lies on a gurney and a man with a chain saw bites into fake chunks of flesh. I shudder and remind myself this isn't real.

Jessie laughs and moves to the next room, her limp apparent. I recoil as I see a bunch of killer clowns lunging toward the door. One of them grips a fistful of Jessie's hair, and she screams while all of us band around her. Why are they touching her? Are these people allowed to touch us?

A bad feeling slithers through my belly until it aches. I want to go home. It's been such a long day, and I didn't even get to celebrate placing second overall. I calculate how long it will take to walk through this place. Thirty minutes? An hour? From the outside, the warehouse seemed endless. I steady myself as Jessie yanks herself free, yelling at one of the clowns who simply looms over her, that distorted face menacing with its plastered-on grin.

This doesn't feel like a safe space, and every ounce of me wants to turn and run the way we came. But my teammates pull me forward, and I follow them, even though something tells me I might never find my way out again.

7

Now

I exit the truck and study my house.

I search the trees, the fence line, and my spacious front porch. The awareness that someone could have been stalking me and Lu, unnoticed, plotting for this very moment, suddenly seems very real.

My entire life, I've been watched: by fans, by critics, by survivors, by true-crime lovers. I filled in the gaps with other things: sitting on boards for charities, traveling, staying small, sliding slowly into a more private life. Through the years, however, people still dredge it all up, especially around Halloween. They never let me outrun my past.

They never let me forget.

I jam the key in the lock and turn it to the left, then shove the door open. It squeaks on its hinges, and I clutch the doorframe, inspecting the house as a cop might. There's a bag of scattered marshmallows Lu forgot to close up before we left for the parade, my coffee cup from this morning, a few stuffed animals and toys. Other than that, everything's tidy, neat, just as I left it.

My gut twists as I think of Lu bounding out of her room earlier today, so excited about the parade. I close my eyes and comb back through our day. I must have missed something. There must be some clue as to who took her from that parade.

As I search my memory, my day with Lu unfolds in vivid snapshots. We had pumpkin pancakes at home. We went into town and saw Mr. Mills at the general store, who gave Lu a lollipop; then we went to see Dave for story time, and I had coffee with Faith while Lu was at the library. My thoughts snag on Faith. She never showed up tonight.

I file that away for later. Could someone have been watching Lu while she was at the library? I think back to what Joe said. How well do I really know Dave? He is single, I think, and practically lives at the library. Could he harbor some secret fetish for snatching little girls?

A violent shudder erupts through my body as I retrain my focus on the task of remembering. We were surprisingly social today. More than normal. Lu had too much energy to burn, and I knew she'd go nuts just staying at home.

I press a hand to my heart, open my eyes, and examine the cabin. Silence greets me, a reminder of what happens when you choose to live in a cabin in the woods. Why did I bring us here?

A sigh tears through my throat as I finally step through the entryway. My parents had been appalled when they heard I'd bought this place. After what happened to me, how could I choose somewhere so remote? A place that was a reminder of my past, not a departure? I tried on new jobs, but they never stuck. Different cities. Different men. It seemed I didn't know how to be normal, how to belong to one place. Except this one. This was home, after all. And after I had Lu, I realized it didn't matter where I was as long as she was with me. My life was once so big, as if other rules applied. Perhaps I just wanted to prove that I was normal. That we were normal.

When my mother learned I moved back, she sent me email after email, trying to talk me out of it. I ignored them, just like I ignored her.

Some of my nerves quiet once I flick on the lamp by the door and drop my keys on the table. It took me years to get used to the dark. For years after that Halloween, I'd slept with all the lights on. Otherwise, I'd hear the screams. They haunted me.

One thing is clear: this is my fault. Somehow, I poked a sleeping bear. I moved home. I awakened something evil, something lurking, and it's up to me to undo it and bring Lulu back.

I glance at our small round dining room table, over to the couch and TV, and then to our Polaroid wall, where I've hung all my favorite candid shots of me and Lu. As I stare at it, I see there's another bloodred card right in the center, trapped behind a pushpin. I move closer. Below it is a Polaroid of an antique baby doll, its dead, glass eyes open and staring at me.

Why did they leave me a photo of a doll? I snatch it from the board and inspect every inch for clues, and that's when I see it: it's dressed like a witch. *No, not like a witch,* I realize with impending dread. Like *Lulu.* Its outfit is her outfit. My body goes rigid before I whip around, as if the person who put this here is standing in my kitchen.

So someone *was* here. Someone knew I wouldn't be home. Before I even look at the card, I pull up my security feed and scan through it, but there's nothing out of the ordinary until the footage hits seven o'clock. Then it goes completely dark. I stare at the app, shaking my head.

This isn't possible. Who could have wiped this?

It's not important, I remind myself. What's important is what the next card says.

I inch forward, step by step, and rip it from the wall.

When I read what it says, my world tilts. The card flutters to the ground before I can catch my breath.

8

Then

In a matter of moments, I lose sight of the girls.

Without Nicole as an anchor, I bump into a wall and cower as a zombie reaches for me and brushes my bare thighs with his chilly hands. I smack him away and begin to whimper, tears stinging my eyes. The world feels like it's closing in. I can't see. I can't breathe. I'm going to pass out.

From behind, someone grabs my waist and yells "Boo!" in my ear. His breath is sour and hot against my cheek. There's cruel laughter, and then the pack of boys from the gym swings into focus, all of them laughing and pointing at me once they see the terror that must be evident on my face.

"What's the matter, Valentine? Get left behind?" One of the guys, Greg, mimes crying by curling his fists below his eyes. "Boo-hoo, Valentine's all alone!" He puckers his lower lip.

"Hey, knock it off," Luke snaps, stepping from the shadows. He towers above the rest of them. Surprisingly, they listen.

"Yo, let's keep going!" Todd motions down the dark hall, and Ryan smacks Luke on the chest to follow. He nods absently at them. Before he leaves, Luke places a warm hand on my shoulder.

"Hey, are you okay, Cora? Did you lose the group?"

I can't even speak, only gulp air. I grip Luke's entire arm, treating him like a lifeline. I don't want to be alone in this place. I don't want to be here at all. It feels like drowning.

"Hey, hey. Breathe, okay? Just breathe. It's all right. Look at me. Breathe with me." He ushers me to the side, out of the way of the throngs of people screaming and whooping down the darkly lit halls. He squats down to eye level and breathes slowly in through his nose and out through his mouth.

I try to do as he says and stare into his bright-green eyes as we mirror each other. To my surprise, it helps.

"Do you want me to walk you out of here? Maybe call your parents to get you?"

Yes! I almost scream. Before I can confirm, the girls burst back into view, running out of a room to the left.

"Ooh, looks like Cora and Luke have a little somethin' somethin' going on!" Laura teases this time, making kissy-faces, just as Nicole did earlier.

I push away from Luke as though he's poison. The hurt flashes across his eyes, but he steps back and shoves his hands into his pockets.

"What are you doing?" Jakayla asks. She stares between me and her brother suspiciously.

"I couldn't find you," I explain. "I—I got lost."

"And what? Luke's making it all better?" Madeline taunts, elbowing Laura in the ribs. Nicole chews on her bottom lip, silent, while Jessie stares between us, calculating just how mean to be.

"They'd actually make the perfect couple," Jessie says now, crossing her arms. "Cora's going to be a big star, and, Luke, you can be her little bitch boy. Since you are already," she mumbles under her breath.

The insult is harsh, and I watch Jakayla waver between disagreeing with her captain and defending her brother.

"Hey, I'll see you later," Luke says, slinking off to find the boys.

Infuriated, I turn on all of them. "What is your problem, Jessie? Why do you always have to be such a *bitch*?"

The hateful words explode from my lips. There is a collective gasp from the group. No one, especially the youngest on the team, has ever talked to Jessie this way.

"What did you just say to me, shrimp?" She towers over me. I can smell the bubble gum on her breath.

"I just mean," I backtrack, taking a step deeper into the shadows, "that you're always so mean. To Luke. Or the other boys. To us. But you're our captain, Jessie. So act like it." I glance at the other girls to see if they'll suddenly decide to be brave and agree, but they stay deathly silent.

"I'll tell you one thing," she whispers, coming within inches of my face. "You better watch your back, Valentine, because I won't forget this," she says. *"Ever."* She sniffs, turns, and stalks off down the hall. One by one, the girls follow along, like minions.

As I wipe away my tears, I realize what I've just said to my team captain. Instantly, I regret it, but there's a small part of me that's proud too. Because the truth is, I always stay quiet, even when Jessie or the other girls cross the line. I never stand up for myself. And because of it, the girls treat me however they want.

Well, not tonight. Not this time.

I waver against the wall. I can try to catch up to the girls, prove that I'm not affected by Jessie's threats, and just get the night over with. Or I can find my way back to the front and wait for my parents to pick me up. Forced with being left alone or following the pack, I reluctantly choose the second option.

I jog to catch up as the girls disappear down another hall.

9

Now

I stuff the Polaroid into my back pocket.

As I attempt to make sense of the card, my screen door bangs open and shut, and I jump a mile, my hands already reaching for my shotgun I keep locked out of reach above the door.

I hear the words before I register who it is, Faith chatting a mile a minute as she breezes past me.

"I know, I know. I missed the parade. So sue me. Tyler and his friends decided they were going to throw a Halloween party without telling me, so I just spent the last two hours teenage-proofing my house. God, I'm sorry, but boys are disgusting. I can't even." Faith has a single bag of groceries in her arms and plops it on my island with a heavy sigh. "I got extra goodies so we can roast s'mores and drink wine. It will keep me from thinking about what atrocities are happening under my own roof." She shudders, then whips around and clocks my expression. "Jesus, Cora. What is it?" Her eyes sweep the room as she lets out another much-needed exhale, one hand on her waist. "Where's Lu?"

My mouth parts to tell her some version of the truth, but I feel trapped. If these people have been in my house and wiped my security footage, then they are probably watching me right now. Is part of this night a test to see who I will tell and who I won't? I think of the Polaroid in my back pocket, some sort of clue I don't understand yet.

When I don't answer, Faith cocks a hip like Lulu often does. "Hello? Earth to Cora!" Faith waves her hand in front of my face, trying to snap me out of it. Since her divorce, her fiery temper flares at the oddest times.

"Someone took Lu." My voice is small and powerless, cracking on the last syllable. It's so faint, Faith has to lean in to hear.

"What did you just say? What about Lu?"

I scoop up the offending red card, join it with the other one, and toss them to her, but she's standing too far to reach. They sift along my hardwood as if caught by a gentle breeze. Faith stoops down to retrieve them with an exaggerated groan. I see her eyes scan the first card and then widen when she reads the second.

"What the *fuck* is this, Cora?" She gestures with the cards. "I'm not in the mood for some stupid Halloween prank. Where's Lulu?"

"She's gone!" I scream. My eyes fill with tears again. "We went to the parade. Someone took her. Someone has been watching us, Faith. Someone has been in my house, and I don't . . . I can't . . ." My lungs gulp for air but once again catch nothing, and that panicky feeling overtakes my whole body again. Almost like an asthma attack, which I used to get when I was younger before my father convinced me it was all in my head and threw my inhaler away. I grip air, and Faith moves to me in three quick strides and leads me to the sofa.

"Oh my God, oh my God." Her hand rests momentarily on my back before she jumps up and stalks back and forth in front of the fireplace. "Where are the police? They'll find her, right? Why didn't you call me! Jesus, Cora!"

Her words jumble together in my brain. I can't deal with her fear and panic on top of mine. It's too big. Faith worries about everything and will somehow spin this into being *her* problem. But it's not.

"I can't go to the police," I say, gesturing to one of the cards.

"The fuck you can't!" she says. Her cheeks are red, her eyes already bloodshot from screaming. "Get in the car. We are going to the precinct right this second." She points outside like she's telling Tyler what to do. But I'm not her kid. This isn't some easily solvable chore to take care of. This is my daughter's life. And there are rules.

Her face is weathered. Her jet-black hair hangs bluntly above stooped shoulders. Deep bags bulge beneath her gray eyes. They appear bewildered now, out of her depth. But I can't carry her baggage tonight. She needs to leave.

"I don't think you should be here." I suck in air, nice and slow through my nose. "They're watching me. They wiped my camera footage. They probably know you're here right now."

"What?" she explodes, turning in a circle. "Are there hidden cameras? Oh my God." Faith begins to tear through the house. I'm too exhausted to tell her to stop. She's a CPA and has a very analytical mind. She's a fixer, a PTA mom, and good with cars. This, however, is out of her league, and we both know it. She can't dole out any useful advice. No one can.

But I'm glued in place. My eyes drift back to the second card. I've already memorized it, it's so ridiculous. I hop off the couch and retrieve it, dragging a finger over the boxy black print.

TO GET YOUR DAUGHTER BACK
YOU MUST TAKE SOMEONE ELSE'S CHILD
WAIT FOR FURTHER INSTRUCTIONS

If these psychos think I'm taking a child, they've obviously underestimated who I am and what I have been through in my life.

Faith bangs through my house, tossing pillows and slamming doors. The more animated she becomes, the more resigned I am. I can sense myself turning off, shutting down, and it scares me. I haven't felt this way in so long, and it took me years to behave like a normal, functioning person. Now, it's like no time has passed. I'm right back *there*, and I need to be *here*.

A few minutes later, Faith bursts back into the living room, her hair mussed. "Let's call Officer Bishop. He'll know what to do."

"Faith!" I scream, ignoring the sudden headache hammering my temples. "Are you not hearing me? I can't go to the police! So stop saying that. You are not helping at all!"

She stops moving, stops talking, her mouth hanging open. Her face turns beet red. Instantly, I feel bad. Her ex-husband used to yell at her constantly, which made her feel like shit. And here I am, doing the same thing. "I want to help, Cora," she says, sliding onto the couch beside me. She's trying to show me that she doesn't take it personally, but her voice wobbles. Yet another thing I need to fix.

"You can't help. You need to go home."

She ignores my request and forges ahead. "Do you think this has to do with what happened that Halloween?"

That Halloween. Something sinister dashes through my heart. "Yes, I do."

She exhales a long, shaky breath. "Okay, okay. So what do we do? What's the next play?" Her eyes roam around the cabin and land on the Polaroid wall, but she stays quiet.

"I don't know, Faith. I need to think." But I don't need to think. I need to move. I need to act.

She leans forward slightly, wedging her hands between her knees. "I just can't believe this is happening." She rocks back and forth. "Poor Lu. She must be so scared." Tears fill her eyes and fall freely.

A fresh wave of terror punches me right in the heart. How do mothers *do* this? Am I supposed to just sit here and wait?

My phone buzzes and makes us both jump. Faith leans over and almost grabs the phone from my hand. I'm too fast. I pluck it from the coffee table, dreading whatever clue comes next.

10

THEN

Once I catch up to the girls, I grope blindly through the dark, nervous as people jump out every few feet in new, aggressive attempts to scare us.

I close my eyes anyway, counting in my head, doing anything to prevent a full-blown panic attack. I think about my routines, how I will have to slightly tweak them for trials next week, how I will have to compete better than I have in my entire life. The thought calms me, strangely, until we approach a tunnel with a clump of people standing in front of it, too scared to enter.

I'm too short to see what all the fuss is about, so I push off my toes in a succession of tiny hops to try to get a better view. It makes me think of conditioning, how sometimes we do hops like this for ten minutes straight with our arms stiff above our heads.

There's a tall man in a horrible mask banging a wide, traditional wooden paddle against the wall across from him. It reminds me of those kids who get yanked into the principal's office at school to get spanked. People have to sprint through the tunnel before the man brings the paddle down again, and Jessie stops and rolls her eyes as she watches people freak out and choose to go another way. An oversize black light buzzes above so that everyone's faces are speckled in white or purple.

"He's not going to hit you!" Jessie shouts to random strangers, arms outstretched. "God, people are such wimps."

I almost mention someone just grabbed her hair, but refrain. Jessie has this way of making you feel dumb or small if you say the wrong thing. I glance at Jessie's knee, knowing that she is most definitely not a wimp. She once cried when she was too scared to do a full-twisting layout without a spot on beam, and our coach humiliated her in front of the whole team and said if she didn't do it, we'd have to condition for an extra two hours. Even though she was scared, she did the trick and fell on the landing, severely twisting her ankle. We had to condition anyway, and ever since that day, Jessie has put on this tough-girl act, no matter what.

When she injured her knee before this meet, none of us even knew how bad it was because she pretended she was fine. But I overheard my dad talking to the coach, and she is far from fine. She might not even be able to compete next week. Though she made it through the meet today somehow, she had to change a lot of her skills, and she didn't place well.

She hobbles forward toward the guy, who is much taller than us. The crowd has thinned to just our gymnastics team, and instantly, I have the urge to run. Nicole grabs my hand and pulls me forward, as if she can read my thoughts. "Let's go through."

"No, let Jessie go first," Madeline insists. "She'll probably scare him so *he* disappears." She tries to force some bravado into her voice, but I can hear how it quakes. Everyone is putting up a front, it seems. Laura and Jakayla hang back and say nothing.

"You think you're so tough with your big wooden paddle?" Jessie says, goading him. She smacks her gum loudly, hands lost in her jacket pockets.

He cranes his head down at her, the stringy black wig falling across his pocked face. He looks horrible, menacing, and my heart is nearly in my throat as he braces the paddle above his shoulder and then whacks it as hard as he can against the concrete wall. It makes an awful splintering sound, but Jessie doesn't flinch.

"If you touch me with that thing, I'll sue you for every penny you've got, buddy, which, judging from your day job, probably isn't much."

She turns to look at us with that signature cocky grin, her lipstick violet under the black light. She steadies herself to go through, but before she can, the monster lifts the paddle again, and this time, he aims it not at the wall, but right at Jessie's bandaged knee.

The scream leaves my mouth before the impact happens, and all of us gawk, horrified, as the paddle makes contact with her knee in the most sickening smack I've ever heard. It's all bones and wood, and then she is wailing in a primal, cawing scream. It reminds me of a goat I heard die once on my aunt's farm, a sound that has haunted me ever since. The man hovers over her, breathing heavily, and lifts the very tip of his mask to spit on her.

"Who's laughing now, *bitch*?" His voice tremors with rage as he disappears into the tunnel. The girls all watch him flee, dumbstruck. None of us knows what to do, but it's obvious Jessie needs help.

One by one, the girls start screaming at the top of their lungs, but it's useless. I glance around, trying to see through my own terrified tears. How is there no responsible adult around, especially in case of an emergency?

Laura looks at me, her eyes wide and terrified. If gymnastics doesn't pan out, she's made it clear she wants to be an actress, and part of me wonders if this is all some elaborate skit. A prank, maybe. Practice for an audition she has coming up. She grips my elbow, and her fingers are like ice. "Cora, go get help. We have to help her." Her teeth are chattering, and she's shaking uncontrollably. This isn't acting. This is real.

I stare down at Jessie, our team captain, clutching her leg and shrieking like someone has killed her firstborn child. It's not just the injury. We all know what this means. An attack like this signifies the end of her career. It is a certainty, a finality. No Olympics. No more gymnastics. An entire life of sacrifices, practices, accomplishments, and pain all wiped away in a single catastrophic moment. A career she began building at three years old is done. Just like that.

"Go!" Laura screams again. She shoves me once, hard, and her face is ugly and contorted under the lights. I want to tell someone else to go. I don't want to wander back through this place by myself. I don't even know where I am. But of course I'm the one they choose. No one cares if anything happens to me. Once again, I'm the outsider. The expendable one. The pest.

Maybe if I get her help fast enough, they will start to value me more. Maybe Jessie will forget what I said to her tonight. I take a few steadying breaths and begin to backtrack, shoving my way through people and looking for someone else who works here that's not in a mask.

I ask people for help as I go, but I'm completely ignored. The panic starts to rise, a buzz in my chest that spreads to my limbs and makes me feel like I'm floating. Finally, I see someone in a black T-shirt with a clipboard, and I grab his arm roughly.

"I need help," I exclaim. "There was this guy who hit my friend. She's really hurt. I think we need an ambulance."

His eyes flick over my head and back to me, as if he's deciding something.

"Okay, come with me. I'll get you to a phone."

I'm not sure if a phone is what I need, but if I don't get out of this haunted house in the next two minutes, I'm going to have to be carried out because I will have fainted. And then where will Jessie be? I tell myself everything is going to be fine and point out things I can see and touch. Things that are real. Things that I know to be true. A wall. My legs. This man. We weave back the same way we entered, but then he comes to one of the draped black cloths and motions for me to follow.

"In here," he says. "It's a shortcut."

For one second, I think about not following him, but I don't want to be blamed for leaving Jessie in such a bind. I can't even imagine how the team would hold that against me later or possibly use it to ostracize me from the group even more. There's that word again.

Ostracize: exclude from a society or group.

I recite the definition to calm myself, mumbling the words under my breath.

The man holds open the curtain impatiently. "You coming or what?"

After a moment, I suck in a breath and slip in beside him.

The curtain drops, and once again, I am left in the dark.

11

Now

I read the text with bated breath, Faith hooked over my shoulder in anticipation.

1445 Seymour Lane. Be there at 9pm. Kill your headlights and park one street over, on Holly. There's a new construction house with no cameras. Make your way to 1445 Seymour via the construction zone, into the backyard. You will enter the residence through the back door, which will be unlocked. Head up to the second floor, first bedroom on your left. You must convince Lennon to get in your car. We don't care how. Drive back to your house and send visual confirmation when it's done.

Lennon. Who is Lennon? I read and reread the instructions before taking a photo of it with the burner phone and texting it to Joe, to which he hastily replies: shit.

I check the time: 8:00 p.m. How is it only eight? I feel like I've been in this nightmare for days.

Faith's sharp intake of breath brings me back to what these people are asking me to do. "Cora, we need to go to the police right now. Bring this to them! They can find her. They have the means that we don't. Maybe they can trace the text."

"Faith, it's a blocked number, and for the hundredth time, I'm not going to the police." But she's right. I need help. I can't leave my daughter's life up to chance, and I sure as hell can't snatch someone else's kid.

"How do you even know Lulu's okay?" she tosses out. She's gnawing on her nails, her eyes wild. "How can you possibly believe anything they say?"

Her words are like an actual slap. My stomach cramps again, and I place my palm over it in an attempt to get the agony to stop. But I'm at the mercy of these people, whoever they are. I have to do as they say. But not before they give me something first.

I lunge for my phone and type out a hasty text. Send proof Lulu is okay. My fingers shake as I type it out and press send.

I wait for what feels like an hour before a grainy photo of Lulu comes through. Tears fill my eyes as I see the close-cropped shot. Her thumb is wedged deeply in her mouth. She's asleep. I send it to Joe and ask if he can pull anything from the shot, though it's such a close-up of Lu, I can't make out anything but the sheets behind her. But it gives me a tiny shred of assurance. It has to.

Faith glances at it. "How do you know that's from right now, Cora? They could have taken that when they snatched her. You can't do what these people ask. You *can't.*"

I bite my tongue to keep from snapping at her. I know she means well, but she's only making things worse. Ignoring what she's implying, I disappear to my room, hurry to the back of my closet, and unlock my gun safe. I need to get my head on straight, remember who I am and what I've been through. I'm not just a victim. I'm also a survivor. There is an entire part of my history I need to tap into now, a strength I haven't had to access in decades.

"Cora." Faith trails behind me as I load my semiautomatic 9 mm and shove it in the back of my jeans. She sees the gun and backs up.

Faith hates guns, refuses to carry them in her home, especially having a teenage son. "What are you doing?"

"Whatever I have to." My voice is sharp, and she instantly quiets. I've also got my pocketknife and about ten years of jiujitsu. Once my knee healed, I took up a new sport, one that could help, not harm. I'm not sure any of that will help me now, but it's something.

My burner phone buzzes in my pocket, and I reach for it. It's Joe.

I'll tail you when it's time.

Roger, I reply. Just knowing Joe will be close by if something goes sideways makes me feel better.

"So what, Cora? You're just going to show up at some stranger's house with a *gun* and take a child?" She gestures to me, then lets her hands drop before scratching her forehead, a nervous tic. "Please just think this through. What happens if you get caught or arrested? What then?"

"Who says I'm going to take anyone?" I say, pulling my hoodie over the gun. The truth is, I have no idea what I'm going to do. My head feels all jumbled, and I'm two seconds away from falling completely apart.

"I know you don't want to hear it, but I really, *really* think we should call Officer Bishop."

"And say what? Whoever is doing this will know I've gone to the police, and then what? What happens to Lu then? Huh?" I'm shouting, and I hate it. None of this is Faith's fault, but her insistence that going to the police is the only answer has me rattled, because what if she's right? What if with me abiding by their rules, Lulu dies anyway?

But the fact is, I don't know where these people are or what they're capable of. Say I go to the police, and they have someone embedded in the precinct? If I defy them again, Lulu will be the one to suffer. And I could never live with that.

I memorize the directions just as I used to memorize words and routines when I was a kid. It's been easier to sharpen my memory since being off grid. While people are constantly crooked over their phones, using apps instead of their brains, I'm teaching Lulu how to think critically. I choke on a sob as I think of my little girl: her bright eyes and sweet lisp, her sticky fingers and fierce hugs. Is she okay? I'm already thinking of after: the trauma she might carry, how it can become trapped in your cells and rear its head at the most inopportune times. If she survives, who will she become after tonight?

I map the address with trembling fingers, which is in a ritzy part of town, a little outside Atlanta. It will take only twenty minutes to get there.

To pass the time, I make myself a pot of coffee—not that I need it with all this adrenaline. Faith fusses around me, pulling out cream and cups and saucers. As the coffee hisses into the pot, I remember Halloween all those years ago . . . when my whole future was on the line, and then everything changed in the course of one fateful night.

Just like this.

Faith pours us both a scalding cup, and I burn my tongue as I suck it down. This night isn't like *that*, I remind myself. This story has a happy ending, with Lulu back home safe and these people behind bars. Justice, after a whole life of none.

Faith doesn't make small talk because there's nothing to say, but I can feel her trying to think of ways to talk me out of it. Her eyes are busy climbing the walls, proof of her anxiety. How was it just earlier today we were at the coffee shop, chatting about the weekend? Now, the mood is fraught with panic and uncertainty. While earlier, there was nothing at stake, now there's everything.

"You should go home, Faith. Be with Tyler. I'll keep you posted."

"I'm not going anywhere," she snaps.

"Faith, you can't do anything here." I motion around. "I don't want to drag you into this anymore than you already are. I couldn't live with myself if something happened to you or to Tyler too." I soften my voice. "I promise I'll keep you posted, okay? Go home." I down the last of my coffee, swipe my keys, and lock up once we're both outside.

She seems rooted to the spot, anguishing over what to do or say. Finally, she pulls me into a tight hug. I know she wants to tell me not to do this. That it's stupid and dangerous. "Please, *please* be careful," she whispers, wiping away streaks of mascara as she pulls away.

I nod, get in the car, and rev the engine again. I text Joe from the burner that I'm heading out.

Copy that, he replies.

I hope Faith doesn't do something stupid, like send Officer Bishop to the address, but I trust that she won't do anything to put Lu's life in more danger. She just stands there, watching me, until I reverse steadily down the drive.

12

THEN

It's so dark behind the curtain, I can barely see.

I'm sick of not having a firm grip on my senses, as I am someone who needs to understand her surroundings to feel comfortable. This place has quite literally become my nightmare. I trip on the edge of something and buckle forward, bumping into the guy, who barks an impatient "Watch it."

I mumble an apology and concentrate on why I'm here: get help for Jessie. I've already memorized how to get back to her and recite those directions to myself now. It would be so easy to get lost in a place like this, but I steady my mind on the sharp turns we're making as the man leads me to a tiny office clouded by cigarette smoke.

He bangs on the glass door, and a fat man with a baby face yanks it open. "Yeah?" He crushes a cigarette into an overflowing ashtray.

"Got an injury, boss. She needs to call an ambulance or something."

The man drags a hand over his face. "Not again. Brian?"

The man shrugs. "No idea." He turns to me. "Did you see the guy?"

I describe the terrifying mask and the wooden paddle.

The man nods. "That's Brian all right. Jesus, Mary, and Joseph, this ain't good." He groans as he leans over his desk to grab a beige telephone with a pudgy hand before dangling the receiver my way. "Who do you need to call, sweetheart?"

I need to call an ambulance, but I choose to call my parents first. I press the number into the phone and wait. They answer on the first ring. "Honey, what is it? Why are you calling? Is everything okay?"

My mother's voice sounds unnaturally tense and worried, and I assure her I'm fine but tell her that Jessie has been injured and needs an ambulance.

"Oh my lord, I knew you girls shouldn't have gone there tonight. Stan, Stan, listen to this! Jessie's been injured by one of those *freaks* at that haunted house."

"Mom!" I practically shout into the phone, because I know that she's spinning a worst-case scenario in her head, like usual. "Mom, will you just call the ambulance, please?" There's a shuffle, and then my dad comes onto the line.

"Cora, honey, are you okay?"

I nod into the receiver, though I know he can't see me.

"Don't worry. I'll make sure they call the ambulance and help Jessie. Just breathe. Can you do that for me?"

He's saying the same thing Luke did. I take a breath and feel my nerves start to settle. Dad always knows just what to do, even when he's hard on me. It's why he makes such a good team doctor, never freaking out when someone gets injured.

My mother bullies her way back onto the phone. "Cora, we're coming to get you right this instant. Okay? We'll be there soon, sweetheart. Just stay calm."

"Okay." Her words have the complete opposite effect. Though I'm not sure anyone could stay calm in a situation like this.

I shiver beneath my clothes and hand the receiver back to the guy. "Will you be able to tell the ambulance where to go? It's in that weird tunnel thing."

"Yeah, yeah, I know exactly where it is. Mike." He snaps his fingers toward the other guy. "Go find Brian, and tell him he's fired. He'll be lucky if he doesn't end up in jail."

"You got it, boss." The man disappears and leaves me with the older guy. Before he can say more, the phone rings, and he answers it.

He groans again and answers. "Yello? Yep. Wait, what? Why?" He eyes me, then turns his back and drops his voice as he speaks in hushed tones into the receiver. While he talks, I spot a nameplate on his desk, Lou Matheson, and wonder who made it for him. The thought makes me almost sad, this guy working in a tiny office in a haunted house with his nameplate, dirty ashtray stacked with crumpled cigarettes, and dented soda cans. After a moment, he hangs up the phone and turns to me.

"You got someone picking you up, hon?"

I nod. "My parents. They'll be here soon."

"Okay, good, good. Look, why don't you come with me? I'll let you out the side door so you don't have to go back through all that mess." He motions toward the warehouse, then waddles to the exit and leads me down a long, poorly lit hallway. I feel bad not going back to the girls, but really, what can I do? I did my part. I called for help. They probably won't even notice I don't return. Despite our fight, I really do hope Jessie's okay.

Lou pushes open a large gray door with a bright-red exit sign buzzing overhead. "Happy Halloween, sweetie."

"Happy Halloween." I hesitate before stepping outside, as I know it will take my parents a little while to get here. Once Lou is gone, I slide down to the floor inside instead and rest my head on my knees. The sudden exhaustion of the day overwhelms me. I am bone-achingly tired. I stretch my legs out in front of me, rolling around my sore ankles. I didn't wear my watch tonight, but I calculate it will take my parents about fifteen minutes to get here.

To pass the time, I review my routines in my head. Vault and floor I feel solid on, but bars and beam need a bit of work. Nicole and I often joke that if we could combine her skills on beam and bars with my strength and power on floor and vault, we'd be the perfect gymnast.

In another five minutes, I decide to step outside, even though it's freezing. I think about propping the door open, but I can't find anything to wedge underneath it. Deciding they will be here soon, I let it close behind me. The echo is loud as I stand in the dark alley. The cold slaps me awake, and I take a big breath, so happy to finally be free of that place.

I find my worry doll in my pocket and hold it tight as my thoughts snap back to Jessie. How devastating. Even if she could have overcome her initial injury, there's no coming back from something as violent as what that man just did to her. My eyes well with unexpected tears at the thought of not having our captain at the trials. Sure, she can be mean, and what I said to her tonight was not particularly kind, but I would never wish an injury like that on anyone.

A pair of bright headlights snakes around the corner, and I relax. They're here. I'm blinded by the lights as the vehicle speeds toward me, going much too fast, but then again, that's my mother in crisis.

As the car approaches, I realize it's a beige van, not my parents' blue minivan. Before I can retreat back up the steps by the door to wait, the van screeches to a halt and the back doors fling open. Two men in ski masks and black clothing jump out and lunge for me.

I'm so shocked, I don't even move. I've seen movies like this, so the image is almost familiar, laughable, even. But nothing about this is funny. They don't say a word as they seize my arms and drape something dark over my head. Finally, I find my lungs, but I'm already shoved into the back of the van when I start to scream. My face smacks into the floor, hard, and I taste blood. The doors close, and the van peels out, the entire ordeal taking no more than twenty seconds.

I expect the men to tell me to shut up or jab a gun into my ribs, but it's eerily silent. I can't see, and it's hard to breathe. One of them wrenches my arms behind my back and secures my wrists with what feels like a zip tie. The van hits a pothole, and I lurch to the right, slamming into one of the men's thighs. He smells like patchouli and pine.

Where do I know that smell?

As I lie on my side, I start to understand the gravity of what is happening: I've been kidnapped from a haunted house on Halloween. I left the girls. My parents are expecting me.

And no one knows how to find me.

13

Now

The drive passes in a blur, though I should really be paying more attention.

Landmarks. Signs. Tails. I search for suspicious cars in the rearview, but the roads are barren in this neck of the woods. I don't see Joe either, which tells me he's doing his job.

Perhaps Lulu is nearby. I try to intuit where she could be. Images of dingy warehouses or scary basements flicker through my mind. I replace those thoughts with something softer, kinder. Lulu asleep in a bed. Lulu watching a cartoon. Lulu sucking her thumb. Lulu back at home. Lulu safe and sound.

As I near the next road over, I kill my headlights and park in front of the construction site. It is a bland, homogeneous neighborhood with overpriced houses, healthy-size lots, and expensive cars in circular drive-ways. It's exactly the kind of neighborhood I sometimes dream of for Lulu in another life, and yet whenever I glimpse kids out playing and parents waving, it feels like some sort of club I'm never going to be invited to.

As I sit there, I'm struck with the overwhelming urge to run. This could be a setup, a way to make sure I never see my daughter again. I drag a hand over my face and try to still my body, but every part of me is buzzing with nerves. I glance around. The neighborhood seems too quiet, like a soundstage. This doesn't feel right.

I fumble with the burner phone and text Joe.

I don't know what I should do.

He texts back almost instantly. I don't like this, Cora. I don't think you should go in. There's got to be another way.

Do I dare text these people back? Tell them no? What will happen to Lulu if I defy their demands? Grappling with my two choices, I finally exit the truck and cover my license plate with an old T-shirt and duct tape I have in the back. The last thing I need is to get caught breaking and entering into someone's home and be thrown in jail.

On the street, I waver once again. Once I do this, once I enter someone else's house, things change. *I* change. I close my eyes, count to ten, tell my brain to shut off. It's what I used to do, what I *had* to do to survive. I'm good at burying pain and terror. I have to do it again now. For me. For Lulu.

I recite the instructions in my head, easily slipping through the construction zone undetected. I check the neighbors' houses on either side of the target, searching for cameras. Luckily, the houses are spaced far enough apart so that anyone could enter a backyard without being seen. I dart through thick hedges and large oaks in the back and search for lights inside the house, but it's completely dark. I know this is the right house, however, because I cruised by it first before circling back to my parking spot the next street over. Maybe whoever it is I'm supposed to meet isn't here?

Lennon. Lulu. The names mix in my head. Is this also some young, unsuspecting child who is going to be ripped from everything they trust and know?

But I'm not a bad person. I would never hurt a child.

I rush past the pool, which glitters under the nearly full moon, and hesitate at the back door, breathing hard. The glass is pristine, and my reflection stops me like a ghost. Dark hair piled in a messy ponytail, intense eyes, prominent cheekbones. After I was taken, the media had a heyday, comparing me to numerous nineties actresses. They tried to get some of the heavy hitters like Alyssa Milano or Jennifer Connelly to play me in the god-awful made-for-TV movie they slapped together about my life but ended up with some B-list celebrity instead.

The door looks like one of those giant sliding doors you can slide all the way open. My hand freezes on the handle. What if there's an alarm?

As quietly as possible, I slide open the patio door and wince, expecting a dog's shrill bark or an angry siren. Not only is the door unlocked, but it is deathly quiet inside, which makes me worry even more. A parent would never leave a young child home alone . . . especially on Halloween.

Carefully, I tiptoe past the oversize kitchen and living room and head toward the stairs. I replay the instructions in my head: *Enter the residence through the back door, which will be unlocked. Head up to the second floor, first bedroom on your left. You must convince Lennon to get in your car. We don't care how. Drive back to your house and send visual confirmation when it's done.*

Lennon. I imprint the name in my head, try to figure out how I'm not going to scare the shit out of some innocent little kid, convince them that even though I'm in their house, I'm not dangerous.

Lulu's face flashes like a neon sign in my head. Yes, I would do anything for my daughter, but this is a line I'm not sure I can cross. With one foot in front of the other, I pad noiselessly up the carpeted stairs and pause on the landing. My ears listen for danger or warning signs. There are none. Pushing forward, I walk three steps and approach the first door on the left. I press my ear to the cold wood but don't hear anything. A low light leaks from beneath the door. A night-light, maybe?

Taking a silent breath, I turn the knob and push. The door creaks loudly. I flinch again and expect an outraged parent with a baseball bat to barrel down the hall in protest, but still nothing. I pan the bedroom, and that's when I see a body, face down on the bed. For a terrifying moment, I think the girl is dead.

Then I see movement: a tapping foot, a ponytail covered by oversize headphones, a head bobbing to the music she's probably listening to. Her thumb scrolls through her phone.

So, not a little kid, then.

My eyes sweep around the low light of her room while she doesn't know I'm standing here. There are trophies on every spare surface and medals hanging from all her walls; leotards balled in random piles; hair spray and barrettes littered across the vanity, along with spare candy wrappers. This girl is a *gymnast*?

I feel like I've been slugged in the face. What is going on? I can't do this. I can't be here. There's got to be another way. Just as I step backward to exit her room, Lennon flips to her back, sits up, and screams when she sees me.

Her chest expands and contracts as she scurries back against her bed, knocking her head against the wall. "Why are you in my room?" She rips her headphones off and rubs the back of her skull with a fist.

Her eyes are determined, but her voice trembles. Staring into her young face catapults me back to a place I don't want to go. Memories usher themselves in, one by one. Another world. Another life. Another era.

I fumble for what to say. How can I possibly explain to a stranger why I'm standing in her room? "I didn't mean to scare you," I say. "I'm . . ."

Her entire face changes as she slides her legs straight and scoots to the edge of her mattress. "Wait. You're Cora Valentine! That gymnast!"

That gymnast. It's never Cora the Olympian or Cora, part of the Magnificent Eight, or Cora the author. No, it's Cora, *that gymnast.* That gymnast who got kidnapped. That gymnast who saved her team at the Olympics. That gymnast who ran away from the limelight and hasn't been heard from since.

"You're, like, famous," she breathes.

I try to keep my movements casual, though I feel like I'm on the verge of having an actual heart attack. "Well, that was a long time ago."

She gestures around her. "Why are you here? Did my mom send you?"

I almost ask her who her mother is, but if I do that, then she'll really know I'm a total stranger standing in her house.

Before she can speak, her phone dings, and she reaches for it. She laughs and texts something back. Now's my moment. To say I've come to the wrong address, fly down the steps, get back in my car, and drive straight to Officer Bishop. Even as I think it through, the risks outweigh my rational brain.

"She did," I hear myself say slowly now, calling her attention back. "Your mom. She sent me."

She rolls her eyes. "Figures." She tosses her phone on the bed and stretches her arms above her head. "I told her I was too old to trick-or-treat, but she thinks I'm, like, pathetic or whatever. But I hate Halloween."

"I hate Halloween too," I say honestly.

"So why are you in my house?" She crosses her arms over her curvy chest and taps her bare foot on the carpet. I can see the outline of a bra beneath her T-shirt, and my heart kicks. Back then, I begged my mom for a training bra. Of course I didn't need one, because I was nothing but muscle, but I remember just wanting something as simple as boobs, or curves, or my period.

I smear away the unnecessary memory and refocus. Lennon is chewing gum, and it reminds me of Jessie. Such bravado for such a young kid. She probably thinks she has the whole world at her fingertips, that it will always be this way: gymnastics meets, long practices, gold medals, and girls who pretend to be your friends. But one injury, and she's done. One bad performance, and it's over. Say or do the wrong thing, and all her hopes are dashed. And as she continues to grow, she won't get as much air. Her landings will be harder. Gravity will take on a different meaning. It's such a conditional sport, I realize now. I don't know how any of us survived it.

"Your mom set up a surprise for you," I say, thinking on my feet. "A gymnastics surprise."

Her eyes flicker with interest, but she says nothing. Her tiny nostrils flare. She is a pretty enough girl, but I can see all the ways she will change: how her face and body will continue to fill out when she doesn't have six-hour practices and isn't chained to a diet, and how she will fight it every step of the way. How her joints will hurt in unimaginable ways, and one day, she will no longer have the urge to do cartwheels or flips. This, perhaps, is the biggest letdown of them all: not wanting to flip.

"What does that mean?"

"She wants me to help you with your routines." Though I'm just guessing, I can see I've hit the jackpot.

"She wants you to help me with my routines . . . on Halloween?" Her thick eyebrows knit together.

"Well, no," I say, trying to spin some sort of truth. "I was supposed to come in this morning, but something came up. She told me to come anyway. Trials are soon, right?"

She snaps her gum loudly and nods. "Yeah. Right around the corner."

"How old are you?" I ask.

"Thirteen."

Jesus. She looks older. Everyone's maturing at a more rapid pace than they used to. So I guess puberty isn't a deal-breaker, like it was in the '90s. That's some kind of progress, at least.

I berate myself for even thinking such idiotic thoughts and try to figure out what I'm even doing. The text said to take her back to my house. "So you're up for it? To chat about your routines?"

I can see her wavering: hang out with some old, washed-up Olympian on Halloween or stay here alone. Before I say more, she shrugs. "I'm not doing anything tonight, anyway. My parents are at a party."

I need to find out who her parents are, and quickly, but I'm more interested in getting her out of this house before they return. I glance around her room, but there are no photos of her family in here. This room is a shrine dedicated only to her sport. Just like mine used to be.

"Wait." She looks at me before pulling on her other sneaker. "Do I need a leo?"

I hesitate. It is clear I have zero intention of actually helping this kid with gymnastics when I'm supposed to be getting my daughter back, but I decide to placate her. "Sure, if you want."

I can see the other questions on the tip of her tongue: Where are we going? What can she possibly learn from me?

I exit her room and think fast on the way downstairs. At the entrance to the living room, my eyes sweep over the walls and shelves, looking for visual clues as to whose family she belongs to. Lennon is right behind me, and I'm turning the corner to head out the back door when I realize I have no reason to tell her why I've parked a street over.

"You know what?" I say, covering my ass. "Do you have any tapes of your routines you want to grab?"

She laughs. "You mean *video*? Yeah, they're all on my phone."

"Oh, right." *Think, Cora!* "Is your gym nearby?"

"Yeah." She snaps a large bubble by sucking in rapidly. "Woodward's. Why?"

Of course. Just hearing the name of my old gym does funny things to my insides. "Do you have a key?" It's a long shot, but a lot of the girls are given keys so they can train at off-hours.

"No, but I know the code."

Tricky. On one hand, moving to neutral territory could be advantageous. On the other, changing plans could be dangerous. "Why don't we head there first so you can show me your routines? That's better than watching videos."

"Right now?" There's a hint of excitement in her voice, and I nod.

"Grab your stuff. I'll meet you out front."

She sprints back up the stairs, and I pull out my phone, hesitating only for a second.

Change of plans, I type to the enemy on the other end of this text chain. We aren't going to my house. We're going to Woodward's. Bring the next clue to me.

14

Then

I'm going to die.

I'm going to die at fourteen. I'm going to die a virgin with no real friends. I'm going to die before I reach my full potential.

The depressing thoughts poisonously drip through my veins. *Drip, drip, drip.* I taste the blood from my split lip. Whatever they have over my head is itchy, like a burlap sack. My wrists ache, the plastic biting into my flesh. I can smell one of the men, that familiar scent of pine and patchouli mixing with something more pungent, like sweat.

The van races through the city streets, and I bump and jostle on the ground. No one says a word. Though I have been trained to stay calm in high-stakes situations, I've never experienced anything like this. My heart punches against my sweater and begins skipping beats, just like it does from the diet pills.

Oh God, I'm actually going to die.

The stark reality smacks me in the face again until my tears mingle with the sharp tang of blood. I choke on my own snot and begin to cough, sucking the thick, rough fabric into my mouth so that it feels like I'm being gagged.

Panic riots in my chest like a swarm of bees, and with my hands tied behind me, I start to hyperventilate and buck my legs. It feels like drowning. Or suffocating. I literally can't breathe.

Bright spots dance in front of my face, tiny black flecks that shift behind closed eyes. I cough and convulse until I'm so lightheaded, my body begins to tingle, and I start to fly away. Perhaps this is for the best. I'll die now, before they can torture me. I won't have to feel anything.

The driver hits a pothole, and I'm momentarily airborne before slamming into the side of the van. My head knocks violently against the metal side. My temple throbs while my skirt hitches up toward my hips, my panties on display to those two perverts. With my bound hands, I attempt to tug the skirt down, but my fingers won't reach.

Despite panicking, I *am* still breathing, I realize. I begin to slow the cadence just like Luke showed me in the haunted house. How I would give anything to be back there right now. But I'm not. So I squeeze my eyes shut and force myself to calm down. I am alive. I am okay. I'm not going to die.

Yet.

The van cranks to a halt, and I wonder if this is it. They're going to rip off my hood and shove a blade through my gut, twisting it like I've seen in horror movies. Or they're going to take turns molesting me. I clamp my knees together as every part of me begins to quiver. Before I can ponder what's going to happen to me, the van peels off again, and I realize we must have only stopped at a red light.

There are so many ways a body can shut down, but there are more ways one can be tortured while kept alive. I just hope, if they do torture me, that I'm not conscious while they do it. Tears continue to leak down my face as I replay tonight's events.

I should have just called for help and gone back to the girls. Maybe this is my punishment for the way I talked to Jessie. Maybe this is my punishment for showing up at all, when I never wanted to come in the first place.

A whimper escapes my throat. I sound like a strangled animal. I sound like a wimp.

I close my eyes and pray like I've never prayed before.

If a miracle exists, maybe I can find a way to stay alive.

15

Now

I don't know what I'm doing.

I'm coercing a girl from her home, and she has no idea why. Filled with guilt, I pull the truck to the curb just as Lennon rushes out the front door.

I check for neighbors, but everything seems quiet. After shooting Joe a quick text of the altered plan, I tell him to keep an eye out. If someone else is tailing me, maybe he can grab a license plate or something useful for us to go off of.

Lennon climbs into the truck and glances around, her eyes snagging on the car seat in the back. "You got kids?"

The tears sting my eyes again before I can stop them, but I clear my throat, thankful that it's dark. "A daughter. She's four."

"She tumble?" Lennon clicks her seat belt into place as we take off down the road.

"Nope. Not interested." What I really mean to say is *I'm* not interested. I never want her part of the sport that almost destroyed me. Not if I can help it.

Lennon rambles on, unprompted, about tricks she's working on. I try to pay attention, but all I can think about is what I've just done. I've taken a child from her home without her parents' consent. Does that make me just like these people? Lennon asks me something, and I try to steer my thoughts back to harmless territory.

"What did you say?"

"What was your hardest trick?"

"Triple full." Now that's small potatoes compared to what these girls are doing. Gymnastics is almost unrecognizable to what it used to be. It's clear I'm going to have to act my ass off if I need to pretend to be any help at all.

As I make a sharp right and head onto the main road, I kill the instinct to check my phone. What if they hurt Lulu because I've changed plans? What if they don't bring the next clue to me like I asked?

I'm terrified of taking the wrong next step. But I'm also not stupid. It's clear these people need something from me, though if it's training an Olympic hopeful, they have seriously overestimated my skill set. I gave up gymnastics and all that goes with it a long time ago. Whoever did this should know that.

Luckily, the gym is close. I drive there from memory, with so much of my life tied to this one place. When we arrive, I'm already exhausted from being in the presence of a chatty teenager. It's like listening to a foreign language. I shove the truck into park and glance around the desolate parking lot. From the outside, the gym looks the same as it always did: an old warehouse converted to hold all the necessary equipment to build potential future champions. I drove by it when I first moved back, which is when all the rumors started that I'd moved home to train Olympic hopefuls.

We walk swiftly to the glass door. I catch our reflections in the glass again and see something dash behind me.

I turn, but nothing's there. My heart thumps madly in my chest anyway as Lennon punches the code in and then tugs the door open. Once again, I hesitate. It's not too late to turn around, get in my car, and find Officer Bishop. But every time I even think of doing that, my mind snags on what the consequences will be.

Inside, I'm struck by the heady smell of the gym: chalk dust, sweat, ropes, and bare feet. It's been decades since I've set foot in this place, and for a moment, I'm immobilized by memory. No, this isn't the 1990s, but it might as well be. It's as familiar to me as breathing.

The front desk is larger than it used to be and has a glass display case with crowded trophies and medals. Lennon walks assuredly ahead of me, flipping on overhead lights. The violent fluorescents jolt me awake, stronger than a cup of coffee.

"I'm just going to change," she says, heading to the back with her duffel slung over one shoulder.

I nod and take in the open space. The floor is white, not blue like it used to be, and the vaults are a completely different shape, but the beam and bars are the same at least. This gives me comfort somehow; like, if I decided to hop up there, my body could still remember what to do. I take in the walls and freeze when I see posters of me with a gold medal around my neck. It makes sense. I was the first Olympian grown from this gym. My eyes pass over other familiar faces and then total strangers. I stopped following the sport a long time ago.

While Lennon is changing, I text Joe to ask if he saw anyone, but he assures me no one is tailing me and that he will stay close by. I let out a shaky breath. My limbs twitch to release some of this terror, so I take off my shoes and step onto the spongy floor. I find myself mindlessly rolling my ankles, wrists, and neck, as if I don't have control over my own body. It's so automatic, so ingrained, like muscle memory has hacked my brain.

I check to make sure Lennon is still in the back, resecure my gun, and do a few cartwheels and handstands. My keys fall out of my pocket, as well as my phone, and I kick them aside as something familiar throttles through my chest. I bounce up and down on my toes, stretch my shoulders, and do a few steps of my old floor routine. Of course, I'm not going to tumble, but as my muscles shake awake, I remember what a good dancer I was, how much rhythm and power I once had, which is why I placed so well on floor.

"That your old routine?"

Lennon startles me as she steps onto the floor in a slime-green leo, her muscles rippling beneath the shiny fabric as she stretches.

"Something like that." Suddenly, I feel embarrassed, ridiculous. My daughter is out there somewhere being held hostage, and I'm doing fucking cartwheels? What is *wrong* with me? But this is what I used to do. Gymnastics was like an antidote to stress. A way to turn off my brain and let my body take over. It's why I constantly practiced, at home, in my yard, at the gym, and in my mind. It became an obsession, really. Routines gave me a sense of safety. When I wasn't tumbling or practicing, anything could happen.

"I've watched all your tapes," she says a little shyly. "Your height on floor and vault was sick."

I don't dispute it, because it's true. It's still a natural talent that might hold up today. I could generate more height than any gymnast of my time, which often led to rock-solid landings. While there were many things that could go wrong in gymnastics, there was rarely a landing I couldn't stick.

"Want to show me what you got?"

"Sure. Should we start with floor?"

I nod and take a seat at the edge, my eyes scanning the door and windows. Could someone be out there, watching? I turn my attention back to the floor. Gymnasts must tumble corner to corner, on a diagonal, and sometimes, with so much power generated, a gymnast can easily fly out of bounds, which causes a deduction.

Everything I once loved comes back to me now in a flurry. Maybe I've been doing the wrong thing by keeping Lulu away from here. I haven't even told her I was a gymnast, haven't told her about gymnastics at all, in fact. But am I doing that for her or for me?

Lennon walks over to an ancient stereo and plugs in her phone with a USB cord. Some modern beat blasts through the speakers as she sprints to get in place and then begins. I find myself holding my breath as I watch her, worried that she hasn't properly warmed up. But if I was nervous about not having anything to offer, now, as I watch, I am judging everything: her own sense of rhythm, which is just slightly off; her toes, which are a hair shy of pointing to their fullest extent; her own power, which pops her out of bounds twice. As I assess, I realize she's got the goods, but something is missing. There's no heart or soul here, no passion. And that can't be taught.

My phone vibrates in my pocket, and I swallow the lump in my throat. Lennon is just about to perform her last tumbling pass, but this is too important. I glance at my phone, and my skin grows cold when I read the next set of instructions:

Make sure she can't compete. Get it done.

I reread the message, stunned. Does this mean what I think it means?

I almost laugh in disbelief as I shove the phone back into my pocket. They don't want me to help Lennon become a champion, I realize.

They want me to take her out.

16

Then

It feels like we drive for hours, but I can't really tell.

I stay alert for sounds. If I can get any sort of clue about where I am or who I'm with, I might have some infinitesimal chance at surviving.

Infinitesimal: exceedingly small or minute.

I repeat random other words and definitions in my head, but they all scramble together. The distraction allows my emotions to shut off, like a faucet. It's what I do in competition. I don't feel. I don't think. I just let my body remember.

I can't think about what might happen once we stop driving. Real dread slithers across my skin like a hostile snake, and I squeeze my knees together again as I begin to tremble. The thought of one of these strange men touching me or doing inappropriate things . . . *no.* I've never so much as kissed anyone.

I say a silent prayer that this won't end with me in a body bag. I'm not going to be pillaged, assaulted, or cut up into tiny pieces. I'm not going to be turned into some teenage cautionary tale or a bad made-for-TV movie. Not me. Not today. I'm Cora Valentine, an Olympic hopeful. I get straight As. I follow directions. This cannot be how my story ends.

I miss my parents.

The faucet turns back on, and everything floods in. A slingshot of memories hurtles through my brain. Hot tears and snot drip into my gaping mouth under the scratchy hood. The men are silent, but I can still smell one of them, that scent so familiar it distracts me just long enough for the tears to stop.

Before I can make sense of anything, the van screeches to a halt, and I buck forward. My shoulder blades pinch together due to the uncomfortable angle they've tied my hands. My head aches where I smacked it.

I try to breathe in and out through my nose again, but I can't. Instead, I'm panting, and I can feel myself preparing to beg for my life. I know that has probably never worked in the history of any person getting taken, but my survival instinct kicks in stronger than anything else.

The back door opens, and I'm jerked to my feet. My body convulses in fear. The men don't make a sound, but there's one on each side of me. My feet drag behind me as I'm lowered roughly to the earth. The cold bites into my exposed skin. I try to figure out anything about where I am, but I can't see a thing. Their strong hands twist into my flesh like rope burns.

I bite my sore lip and will myself to stay quiet. Not being able to see makes everything scarier. I count my steps from the curb or driveway to wherever it is we're going. Fifty steps. We head down a flight of stairs. Ten steps. Am I going to a basement?

Oh God. I hate basements. Ours is so dark and creepy, I've been down there exactly twice in my entire life. The men pause. I hear a set of keys. So I'll be locked in? Hopefully that means they aren't going to torture and kill me first.

I can't tame the absurdity of my own thoughts. This is happening. This is *real.* I think about kicking one of them and trying to run, but I don't know if they have guns. And not being able to see would render me almost completely helpless.

Helpless: unable to help oneself; weak or dependent.

Instead of making a move, I just stand there, trembling and cold, my teeth chattering loudly underneath the hood. After a moment, I'm shoved inside a room. I smell mildew. It's warm, at least. One of them cuts my hands free, and instead of going on the attack, I stand there dumbly. There's the click of the door being shut again, keys shoved into a lock from the outside, and then nothing. I wait for a moment, uncertain of what's going to happen next, before ripping the hood off my head and sucking in full breaths. My eyes itch from the hood, and I scrub my fingers over my skin. After a few moments, I blink into the darkness.

There's no light, and it takes my eyes a moment to adjust. It's a small room. There's a mattress shoved against the back wall, a tiny door I pray is a bathroom, and the main door I just entered through. The whole place is no bigger than a bedroom. A sliver of moonlight shines through a window that's too high to reach.

Stupidly, I try the door, but, of course, it's locked. I run my fingers along the seam of the lock, then find the hinges at the edge of the door. I wonder if I could somehow pry them off?

My mind starts to settle for a moment. I know once the adrenaline leaves, I'm going to want to sleep. But there's no way I'm sleeping. Not when my life is at stake.

I shuffle to the other door. Inside is a small bathroom with a toilet, a sink, and a grimy shower. There's a single bar of soap, still in its wrapper. How long do they plan on keeping me here?

I begin to quiver again as I enter the main part of the room and lower myself to the mattress. There's no sheet but a thin, scratchy blanket, which I wrap around me now. It smells old and musty, just like this room. I reach into my pocket for my worry doll but find that she's not there.

"No, no, no." I turn the pockets of my jacket inside out and realize it must have flown out in the van. It's such a small thing, losing that doll, but it's a tether to home, a way to stay calm in an impossible situation.

My eyes fill with tears again. I think about my parents—my father in particular. What will happen when I don't come out of the haunted house? When they can't find me? There will be panic. I can see the headlines now: Olympic Hopeful Cora Valentine Disappears on Halloween. It's probably every parent's worst nightmare.

I swallow the lump in my throat and vow to stay strong. If I can keep myself together mentally, maybe there's some small chance I'll get out of this alive.

But first, I have to survive the night.

17

Now

The routine ends, and Lennon jogs over to stop the music.

She's panting hard but seems pleased enough. I try to arrange my game face and forget what I just read in that text. I assumed her parents could somehow be involved in this . . . now, it seems it could be a jealous competitor. Or another gymnast's parents. The familiarity of my own story rears its ugly head. I've always thought whoever kidnapped me wanted to take me out of the Olympics, but their plan backfired.

Not only did I qualify, but all of America rooted for me. It was a story I would have done anything to undo, of course, but this whole thing is striking a bit too close to home. Someone is either trying to copycat my kidnapping or has a serious vendetta against Lennon's parents.

Or maybe it's the same people who took me.

I catch my breath as that possibility clicks into place. They never found who took me, and after a while, the case went cold. But I haven't forgotten. I've *never* forgotten. How could I? Every place I've lived, every job I've taken, every phase of life I've endured has been like running from an abusive ex-lover. No matter how far I go, I never feel completely safe. Which is why I came home. I got tired of running. And now it seems they've found me anyway.

Whatever this is, or whoever is responsible, I have to figure out who Lennon's parents are and what enemies they have. Because there's no way that I'm injuring this girl. I know how devastating that can be. On cue, my knee aches, and I massage it absentmindedly. Lennon notices.

"Well"—I clear my throat—"your power is both a gift and a curse. I was the same way."

She rolls her eyes and takes a long sip of water from her squeeze bottle that has the gym's logo on it. "Tell me about it."

I go down the list of things she did well—good timing, strong tumbling, decent showmanship—but then I fill her in on what could be improved. Instead of whining, she nods, seeming to take mental notes.

"Again?"

I'm surprised she wants to do her routine again so soon, but I nod. "Actually, let's work on it in chunks. Take it after the first tumbling pass. Let's focus on your toes and putting some feeling into it."

"Feeling?" She's already walking back over to her phone. I join her so I can press play.

"Yes, feeling." I search for the right way to connect. "For instance, tell me why you picked this song."

"I like it," she says, cueing it back up on her phone.

"But that's not enough," I say. "Music has the opportunity to make people feel something, right? A mood. An emotion. A memory. You want the audience to experience every move, to hold their breath on each tumbling pass. You want to tell them a story they never want to end." I'm saying all the same things my coach said to me. Lennon's eyes are glued to my face. "Does that make sense?" I add.

"Yeah. I think I picked this for speed, but what about . . ." She flicks through an approved list. "This was the other song I wanted, but then a guy I liked started hooking up with my friend, and I listened to this, like, a million times, so it made me sad for a while." She rolls her eyes as her cheeks redden.

"So use it," I say, asking for the phone. "That sadness. Show me exactly how that feels." As she gets into position, I ignore the itch to scroll through her texts and photos. "Ready?"

She gets into position, splayed on the floor with her back arched and her arms crossed in front of her. Her legs are crossed, too, toes now perfectly pointed. When I press play, she springs to life, and despite this insane situation—my daughter is missing, and I have no earthly idea what I'm doing here or why—my mind focuses as I watch her. The song changes everything. She takes my notes, absorbs them, and infuses more feeling into the routine than I anticipated. She's looser with her dance moves and more accurate with her tumbling. When she's done, I release a deep breath as she jogs over, a silly grin plastered to her face.

"I've never done my routine like that," she says, almost in a state of disbelief. "That felt way different."

"Who's your coach?"

She makes a face. "Ryan Specter. He was a gold medalist like a gazillion years ago. I think, like, right after you? He's *so* stuck in the past. We finally got him to bring in a choreographer from this century to help us at least."

I try not to take the dig personally. I'm also an ancient gymnast in her eyes. I shuffle through my memory. Ryan Specter. The guy who grabbed my waist at the haunted house? The cocky gymnast. He made it to the Olympics four years after me.

A small protectiveness flares. With the right coaching, this girl could actually *make* it. I shake my head and remind myself that I'm not a damn gymnastics coach, and after tonight, I'll hopefully never see Lennon again.

"Let's do it one more time," I say. "Make your body remember."

I watch her with a little more detachment as I think through my next steps. These people want me to injure Lennon, but all I can think about is Lu. It's well past her bedtime, and my heart nearly capsizes. Where is she? Has she eaten? Is she cold? Is she being mistreated? My stomach bucks in protest as I think about anyone hurting my sweet-natured daughter.

As she completes her routine for the third time, I shove the heels of both hands into my eyes and vigorously rub. The chalk dust is getting to me, just as it always did as a gymnast.

Next, we move to vault. She adjusts it to the proper height. I think back to the Olympics when Kerri Strug destroyed her ankle but clinched the gold with her full-twisting layout. It was a sensational moment for our team, but it also prevented her from competing in the individual competition, which is where I stepped in and won gold. I'm curious to see what vault Lennon throws, as I know it will be a million times harder than anything I've ever attempted.

She sets up silently, adjusting the board, chalking her hands, and then doing some practice runs. Sprinting toward the vault used to be my favorite part of gymnastics. Vault isn't something I could ever think about—exactly where to put my hands, or even *how* my body could do a roundoff back handspring onto an object so far off the ground. It defied gravity, and yet somehow, I could do it. It was the one apparatus where I could simply switch off my brain and *go*.

As I watch Lennon now, she does some ungodly number of twists and flips and pops out of bounds. There's that power again.

I hold tight to the image of Lulu, asleep and safe, to keep my mind focused on the task at hand.

"Again," I say, as if I've been trained to do this. Watching her now gives me a small pause. Why *didn't* I ever devote time to helping other gymnasts? I certainly could have. Instead, I just ran away, hiding from my own fame and success, almost apologizing for it. I thought that part of my life was over because it represented so much pain. But instead of hurting now, all these years later, I find that I do have an eye for this. I know what I'm talking about, and it's just like riding a bike, even if the bikes are bigger, harder, and faster. But it's still a bike.

"You're popping off the horse just a touch too late," I say. "Come off a second before you think you have to." Telling her to release her hands before it feels safe to do so seems counterproductive. Yes, it can make all the difference, but once you've trained your body to do something, it's hard to undo.

"Got it." She preps herself at the end of the runway by extending her arms above her head, pulling them to her chest, twisting, and mumbling to herself. All gymnasts, when you come down to it, are the same. Endless hard workers. Tough. Sometimes superstitious. And usually there's a world of physical and mental hurt lurking beneath those bright leotards and tight ponytails.

Before I can say anything encouraging, she's off again, hitting the horse at the exact right angle. I hold my breath as she pops off just a second sooner, spinning and rotating through the air with perfect precision. The hard smack of her ankles against the mat makes me wonder if I'll get lucky, if she'll naturally roll an ankle or injure herself just because it's late and she's not properly warmed up. But that's not what happens. Instead, she sticks the landing.

She turns to me, mouth twisted into an astonished grin. "I think I just found my secret weapon," she says. "You're way better than Coach Specter."

Despite this insane situation, it's nice to receive the compliment. Maybe in another life, I could have found my way here, but this isn't another life. I'm not a young, naive gymnast who thinks my life is going to be great. I've lived a thousand lives since then, and gymnastics no longer fits.

I tell Lennon to take a quick break and excuse myself to the bathroom. Under the bright lights, I take a snapshot of the cryptic text and send it to Joe, then type back a reply to the kidnappers:

Not happening. Come up with a new plan.

I know I'm in no position to say what I will or won't do, but I would never purposely injure an athlete.

Take Lennon out or we take Lulu out, someone types back almost immediately. The choice is yours. And if you need a little incentive, there's a reminder on your truck.

My fingers freeze on my phone. I catch my own terrified reflection in the mirror, then burst out of the bathroom and tell Lennon I have to grab something from my truck. Outside, I check the barren parking lot, expecting someone to jump out. My truck sits alone in the abandoned lot. I can hear my own shallow breath as I approach it slowly, panning left and right, not knowing what I'm going to see. My breath clouds in front of me, then evaporates.

At the truck, I inspect the tires and the bed, peer through the glass inside the cab, and circle toward the front. Once again, there's something trapped beneath the windshield wiper. Another Polaroid. I pluck it free and shine my phone light on it so I can see in the dark.

"Oh my God." I smother my words behind my palm as I slap it against my mouth. It's another photo of that creepy doll, still dressed like Lulu, except now it's missing its left eye.

My phone buzzes in my hand.

Get it done, or your precious daughter loses more than just an eye.

A primal sob flies up my throat and echoes around the empty parking lot. The asphalt tilts as I grapple for balance. I slump against the truck. They took her *eye*? No.

I spin off the hood, tears hot on my cheeks, rage a festering knot in my gut. They're watching me right now. They have to be. I search every possible place I can think of, but I don't see anyone. The gravity of this night and what's at stake comes fully into focus. Faith was right. I should have gone to the police first. But maybe then they would have done something even worse.

I brace a hand against the truck. Another buzz in my pocket. I don't want to look. I feel sick.

Tick tock, Cora, the next text says. We're waiting.

Enraged and disgusted, I walk back to the gym. *Lulu.* They have tortured my child. And now I have to hurt Lennon.

75

I put on my best game face and point to beam. "Let's see what you've got there, hotshot." My voice is shaky, but Lennon doesn't seem to notice.

I know, even as she trots over and begins chalking certain spots on the beam, that if an injury is to happen, this is one of the easiest places to do it. And because she's not hurtling ten feet in the air like on floor, maybe it won't be as devastating. Enough just to placate these psychopaths to stop hurting my daughter.

"You ready?" She hops onto the beam and gets into position.

I lick my lips, my mouth suddenly parched. All I can think about is the image of that doll, one of its eyes plucked clean.

Am I ready?

I have no choice.

I nod, and she begins.

18

THEN

The night is endless.

My eyes are gritty from being awake so long, and my body seems to have a mind of its own. Not knowing what's going to happen is worse than any torture I can possibly imagine. My brain runs through worst-case scenarios every five seconds, and I can't seem to focus long enough to figure a way out of this mess.

There's no exit from the bathroom, and the main window is too high to reach. The main door seems to be my only hope, but there's literally nothing I can use to start working on the lock. I'm kicking myself for not having any bobby pins in my hair. I took them all out after the competition because they were giving me a headache.

But I need something sharp. I've run my fingers along the baseboards, trying to feel for a nail or screw. It seems they've swept the room completely of any potential weapons.

Left with time to think, I just can't make sense of any of it. Why me? Why that van? It's like they *knew* I'd be standing there . . . though *I* didn't even know I'd be standing there until I decided to step outside. Could the men in the haunted house have set it up? Lou Matheson with his sad nameplate, baby face, and cryptic phone call? Could he have shown me that side exit because he knew what was waiting for me on the other side?

Is this about money . . . or something else?

I grip my head. It pounds from lack of water and food. Food! I look up. They'll have to bring me something to eat, won't they? I shiver in my clothes. If they want to keep me alive, they will. What if they starve me? What if I'm just going to die a slow death no matter what? I almost laugh. My current diet is pretty much like starving anyway.

Something sparks in my head as I think of the gym. I'm so close to all my dreams . . . What if I don't get out of here in time for trials? I scurry to my feet as the thought lands. What if I die and I never get to show everyone what I've really got? What if all I've worked for the last decade disappears along with me?

Outrage as hot as an ember launches through my chest. It overrides the fear of not knowing. It masks any worry about what those two men might do. This is gymnastics we're talking about, my entire world. I have to get out of here. There has to be a way—

The lock jiggles, and I fly back against the wall, flattening myself in the shadows. I scan the area for a weapon again, but other than the space heater, I am totally defenseless.

The door squeaks open, and a tall man in a mask stands there, panting from the cold night. He is shapeless in the shadows, but I can see his breath whip into the room through his mask's mouth hole, moving toward me like smoke. There's something in his hands, but I can't see what.

Oh God, oh God, oh God.

He takes a step forward, and I try not to breathe. I don't know if he can see me. Will he speak? Should I?

I watch the door. Did he relock it behind him? Could I somehow knock him down and make a run for it?

His masked face disappears from sight as he lowers himself into a deep squat and then shuffles back toward the cracked door. He shuts it behind him, and I take off running, then grab the doorknob. He hasn't locked it yet, and I wrench it to the left. Surprisingly, it twists open in my hand. He stands on the other side, shock in his eyes as I stare up at him in the full moonlight. I tell myself to move, to scratch his eyes out, to *go*, but after a moment, he shoves me in the chest with the heel of his hand, hard, and I fall back inside onto the floor as he slams the door and locks it from the outside.

My chest aches, and my breath comes in rapid, audible gasps. I fling myself forward and bang my palm against the door anyway, knowing the louder I get, the angrier they'll probably be. When my voice tires, I rotate back to the middle of the room. What did he come in here for? I crawl around on my hands and knees and bump into a tray. My hands find a lumpy sandwich, an apple, and a bottle of water. Do I drink it? What if it's drugged?

I'm so thirsty, I don't care. I twist off the top of the bottle and suck half the water down in a greedy gulp. I know I need to save some in case they don't come again. The heater sputters behind me. If they wanted to torture me, why would they have this place heated? Why would they leave me a bar of soap and a blanket? What is actually going on?

I smell the sandwich: turkey and cheese. I haven't had a turkey sandwich in ages. I bite into it and moan. Mayonnaise coats my tongue. I pluck off the piece of cheese and roll it into a tight coil in my fingers, chomping it down in two large bites. I didn't realize how hungry I was . . . how hungry I always am. My stomach cramps as I finish the sandwich. I decide to save the apple for later.

I'm so used to rationing my food. Some of my teammates eat their meals and throw them back up again to stay thin. I hate throwing up, so instead, I have to make sure I pay attention to portions. We all have to keep journals, count calories, and get weighed daily. Our coach makes us, and my dad isn't much better, always reminding me that lighter is better for this sport.

It never makes sense because I always feel better if I can eat a good, healthy meal, like in the offseason. It gives me energy. And don't I need energy if I'm exercising all the time?

Rea Frey

I don't know why I'm thinking about any of this now. None of it matters if I don't survive. I need to think about getting out of here. I move back to the door to examine it. Maybe I can wait right here until they return. The man moved all the way inside before he shut it. Instead of trying to attack him, what if I just sneak out quietly the moment he steps inside?

I calculate the risk. It's high, but I might be able to pull it off.

I move to the right of the door so that when he opens it and the door swings to the left, I can slink out undetected. I glance at the bed, then rush over and arrange the blanket in a giant heap to make it look like a body.

After walking back to the door, I close my eyes.

The next time he comes, I'll be ready.

19

NOW

Beam is her best event. She doesn't waver, doesn't shake. Not even once.

I can feel time running out, the urgency of doing what these people say . . . *or else.* I motion to bars. "Are you too tired to show me your routine?"

"Nope. I'm just going to go grab my grips."

Once she's gone, I whip out my phone to see if they've sent me anything else. They haven't. I stare at the Polaroid again in utter disbelief.

As soon as Lennon reemerges, she unselfconsciously picks a wedgie, cementing her leotard back in place. I help her set the uneven bars and hesitate before I tighten the spread cuff. Now is my chance. Make a dumb mistake. Leave it loose. She gets hurt. I get my daughter back.

I hold my breath. Do I really think these people are going to return Lulu if I injure Lennon? It's like an invisible clock is ticking, and this is my last chance. But as I stare at her, at this young Olympic hopeful, even with my daughter's life hanging in the balance, I can't do it to her. I just *can't.* I'll get Lu back another way.

I tighten the bars and step back as she reaches into the chalk bowl and coats her grips. A cloud of white hides her face as she claps a few times. She adjusts the dowel and finger holes, takes a deep breath, and begins. *Here it is,* I think. *Her Achilles' heel.*

I know it even before she mounts the bars. It's not that she's bad, but she doesn't move with the same confidence or attack them like the other events. Her form breaks on more than one giant, and there are those damn flexed toes again. I clock the mistakes—one too many—but she still sticks the landing.

I don't say anything as she trots over, but I can tell she's not happy.

"So this is where we work," I confirm.

"I don't know why it doesn't come easy to me," she says. "But it just doesn't."

I place a hand on her shoulder. "Relax. Every gymnast has a weak spot. This is yours." I glance at my watch. "How about I go pick up some food, and by the time I get back, you tell me ten ways we can improve this."

"Got it, Coach."

What I really need is time to stall. Time to think. Time to ensure these people don't do anything else to Lulu. I grab my keys next to her gymnastics bag and wave. "I'll be right back," I say.

When I'm in my truck, fingers trembling, I call Joe and tell him about the photo. He's gobsmacked into silence.

"They're probably watching me right now," I whisper. "They'll know I didn't hurt her."

"Of course you're not going to hurt her," he snaps. "God, this is just too much, Cora. I'm sorry."

I exhale. "Did you find anything useful?"

"Yep." I can hear him typing in the background. "Lennon Murphy. Thirteen. Originally from Atlanta, Georgia. Daughter of Jessica and Richard Murphy."

I freeze. "Jessica *Bateman*?" I ask, nearly breathless. "Is that her maiden name?"

My heart pounds in my ears as I wait.

"Affirmative," he says. "You know her?"

"She was my gymnastics team captain," I say. As soon as I saw Lennon, Jessie instantly popped into my mind. Now I know why. Jessie is her mother. Her career was ruined that Halloween night thirty years ago.

"Well, I guess someone has it in for her or her daughter," he says. "Wants to knock her off the competitive circuit."

"Which means," I continue, "that whoever is behind this is probably the parent of someone on her team." But could a parent assault a child? Who would do that? But still, hope bubbles in my chest. Maybe we can find who's responsible. Maybe this will all be over sooner than we think.

"I'll get you a list of the girls on the team. I'll text you when I have it."

I start the car and find the nearest drive-through. I don't know what kind of eating restrictions Lennon has, but hopefully what I grab will do. I'm back in the parking lot in minutes, and I take a moment to steady myself. It's late, I'm exhausted, and despite the situation, my stomach growls. My phone buzzes, and I jump, but it's just from Faith.

TELL ME WHAT IS HAPPENING!!! ANY UPDATES?

I ignore the text, then kill the engine and the headlights. I'm not sure how long Joe is going to take, but I head back inside to find Lennon still hard at work on bars. She definitely has a solid work ethic—I'll give her that.

I hoist up the take-out bag and shake it. The scent of burgers and fries fills the space, and she hops down and joins me on one of the benches. I expect her to ask what's in the bag, but she sinks into it with a mumbled thank-you and devours the food unselfconsciously. I got her a milkshake, too, which she slurps down in two minutes flat.

"Are you close to the girls on your team?" I ask, taking a sip of my own sickly sweet strawberry shake. I can barely choke it down, my stomach is in so many knots.

She shrugs. "Sometimes. There's this one girl, Kayla. She hates me."

"Why?"

"Because we're the two best girls on the team, and she thinks there's not room for both of us." Lennon's cheeks redden as she talks about it, and I wonder if there's more to the story than she's letting on.

"She probably gets that from her parents," I nudge. "That type of competitive spirit sometimes isn't even coming from the kid. It's learned."

83

She sucks on her straw and nods. "Maybe."

"What are her parents like?"

"I don't know," she says. "It's just her mom."

My phone buzzes. Not the burner. Dread pools in the pit of my stomach as I take it out and read the message.

Except it's not a message. It's a photo of another Polaroid, this time depicting the creepy doll with a missing left hand.

I cry out and slap a hand over my mouth, startling Lennon.

"Everything okay?"

I jump up, barely able to see through my tears. They can't do this. They *can't*.

You have five minutes to send visual confirmation that Lennon is hurt, or Lulu's foot is next.

They are dismantling my child, bit by bit, like some sort of horror movie. I glance out into the night, pressing my face against the windows, but the parking lot is bare.

"Is someone out there?" Lennon asks.

"Thought I heard something," I manage to choke out. I turn to her and do my best to rearrange my face to neutral. "Sorry. I just got some bad news." I wave the phone in the air and then pocket it. "How about we finish that routine?" The blood whooshes through my ears. I don't know how to do this.

"I need a few minutes," she says, patting her flat, muscular stomach. "I don't want to barf."

"That's fine," I say. "I need to make a quick phone call anyway."

I step outside. The cold sends a surge of chills through my body. Enough is enough. I can't just sit here waiting for texts and threats and warnings.

I take a breath and call the mystery number, expecting no one to answer, of course, but when I hear the voice on the other end, all the hairs on the back of my neck stand up.

"Hi, Cora," the voice says. "I was wondering when you'd call."

20

THEN

The minutes seem to creep by.

My stomach complains from the rush of processed food. I'm usually asleep by ten because I have to be up so early to train. Everything about tonight is wrong, and I worry it could be my last.

Even with that horrifying thought trampling my brain, I would still kill for a shower and a good night's sleep, but I know I have to stay awake. I have to wait for one of the men to come back so I can make my move.

I adjust next to the door and replay the events of tonight, from standing in line to losing the girls to Ryan grabbing my waist and Luke coming to my rescue. The girls making fun of him. Me snapping at Jessie. Jessie getting injured. Me running for help. Lou leading me out that side door. All seemingly random events that led me here, to this very room.

My eyes snake around the perimeter of the small space again. It is so dark, my eyes play tricks on me. Shadows seem to morph into shapes. I pull my knees to my chest and drop my cheek against them, nursing my swollen lip with my tongue. I've been injured plenty of times in gymnastics. I've had busted lips, a chipped tooth, sprained ankles, bruises, even slipped discs in my back.

As a doctor, my dad has told me horror stories about the things he's seen—girls who've landed wrong, girls who've broken their backs or their necks—but somehow, when I'm upside down with no safety net, I never feel scared.

Instead, I feel safe.

It's being here, feet firmly on the ground, that feels so unnatural. Even with how tired I am, I itch to move, to flip, to have some semblance of a normal routine. To distract myself, I spread my legs into a straddle and begin to go through my series of stretches and warm-ups—if nothing else, to increase body heat. Before I know it, a thin line of sweat trickles down my forehead. I move on to push-ups and crunches, my body so tired from what it's been through tonight I feel dizzy.

But I think about the calories I just ate and calculate how long I need to exercise to burn them off. It's hard having to stay so light, but I can't gain an ounce before trials. Even a pound can throw my weight off on bars or vault. I need to stay just as I am. I need to be lean.

I lose myself for what feels like an hour, moving until I'm spent, lying flat on my back on the mattress after. Instantly, I realize what a stupid idea this was. I need to preserve my energy, not drain it. I need to be prepared to fight or run.

My eyes keep tracking back to the door. What will I do the next time one of the men comes in? Looking at the door from here, I don't think it's likely I can just sneak out without him knowing. Despite being a gymnast, I don't know any self-defense. Maybe I can flip my way out of here? The preposterous thought almost makes me laugh out loud and brings me a bit of comfort. Man enters room. Girl takes off in a roundoff back handspring that connects with his face and knocks him out. Then she flips her way up the stairs and out into the unknown.

Faced with nothing else to do, I begin to gnaw on my nails and spit the tiny half moons onto the worn carpet. I shuffle closer to the heater and let the thin, warm air and gentle hum placate me somehow.

There's no getting out of this, a small voice says in the back of my mind. *You're going to die here.*

I shake my head and place my hands over my ears, as if I can cease my own thoughts. I have to stay strong. I have to stay alert. I begin reciting states in my head, first going alphabetically and then from *Z* back to *A* again. I recite them in English, then Spanish, then French, the monotonous memorization calming me just enough to regulate my breathing.

Once that's done, my mind begins to spin back to reality. What if they never come back? What if I starve to death? What if I die of thirst? What if the heater stops working and I freeze before they find me?

All at once, the calm I created vanishes. My breathing becomes shallow again, my fingers and toes twitching with worry. I move on to my cuticles, chewing them as if they have all the answers. They don't, and neither do I. The sharp tang of blood causes me to stop. I can't logic myself out of this one. I can't think my way to any sort of freedom.

I'm not sure what's worse: knowing what's coming next or not knowing. Either way, I'm trapped.

21

Now

It's the same voice from the 911 call, but I don't recognize her.

"Please don't hurt my daughter." My voice sounds weak, pleading.

"Too late," she snaps.

Even with the agony that statement brings, I try to place this mystery person. Who would harm a four-year-old? But I already know the answer to that. After my own kidnapping, I became obsessed with other kids who had been taken too. Apparently, there are all kinds of people who want to hurt children. I swallow the painful lump in my throat and continue. "Just tell me what you're really after."

After a beat, she responds. Her voice changes, deepens. "Your darling daughter is in a lot of pain, Cora, and I know you don't always follow directions, so know this: I'm not bluffing. Either injure Lennon, or Lulu is going to continue to get carved up like a fish. Three minutes." The line goes dead.

I stare at the phone, panting, and turn back to the gym. Inside, Lennon is making her way to bars.

I stand on the other side of the glass door, watching as she takes a breath and starts her routine, going over the first part a few times. I feel like I'm underwater, sinking faster and faster, when I need to stay afloat. I search my brain for any sort of memory of that woman's voice, but there's nothing. I've erased so much of my own life from those earlier years, sweeping it all under a rug I dare not lift.

With my hand on the door, I open it. The jingling bell seems to startle Lennon, but she continues circling around the top bar in a series of giants before doing an easy layout dismount. I calculate my options. I have mere minutes to make sure she falls off the bars or hurts herself some other way. I gnaw on my bottom lip as she turns, rechalks her hands, and then claps so the excess shakes off her grips.

"Can I see your routine?" My voice shakes. The three-minute countdown begins in my head, my heart pulsing wildly in my chest. I can feel it in my ears. She performs her routine on command. The skills are sloppy. Her toes flex, her form breaks. She sighs as she completes her dismount with a stumble and a hop.

I eye the bars. "Let's adjust the bars."

"Really?" She places her chalked hands on her hips. "Coach says this is where I need to be."

"Do you feel good about that routine?"

She rolls her eyes. "Well, no."

"Then let's adjust." I tell her we should lift up the high bar one notch. As I pull over a block to stand on and loosen the knob, I know that this is where I make my choice. This is where I cross the line or don't. Where I decide what Lulu's life is worth.

We lift up the high bar, but I don't let it click into place and only pretend to tighten the knob. I stand back, feeling like the worst human on earth. If she falls during her handstand, maybe it won't be so bad. Maybe nothing will happen at all.

But then where does that leave me?

I stand back and whip out my phone to press record. Lennon doesn't even look my way as she mounts the bars and goes through the motions. When she gets to high bar, I hold my breath as she completes one giant. At the top of her handstand, the right side of the bar slams down suddenly since it wasn't locked into place. She lets out a yelp of surprise but maintains her composure, though her form breaks. I keep recording as she arches her back in her handstand. Her legs bend to counterbalance, but she overcorrects. Before she can swing back down, her right hand slips from the bar, and she comes crashing down, but not before circling again and nailing her spine on the lower bar. She smacks the mat with enough force to knock the wind out of her. I press stop on my camera and sprint toward her, my heart in my throat.

The guilt is a hammer, pounding every inch of my flesh. Lennon's face is scrunched in agony, her eyes closed. I hurriedly shoot the video to the mystery number before dropping to my knees to assess.

"Lennon, are you okay? Can you move?" My words are a betrayal. *I* did this. This is all me.

The wind literally knocked out of her, I have to wait until she catches her breath. I examine her limbs. There's nothing at odd angles, thankfully. Finally, she rolls to her side and sits up, gingerly touching her back.

"How did that just happen?" She gasps.

"I have no idea," I lie.

She closes her eyes and pushes up to her hands and knees. Her stomach begins convulsing, and before I can offer her help to stand, she vomits up a chunky pile on the bright-blue crash mat.

"I shouldn't have eaten so much."

My guess is that she never eats like that at all. Suddenly, I'm furious. Furious at this night. Furious at Halloween. Furious at the enemy on the other end of my cell phone. Furious at a sport that makes its athletes eat, behave, and look a certain way when just *one* injury or mistake can render you completely obsolete. Furious that I can't save my daughter, that I have no idea where she is, that I might never see her again. Furious that I have just helped injure an innocent girl. Furious that my daughter is out there somewhere, hurt.

"Can you stand?"

"I don't think so."

I jog to the bathroom to get her a cold washcloth and fist a giant wad of paper towels to clean up the mess. My phone dings when I jog back to the bathroom to throw away the clumpy mess.

Good girl, Cora. Now take her to your cabin. Wait for next steps.

I almost chuck my phone against the mirror. I'm over this. I can't do this. I can't be part of this person's sick master plan. But what choice do I have? Back on the mats, I help Lennon to her feet. "How does your back feel?"

"Not good." All the color has drained from her face.

"Let's get some ice on it and let you rest. Your parents will pick you up from my place, okay?"

I can tell she's not really listening. Otherwise, why wouldn't I just bring her straight home? Why would she need to come to my house? I help her into the car and gun it back toward my cabin. I don't know what's awaiting me there, but it better be the final steps to get Lulu back. I did what these people asked. Now it's their turn to come through.

On the short drive back, Lennon doesn't say a word. I lower the window just in case she gets sick again. The cold air seems to help her queasiness.

"How's your back?"

"Hurts," she says. "But I'll be okay." There's a hardness I didn't see before, which tells me this isn't her first scare. It reminds me of when Jessie injured her knee—how she ignored it until she couldn't. How I'd done the same with my ankles and then the knee injury that eventually took me out. I knew it the moment it happened. My whole big sensational career deflated in on itself like a punctured parachute.

One moment I was on top of the world. The next, I was mostly irrelevant.

I've spent a lot of years in therapy trying to understand that very fact: how, when you're a professional athlete—an Olympian, no less—your life is up for public consumption. People can tack posters on their walls and put you on their cereal boxes and engage in heated conversations about your routines. Complete strangers watched me perform impossible feats in little more than a bathing suit and then stand on a podium, flashing my gold medal for all to see. There was such a sensational story attached to that win; it felt like America had survived what I survived. But no one knew the whole truth. No one knew what happened in that cabin. What I saw.

What I left behind.

Regardless of my secrets, I was a survivor. But then it all came crashing down like Lennon from high bar.

I kill the headlights as we bump into my driveway. My eyes pan protectively over the trees, just as they always do. Part of me expects Lulu to come banging out the front door, shouting, "Surprise, Mama!" What I wouldn't give for this to be some cruel prank.

The cabin is dark and ominous. Once I park, I rush to the passenger side of the truck to help Lennon down. She hobbles, crooked over like an old woman, and the mother in me really hopes she's okay. Inside, I can still smell the fire I burned earlier today. It's cold, so I get Lennon situated on the couch and then quickly start another one, though I'm not sure how long we'll be here.

"Your place is cozy," she says, taking it in. "Like stepping back in time."

"I like simple," I say. Isn't that an understatement. One of my shrinks thought my subconscious literally got stuck in the 1990s, which is why I'm so resistant to technology and the fast pace of modern-day life. It's not that my maturity got stuck. It's that my whole life went from building toward this one thing to receiving it in an unpredictable way, and then, once it was over, it never dawned on me to build a new life with new interests. Though I tried. But I could only remember the girl I was. I was defined only by what happened to me *then*. There was no after. Not until Lu.

My mind is like a Ping-Pong ball being whipped back and forth across a table. It's clear I'm not focused, and I need to be. I get her some ice for her back, make both of us some hot tea, and scan the room, looking for more clues. A card knifed to a wall. Another terrifying photo. The next reminder of what's at stake. But the place seems untouched.

"Where's your daughter?" Lennon asks.

Her words are like a blade. "With a friend," I hear myself say. I want to scream at her that this is deeper than she can possibly know, that there's real danger here and she could be the key to getting my daughter back. Before I can say more, she changes subjects.

"Tell me about that night." She shifts again and groans in pain. "The night you were taken."

Not this again. Though I haven't talked about it in years, it's still all there, as fresh as if it just happened. I hesitate. "What do you want to know?"

I squeeze a healthy amount of honey into our tea, add a splash of cream, and bring one over to her. She murmurs a thank-you.

She takes a tentative sip of the scalding tea. "Were you scared?"

"Of the kidnapping or the Olympics?"

She shrugs. "Both."

"Shitless," I respond. "It's hard to describe."

"Will you try?" She suddenly seems like a little girl in need of a bedtime story. I check the time—late—and know I have to bide my time until these freaks give me my next clue. Maybe if I tell her something, she can tell me something. A trade, of sorts, until I can figure out who's on the other end of my phone.

"Well, which do you want? The Olympics or the kidnapping?"

"Let's start with the kidnapping," she says. "And how you escaped."

22

THEN

I wait all night by the door, but no one ever comes.

I'm too afraid to move or even blink. The sun is just rising, and I take advantage of the early-morning light to absorb my surroundings more fully. The room is mostly like I envisioned last night. My eyes drift up to the window above me again. If only there was a way I could reach it . . . as I stand, my body aches all over. I'm not sure if I've ever stayed up the entire night before.

The room is quiet. The coils from the heater burn orange in the soft glow of morning. My eyes linger on the tray from last night. There's a plate from my sandwich and apple. I rush forward to examine it. Is it plastic? I turn it over in my hands. It's real. Maybe I could break it and use a jagged edge as a weapon? Even as I think about it, I falter. Could I *really* stab someone? Am I even strong enough? I glance around. If anything breaks, I'm sure someone would hear.

I'm desperate for a shower, but there's no way I'm getting naked in a place where two grown men could barge in on me at any second. I examine the bathroom door, but there's no lock. Of course there isn't.

After I splash some water on my face, I stare into the mirror. I look exhausted and scared. I scrub off the makeup from last night and sigh.

Tears and mascara burn my eyes, but now isn't the time to fall apart. I can bawl my eyes out once I'm free from this place.

Behind me, I crank on the shower and flip on the air vent. I'm not sure if they have hidden cameras in here or if there's someone standing guard right outside, but I don't want them to hear. I slink back into the main room and grab the plate, then shut myself in the bathroom. After counting to three, I bring half the plate down on the edge of the sink, and it cracks into two giant chunks. I crouch to examine the sharpest piece. Will this work? I jab it into the skin of my forearm, but it's too dull.

I shove the piece into my jacket pocket anyway and bury the other part in the trash can. After I crank off the shower, I exit the room and pause, my heart hammering in my throat.

In the middle of the room is another tray: a banana, a bowl of oatmeal, and a glass of orange juice. My eyes swing toward the door. How did they know I'd be in the bathroom just now? My eyes pan the room again, now that it's brighter. There must be a camera in here . . . which means they might know I have the plate.

I poke the sharp end in my pocket. Maybe they don't have cameras in the bathroom. It could still work. My stomach grumbling, I lower myself to the dingy carpet and take a bite of the lukewarm, sugary oatmeal. I down the orange juice, then chew numbly on my food.

I try not to think about what's going to happen next, why I'm here, or how awful my parents must feel. Has it been on the news? The thought makes me sick. Though I am a gymnast and I want to make the Olympics, I've never liked taking center stage, and the last thing I want or need is this kind of negative media attention.

My appetite disappears at the thought of being kept here for days, weeks, or even months. Missing trials. Missing my one shot at what I've worked my whole life for. It cannot happen.

I shove away the food and sigh. What I need right now is a plan: a plan for how to get myself out of this situation. I poke the end of the plate again, and it brings me a small sense of comfort.

My stomach aches along with my muscles. I am so tired, I feel drunk. Not that I know what that's like, really. I went to a party once and had a few sips of tequila, felt queasy, and vowed to never drink again.

My mind trips back to last night. I wonder how Jessie is and what happened after I was taken. If only I had stayed with Luke or let him guide me out—I wonder if any of this would have even happened.

Are the girls worried about me? I squeeze my eyes shut. Who am I kidding? The girls have never cared about me. When I first joined the gym, they would make fun of my clothes and shoes, whispering, "Cora the Poora." It was a terrible joke—that I was poor—but it still made me self-conscious. I worked hard to save up my allowance so I could buy clothes like the other girls, but honestly, I didn't really care how I looked. I just wanted to train. I wanted to fit in, but the more I tried, the more I stood out.

Now, after this, I'll never blend in. I groan and grab the blanket, then situate myself back in front of the heater. The airflow is weak, and I shiver. My legs are bare and cold.

Think, Cora.

I need to replay every moment of last night, from the time I arrived at the haunted house to the time that van rolled up. Was it all random, or could it have been premeditated?

Premeditated: done deliberately; planned in advance.

Who would want to sabotage my chances of attending trials? I think of Jessie again. Did someone sabotage her chances too? Did that man in the mask know her, or was he just some random psycho? Last year, Nancy Kerrigan's knee injury was all the rage. What if someone is doing the same thing to me? Or targeting elite gymnasts? Like a copycat?

Before I can continue down this train of thought, there's a commotion on the other side of the cabin wall. I scramble to my feet. Another door slams, and then I hear a girl scream.

Every hair on my body stands at attention as I rush to press my ear against the thick wood. Is there another room? I snake my palms along the east wall and listen.

"Help! Help me, please!" The girl's voice is muffled, but she sounds terrified. Just like me. After a few moments, her voice dies down. I glance at the main door, then bang softly on the wall, firm enough that she can hopefully hear me.

I hear her gasp. "Hello?" she asks. "Is someone there?"

"Hello? Can you hear me?"

After a moment, there's more commotion; then her voice sounds closer, like it's directly opposite mine. "Oh my God, yes, I can hear you! Who's there?"

I have to strain to hear. Everything is muted, as if trying to communicate underwater, but hope pricks in my chest. I'm not alone down here. There's someone else! "Who brought you here?" I ask. I'm desperate for more information, desperate to know who is behind this and why.

"I was at a party," she cries. "Two men grabbed me. I'm . . . I have no idea where we are. Are we going to die?"

"I don't know," I say honestly. But hearing someone else's voice is like a shot of adrenaline. I'm not alone.

Maybe if we work together, we can find a way out.

23

Now

Before I can start talking, there's a noise outside.

I jump from the couch and rotate toward the window.

Lennon notices and shifts the bag of ice on her back. "Is that your daughter?"

"Stay here. I'll be right back."

Part of me wants to pull my gun, but I don't want to alarm Lennon if I don't need to. Outside, I close the door behind me and suck in a cold breath. My eyes adjust to the night, and I'm reminded of that one-room cabin, where I spent all that time contemplating the myriad of ways I might die.

I travel toward the trees, gun in hand. I know I heard something. I walk toward my favorite group of pines and stop. There, nailed to the tree bark, is another red card.

"Son of a bitch," I say, pocketing my gun. How do I keep missing these people?

I rip it free and shine my phone light on it.

> A MILLION DOLLARS
> FOR LENNON'S LIFE . . . AND YOUR
> DAUGHTER'S.
> YOU HAVE UNTIL 2:00 A.M.

I think of the red cards so far, the mad goose chase up until this point. The cryptic, cruel Polaroids. The texts and phone calls. Wondering what this is really all about. I should be more shocked, but I'm not. Somehow, things always seem to come back to money.

Tonight's strange events cement more into place. If Lennon is injured and can't compete, that makes room for someone else. But there's something going on much deeper than a strong competitive streak. They have my daughter, and because of that, they will get me to do pretty much anything, pay anything. Two lives for the price of one.

I hesitate outside the door. What if I just decide to come clean and tell Lennon everything? Would she freak out? Would she help in some way?

Back inside, I glance at the TV. Somehow, Lennon has found my stash of Olympic tapes and managed to figure out my ancient VCR to watch them.

"This is so sick," she says, glancing back at me from her position sprawled on the floor, the ice pressed against her lower back. "Some of these moves could still hold up today, you know."

I can't concentrate on what she's saying. My mind is switching back and forth through options and scenarios. I need to talk to Joe. While I think, my eyes drift to Dominique Moceanu's floor routine. As I watch her tiny frame explode through the air, the words from the card flash through my head. A million dollars. I check the time. There's not enough of it.

"Why did you quit?" Lennon pauses the tape now and turns to look at me. "You could have made it for one more Olympics, maybe even two."

I attempt to focus on what she's saying. I want to scream that these people have my daughter, that they have hurt her, and that they are probably going to hurt Lennon even more unless I do what they say. But as I stare into her hopeful face, I realize she's just an innocent kid in all this. And if I can, I'm going to keep her safe.

"I injured my knee," I say to placate her.

"Just like my mom," Lennon says.

That memory tugs me from the present moment, if only for a second. "I'll never forget that night," I say absently.

"Night?" Lennon scrunches her nose. "It was during trials. She was devastated."

I open my mouth, then close it. Is that what Jessie told her own daughter? That she made it to trials? "No, that's not what happened," I clarify. "Your mom never made it to trials."

I have her full attention now. She turns to me, wincing from the sudden movement, her eyes wide. "What? What do you mean?"

"Your mother hurt her knee weeks before trials. But then, on that Halloween—the night I was taken—she got injured at a haunted house. I saw it happen."

Lennon tosses the remote against the carpet, and it lands with a dull thud. She struggles to sit upright. "What? She was *there*? The night you were taken?" I can see the confusion and excitement on her face. "Why didn't she ever tell me that?"

"I don't know," I say. "But she was definitely there." I explain what happened with that creep, Brian, and then give her the truncated version of the kidnapping and everything that happened to get me to the Olympics.

The latest clue is burning a hole in my pocket. As I look at her, I wonder what I should do: Tell her what's happening, or keep playing this silly game? Alert Jessie to the ransom demands?

"Did you blame her? My mom?"

"Of course not," I say, desperate for this conversation to end so I can think rationally. "I felt terrible for her. But . . ." But after I escaped and qualified for the Olympics and she didn't, she made my life a living hell. "Your mom wasn't very nice to me after that."

"What? Why?" I can see I've genuinely piqued her interest. It must be strange to hear someone else talk about a version of your parent you won't ever know.

"Because I qualified, and she didn't. In fact, I made enemies of almost everyone on my team." It was one of the reasons I moved gyms.

"Huh." I can see her wheels spinning. "They weren't happy for you?"

"Would you be happy for Kayla?"

She makes a sour face. "Point taken." Gingerly, she stands. "Bathroom." She disappears down the hall, and I call Joe.

"We have a problem," I hiss into the phone. I tell him about the ransom note and ask him what I should do.

He's silent for a moment. "I guess you have to decide if you're willing to play their game, Cora."

"This isn't a game," I bark. "This is my daughter's *life*." And Lennon's, apparently.

Joe rattles off Jessie's number if I need it, having done his own digging. "Maybe she has that kind of money?"

I don't respond. It doesn't matter if Jessie has that kind of money, because I do. I tell him I'll call him back. I have a choice to make, a million dollars to secure, and barely any time to do it.

Once Lennon is back in the room, I weigh my options. "Do you think you can call your mom to come get you?" *That's it, then,* I think. I've decided. I'm bringing Jessie into this. If her daughter is in trouble, she should be aware of it.

I think of the Polaroids again and shudder. God forbid something happen to Lennon, too, other than a sore back. Tears fill my eyes again at the realization that I'm responsible for her injury and that I'm also the cause of Lulu's pain.

Lennon texts her mom, gnaws on a cuticle, and then waves her phone in the air. "Cool. She's on her way."

"Great." I busy myself in the kitchen, secretly studying the Polaroids again. I try to channel the terror I feel into nothing but rage, nothing but revenge, nothing but finding these people and making them hurt the way they've hurt Lu.

I never found my kidnapper then, and it has plagued me all these years, following me around like a ghost. Like a tumor you can't physically see but know is there. Like torture. Like the end that is coming for all of us.

I'm not a violent person, but if I find out who did this, they will pay. No matter what.

24

THEN

Despite how tired I am, my mind is alert.

The girl gives me just enough details to make me think that this isn't premeditated. Two girls, at two random places, both kidnapped on the same night. If this isn't personal . . . maybe it's pathological?

Pathological: compulsive, obsessive.

I whimper against the wall. The girl, Evie, has been quiet for a while, and reluctantly, I pull away, my ear damp from the pressure. If she's fallen asleep, I want her to rest.

While I try to file away this new information—that I'm one of *two* people kidnapped—I keep my mind busy with rewinding the entire last day, like a videotape. Maybe if I retrace my every step, I can figure out who did this.

I think back to early yesterday, during the competition. Could someone have been watching me? There were so many people there—people with posters and homemade fan art. It's something I'm still not used to because I was once the one in the crowd, waving my posters and dreaming of the day when I'd be an elite gymnast.

Even as I recall every step of my routines yesterday, nothing feels out of place. There were no odd comments or people who shouldn't be there. The girls were supportive, putting on their usual friendly faces for the cameras and interviews. Once upon a time, I would soak it all up, pretending we were all best friends. But the moment the competition was over, they'd close up and push me out, and it made me wonder, as I watched all the other teams, if everyone was always just pretending.

If anything was real.

Luke flits through my mind again: his fierce green eyes, his kindness, how he always sticks around to help, even when the girls are mean to him. In a lot of ways, he reminds me of myself. A small flutter worms its way through my gut. Do I *like* him? It's not something I even know how to identify, as I've never had a crush on a boy. Celebrities or musicians, sure, but not anyone from my real life.

I squeeze my eyes shut again and remember Luke's warm, comforting hand on my shoulder. Could I imagine holding his hand or kissing him? I'm shocked to find the thought isn't entirely awful. It allows my brain a little space, something to look forward to if I get out of here alive. Maybe I can put more energy into finding a boyfriend. Maybe I can have my first kiss. Maybe I can still make all my dreams come true.

Intellectually, I know what I'm doing. I'm trying to find hope in a hopeless situation. If I can imagine myself outside these walls, then maybe I can get there. If I can imagine myself living a big, shiny life, then maybe this will simply be a story I tell someday.

I let my mind wander back to trials, which are in exactly one week. My parents and I are going to fly down there two days early to acclimate to the gym and meet everyone. So really, I have only five days until trials.

My heart gives another violent kick. After last night, I was going to take two days off, get some much-needed rest, tweak my routines, and then fly to Boston completely ready. I have five days to find my way home. To get myself and Evie out of here. Or be rescued.

I glance around the tiny room again. I have to train. I have to stay sharp. Closing my eyes, I start to envision my routines on each apparatus, starting with floor, then moving on to bars, beam, and vault. I practice the moves so many times in my head, it almost feels real. I make mental corrections and wish I had something to jot down notes on exactly what I'm going to change.

I know I need to exercise, but I'm still exhausted. My eyes begin to flutter closed, but I jerk them open. Yet the hum of the heater is so comforting. I snuggle under the blanket a bit more and let the warm air caress my face. I think of my mother and father. I think of my bedroom. I think of the men in the van. I think of Evie.

What if I never see home again? What if everything I love in my life is taken away? I shiver. I remember in the late 1980s, there was a slew of young girls who were kidnapped and killed. For a while, I was terrified to even go out into my front yard alone, but over time, I'd forgotten about it.

And now here I am. Here *we* are.

Victims.

Have I ever taken the time to realize those girls were real people with full lives and friends and families too? No, I hadn't. It's like my brain couldn't hold on to the possibility of something like that ever happening to me. Kidnapping is something reserved for other people.

I blow warm air into my cupped palms and then flatten them in front of the heater. I wonder if the shower even has hot water. Maybe I could take a quick one . . . just stand under the hot spray. If only to feel human.

Even as I imagine it, I think of a camera watching me or one of the men bursting in and taking advantage of me. I wrap the blanket more firmly around me, tucking it around all the exposed spaces, just like my mom used to do when I was a child. No. No one is touching me.

I slide my thumb over the edge of the plate again and close my eyes. I start to replay my routines once more, starting this time with beam and working in a different order. You never know what event you're going to start with. You always have to be ready.

By the time I get to floor, my brain is mush. I can feel myself careening toward sleep, but I need to stay awake. I have to. I strain to hear sounds next door or Evie's muffled voice. There's nothing.

As I wait, my body seems to know what it needs more than my brain. Before I know it, I'm being tugged toward sleep.

After a while, I give all the way in.

25

Now

While we wait for Jessie, I debate what to do.

Joe has texted the list of other teammates, and I scan through them quickly, but none of their names rings a bell. Faith has texted again, too, more frantic than her previous messages. I ignore them both. Every moment is a stark reminder of what happens if I don't get the money.

I don't know if bringing Jessie into this is the right thing to do. I know I have Joe and Faith for support, but this feels like a decision I need to make on my own. With just one clue, the stakes have shifted. This isn't just some note left on a car or pinned to a tree. This is my daughter's life. And Lennon's. No more playing games.

"How's your back now?" I try to anchor myself to the moment. I'm in my cabin. Lennon is on my couch. The kitchen island is firm beneath my palms.

Lennon winces. "I don't know. I probably need to see the team doc to make sure everything's okay."

I nod, but that only makes me think of my own father, which I promptly ignore. I glance at my phone again, expecting some new clue or evidence that these people are harming Lu, but thankfully, there's nothing. I close my eyes for a moment and try to place the voice I heard.

I have to know her somehow. The connective tissue between *then* and *now* is there; I just don't see it yet.

"How long has it been since you've seen my mom?" Lennon asks.

I struggle to remember. "A long time." After the Olympics, I went back to Woodward's. With her knee, she was done competing, but she would still show up sometimes to coach the girls. I don't go into detail about how horrible she was to me. That, while all the other young hopefuls treated me like some sort of god, Jessie acted like I was scum. Beneath her. A pest to be stomped and trampled, even though I was the one with a gold medal hanging around my neck.

Beyond her apparent jealousy, I never understood why she treated me that way, especially since I was the one who got her help the night she was injured, and because of that good deed, I was taken. But none of the other girls saw it that way. Instead, they viewed it as my meal ticket. Though my coach encouraged us to move gyms post-Olympics, the decision was a lot easier once I saw how I was received by the girls.

There's a tentative knock on the door, and I take a shaky breath. Jessie always made me nervous. Even though she could be cruel, the need to impress her was always there; it was like this pressing desire to be accepted and liked by my team captain was more important than how she made me feel. But she and I aren't kids anymore. She's no longer my captain, and this situation goes so far beyond who we were then. We're both mothers now. We both have daughters to save.

I move to the door, steady myself, and open it. Jessie's face registers complete shock as she takes me in from head to toe. I do the same. She is older, sure, but looks mostly the same: short, fit, with that same curly hair that still looks crisped at the ends and skin covered by heavy makeup. Fine lines exist beneath the thick foundation, revealing the passage of years. I resist the instinct to shrink. Instead, I stand up straight.

"*Cora?*" Her mouth literally drops open as she looks at me and then sees Lennon behind me. "Why is my daughter here?" The shock gives way to accusation, and all at once, I remember. The way she could spin a truth. The way she could get others to gang up on you. The way she could turn everyone against you in a heartbeat.

I open the door wider, already exhausted at the mere thought of trying to explain what the hell is going on. She steps through tentatively and eyeballs the place.

"Hey, Mom."

Jessie rushes over to Lennon as if rescuing her and then turns back to me. "Why is my teenage daughter in your *house*, Cora?" She glances at the ice pack. "And why does she have an ice pack? Are you injured?" She turns to Lennon and gingerly touches her spine before ripping her gaze back to me. "Is she injured?"

"You might want to sit down," I say.

"Why?" She removes her coat but does as she's told. I take in her compact frame, her expensive clothes. A diamond the size of the moon glints on her left hand. As she sits, she favors her bad knee, and that night comes hurtling back to me. I see Brian swinging the paddle toward her knee. I hear the sharp crunch of her patella shattering into spiderweb shards of bone. I watch her fall and make wounded sounds that still rake nails down my spine. I will never forget her screams.

After ramming that image into the closet with the rest of my unpleasant memories, I give Jessie the highlight reel of tonight. From the cards and text messages to where we are now. Hopefully I'm not putting Lulu in danger by being so forthcoming, but I'm out of options. And if these people are really after a million dollars, then I'm assuming they don't care who I tell or where it comes from as long as they get their money by the end of the night.

"Is this some sort of sick Halloween joke?" Jessie glances up at me with those dark, beady eyes, and I shake my head.

"I wish."

I search the recesses of my mind for a better way to explain what's happening but come up empty. "Can you think of who could be behind this? Any enemies either of you might have?"

She scoffs. "We don't have enemies. Just competition." She motions to Lennon. "But trust me when I say there's no one on her team who has the brains to pull off something like this." As if realizing what she just said, she shrinks a bit, but I can still see that inner bully straining to break free. "You know what I mean."

"Are you friends with the other parents?" I ask, knowing *friends* can be a very loose term. She wasn't really a friend type of girl back then. She had groupies or followers. People who obeyed her. People who didn't want to disappoint her. I don't think I ever saw her interact with someone she would deem her equal. Maybe she preferred it that way. Maybe she still does.

She shrugs. "Yes and no. You know how it is. Such a fine line between who we were then and who we are now." She laughs, and it sounds like a smoker's laugh, thick and wet. She sighs and adjusts her expensive watch. "We put stock in our kids, right? And I'm not just saying this because I'm her mom, but it's clear Lennon has the best shot out of all the girls, so . . ." Her voice drips with pride at that, but it makes me sad. It makes me sad that parents push all their unmet dreams onto their kids as though they are our puppets, our do-overs, our second chances.

"But someone wanted to make sure Lennon couldn't compete, Jessie." Lennon visibly flinches while Jessie's nostrils flare. I show her the text chain before she can question me.

"You *hurt* her?"

"They tortured my child and gave me no choice. Lennon fell on bars. I think she'll live."

Jessie stares right through me, too shocked to speak.

I move on to the real issue. The money. "Do you have that kind of money?"

She evades the questions. "Who has a million dollars lying around?" She smooths a hand through her hair and sighs. "And how do we know this has anything to do with me? What about your dad's lawsuit?" She's suddenly a haughty teen all over again in her jean jacket with her glitter eye shadow and pink bubble gum.

Just the mention of my father feels like a poisonous spider traversing my skin. It's something I don't like to think about or talk about, and when the trial happened five years ago, I disappeared for good.

"But he's done his time," I say. "The girls who testified got their money."

"No," she says, shaking her head sadly. "Not everyone." I don't think Jessie was one of the girls from our team who accused my father of anything, but she must have known what was going on. She was our captain. She saw everything. Though I was his daughter, and I didn't have a clue.

"Who didn't get their money?" I think about what an ugly ordeal that turned out to be. After the Olympics, the rumors started that my father was forcing girls to starve themselves by giving them diet pills and then pain pills to cover up their injuries. Some of the girls got addicted, and he inadvertently became a drug dealer.

A few girls, whose names were kept private, came forward from my original team. I was stunned. I'd always known my father to be professional. He loved his job and kept clear boundaries intact. But then I remembered how he'd forced me to throw my inhaler away, how he portioned my meals and was always on me about my weight. He gave me diet pills too. I thought it was just part of being the team doctor. I was oblivious to his relationships with the other girls, and when he finally got in trouble, I was ashamed to admit that part of me wondered if it was some sort of vendetta against me.

That the girls were punishing me for my success by going after my father all these years later—going after a man I'd always known to be firm but kind. What did they have to gain all these years later? The way they painted him, the stories they told . . . it brought my name back into the public sphere when I had worked so hard for anonymity.

But instead of fighting the charges, my father was so mortified, he pleaded out almost immediately to make the accusations go away.

His reputation meant more to him than anything, and yet in a single moment, it was forever tainted. An illustrious career dragged through the proverbial mud. And the fact that he took a deal proved his guilt in my eyes. That was the most crushing blow of all. Wouldn't you fight if you were innocent?

Jessie's voice snaps me back to the present. "Madeline is one of the moms on the girls' team," she says, surprising me. "She was also one of the people who testified."

"And?"

"Rumor is she didn't get a settlement," Jessie explains. "Maybe now she's come to collect."

26

THEN

I must sleep for a while, because the next thing I know, the door opens, and another meal is replacing the morning tray.

My heart thuds viciously through my ears. It's like I've been splashed with ice water. I sit up and find my voice. "Wait," I say, my throat scratchy. "Please." I still have the piece of plate in my pocket, but I know it would take every ounce of strength and exact precision to inflict any sort of damage.

This man is the tall, thin one. He takes a few steps back and glances over his shoulder as if expecting someone else to join him.

"Please tell me why I'm here. Are you going to kill me?" I can't believe the question actually leaves my lips, but it does. "Are you going to kill *both* of us?" I don't know why I mention Evie. I regret it the moment the words are out of my mouth.

The man doesn't acknowledge the question. He simply exits back out the door as if I don't exist, as if I'm not worth answering. I'm left alone again, and as I hear the click of the lock, I have the urge to scream. Then I think of Evie. She screamed, and what did that get her?

Just as I'm figuring out what to do, I hear movement next door. There are raised voices. I crawl to the other side of the room and press my ear to the door. I can hear Evie say something, her voice getting higher pitched. Then, there's a cracking sound and anguished screams. Just like Jessie's screams.

I cover my mouth with both hands, and my eyes instantly fill with tears. Did they just *hurt* her because of what I said? Is this my fault? My eyes swing back to the door. Are they coming for me next?

I grab the plate in my pocket, though my fingers are trembling so violently I can hardly get a good grip. Evie's door slams, and finally, she quiets enough that I try to talk to her.

"Evie? Evie? What happened? Are you okay?"

There's some shuffling and sniffling, and then I can hear her, pressed up against the wood like me. "Cora, they . . . they just broke my ankle! They came in with a hammer, and they hit me! Oh my God! I'll never be able to cheer again."

So she's a cheerleader? She dissolves into crying again. I bite my lip so hard I taste blood. Somehow, I can feel her pain and absently massage my own ankle. Am I next?

"Why would they do that?"

"Because I tried to run. I tried to push past them yesterday. I fought them. And now I can't run. I can't escape." She begins crying again. "You have to do what they say, Cora. Play along, and maybe you can find a way out."

I recoil from the wall. I'm certainly not leaving her here. If there's a way out, then we're *both* getting out. I make that promise to myself and then to her.

I tell her who I am. That trials are in four days. That I'm sure our parents have already gone to the police, that people are looking for us, that we will be rescued. I tell her that my dad has an important job and knows important people. They will come. I talk us both into calming down, staring at the sandwich on the tray. My limbs are restless. I don't want to spend another second in this place.

"We're going to get out, Evie. We are."

She's silent from the other side. I close my eyes, try to think. With schoolwork, there's rarely a problem I can't solve. It's another reason the girls don't like me very much; they call me a teacher's pet because I'm always jumping in to answer questions that our tutor asks. But I love learning and don't understand why anyone would make fun of someone who enjoys getting an education.

I begin to study the room like a geometry equation, noting the angles and the perimeter and looking once again for exit points. I don't know what time it is, but I assume one of the two men will be back for dinner. He will come when it's dark, and this time, I will be waiting. With my jagged edge of the plate, I could stab him in the neck, find the keys, and open Evie's door, and then we can make a run for it together. My limbs surge with adrenaline at the mere thought of getting outside these walls. But then I remind myself that Evie's ankle is broken, so she can't run.

Tears trickle down my cheeks as that plan dissolves. I place my back against the wall and draw my knees to my chest. Maybe I can escape and get help for Evie. If the thin man comes tonight, I could stand a chance going toe to toe with him.

I keep the jagged plate ready, my eyes on the door.

27

NOW

"So Madeline is mad she didn't get her money and is coming to collect from us five years later?" I shake my head. "That doesn't add up. I haven't seen Madeline since we were kids."

Jessie shrugs. "Maybe she's using Lennon to get to you? Or maybe she's punishing *me* because she's jealous of Lennon's chances? Who knows?" She glances at Lennon and then back to me. "Or maybe it's because your dad is finally out of prison? I mean, isn't the timing kind of crazy?"

My body feels like it's floating, as if my brain is disconnected from the rest of me. It's true my father was just released from prison. My mother called to see if I would come visit them, at least have a conversation. I said no. I couldn't look at him, even all these years later. I couldn't face what he'd done.

After the trial, I felt like that often, sickened by photos of my own father, a man I once adored and respected. Despite my mother's incessant pleas that I give them a chance, he's never even met Lulu. As his daughter, I've lost all trust in someone who was supposed to be there for me, for all my teammates. Looking back, I feel like my entire childhood was built on a dangerous lie. And I don't want to expose Lulu to that kind of person, even if he is her blood.

Even now, it's hard for me to wrap my head around. My father, guilty of pushing pills to young girls. Is this why someone took my child? To make me hurt the way my father hurt them? I take a sharp breath. Could it be that simple?

"What do you know about Madeline? Anything useful?"

Jessie smooths a hand over her long skirt. "Her daughter is on the Olympic track, like the rest of the girls." She glances proudly at Lennon. "The girls were friends for years, and then things got competitive." Her hand reaches involuntarily for her knee. "Laura also has a kid on Lennon's team. But like I said, I can't imagine any parent would do something like this."

I think about the rest of my former teammates: Nicole, Laura, and Jakayla. Last I heard, Nicole moved to Seattle after the Olympics, Laura moved back here after trying to make it as an actress in Los Angeles, and Jakayla died in a tragic car accident in the nineties.

"Tell me more about Laura."

Jessie scoffs. "Since her acting career died, she funnels everything she can into her daughter. I don't think it's her."

I understand that. Everything I've done, I've done for Lu. Though I lived in Manhattan, when I got pregnant, it felt too frenetic to raise a child there. I could have gone anywhere in the world, but for some reason, I chose to return to my roots. Just like some of the other girls I grew up with, apparently.

I chew over my next question. "What about the money?"

Jessie wrings her hands in her lap. "Well, my husband, Richard, owed Madeline some money." She flicks her left hand in the air, her gigantic engagement ring catching the light. "A real estate thing. Madeline is an agent. Richard sells commercial real estate. They had this huge deal that apparently blew up. She lost out on a giant commission. Maybe she's pissed?"

Panic swirls in my chest. "And you're just mentioning this *now*?"

"I just remembered," she says.

"How much?"

She eyes my fireplace, then looks at me. "No idea."

So perhaps this is about more than gymnastics or a lawsuit. Could this be about business? If so, why do it through me? Why harm *my* child? Why go to all this trouble? I try to remember if Madeline and I ever had issues. So much of that time is a blur, only key moments sticking out with the girls on the team. I remember that she always blended in, never really spoke up. And she worshiped Jessie. So what's changed?

"I guess the real question is, can you get the money? Or some of it?"

She sighs. "Cora, I don't have access to Richard's funds. I definitely don't have that kind of money personally, and there's no way in hell I can get it tonight." Her eyes are remorseful, and I'm not sure if it's for Lennon or for my child. "But I can try."

The thing Jessie doesn't know is that I *do* have access to that kind of money, and I have it in cash, buried in a safe on the property. And I won't think twice to hand it over to save my daughter, but how can I trust I will even get her back?

"You'd recognize Madeline's voice, right?" I ask Jessie now.

"Of course."

I dial the number and motion for everyone to stay quiet. I put it on speaker.

"Get the money already?" a woman asks. This time, the voice is altered, like one of those voices in a scary Halloween movie.

"Not quite," I say, annoyed at the sudden shift. "I want to speak with Lulu. Or this whole thing's off."

There's silence on the other end as the woman contemplates what she might assume is nothing more than a bluff. "You're not really in the position to make demands here, are you, Cora?"

"I don't know," I spit back. "If you want your money, you'll let me speak to my daughter. Right now."

"No can do," she finally responds. "She's a bit . . . indisposed at the moment. Get the money, and don't call this number again."

The line goes dead, and bile rises to the back of my throat. I call the number back, but it's been blocked. "Damn it."

I pull up the earlier photo of Lulu again, studying the starry sheets. I examine every curve of her unharmed face, and that's when I see it. I nearly drop the phone.

"Oh my God."

"What?" Jessie asks.

But I ignore her, zooming in on the photo. When I studied it earlier, it didn't register. In this photo, Lulu is clutching Bun-Bun. I can see the top of his ears tucked beneath her chin. But Lulu doesn't have Bun-Bun because she dropped him at the parade. Which means this photo isn't from tonight.

Nausea burrows deep into my gut. My eyes blur, and both Jessie and Lennon fall silent as I grapple with this new truth.

I stumble outside and eye the darkness. I know where this photo was taken.

It's from Faith's house.

28

THEN

I'm freezing.

It's dark again, which means I have been sitting here, staring at the door, for most of the day. I wait for my eyes to adjust to the swiftly blackening room. I sidle up to the wall and listen for Evie, but I don't hear anything.

"Evie?" I call, my throat scratchy. "Evie?"

I wait, but she doesn't answer, which makes me feel even more panicked. What if she passed out from the pain? I move toward the heater and extend my hands, wishing to God I had thought to wear jeans and several layers to that haunted house, not a skirt and cropped sweater.

The heat warms my exposed flesh. After a few minutes, I hear her voice.

"Cora?"

I hurl myself back in place, snuggling my ear against the wood. "Are you okay?"

"No. My ankle is so swollen. I think I passed out from the pain."

"I'm sorry." I think of what else to say. I have so many questions. Why did they hurt her instead of me? What are they planning for us? How can we help each other? "What's in your room?"

She describes roughly the same setup as mine. I tell her about the plate.

"Is it sharp?" she asks. Her voice sounds weak.

"Sort of." I exhale a shaky breath. I want to tell her that I have an idea of how to get outside these walls, but I'm afraid if I tell her, they might find out. Or hurt one of us. Or both.

"Tell me about your life," she says now. "What you want to do when you get out of here. Besides gymnastics."

I'm thrown by the question. For so long, it's been only gymnastics. But didn't I just think about what it might be like to have a boyfriend or make real friends? Maybe go to college, study something useful? I think of the other girls on the team, the only girls I ever hang around. Only Laura has ambitions beyond gymnastics. What else could I do? I rack my brain, but nothing comes. Shouldn't I have bigger goals? Other interests beyond the Olympics?

As I figure out what to say, I close my eyes and let the words tumble out. "Ever since I was three, it's been about gymnastics. At first, I thought it was fun, but then when my parents realized I was good at it, my dad took the reins. He's the USA Gymnastics team doctor, so it was always going to be in my future." I pluck a frayed thread from my skirt. "I really did love it. I *do* love it. But you work your entire life for this one thing, and now I might miss the payoff." The panic swells in my chest again, and I take a steadying breath to stay calm. "Even if I make the Olympics, what comes after, you know? College, I guess. I like school, but I'm not really good at anything else."

I fall silent, suddenly embarrassed by sharing so much. When she doesn't respond, I fear I've been too open.

"Maybe because you haven't had time to figure out if you're good at anything else. But there's a whole life out there beyond gymnastics, you know?"

For the first time, I wonder how much older than me she is. She sounds like an older sister, someone good with advice. Despite our situation, her words are a comfort. "What about you?"

"Well, I love cheerleading, but now with my ankle . . ." She trails off. "My dad is a physicist, so that's kind of cool, I guess. I'm not really sure yet."

I find myself nodding along. I realize it's okay not to have everything figured out. It's okay that I've focused on only one sport. It doesn't mean I can't find anything else. I glance around the room again, almost forgetting where I am. Is this what it's like to make real friends? To sit in a room and swap stories?

Suddenly, I feel robbed that I haven't had these opportunities. I can't blame it entirely on gymnastics or my parents. It's me too. There's a desperation I feel when it comes to making friends. I'm sure the other girls can tell. Before I can wallow too much in my own loneliness and what might have been, I hear the door bang open next door and a man yelling.

Evie yells back, but I can't hear what they're saying. I gasp and scramble to my feet as their voices escalate. Something slams against the wall. The force of it vibrates all the way to my fingertips, and I keep my ear pressed against the wood, even though I'm shaking. My heartbeat rushes through my ears, a hammering pulse.

"No, please!" Evie's voice rises as another sharp crack, similar to the first, reverberates through the wall. Something crashes, and instead of Evie's screams, there's nothing. The door slams, and I push away from the wall, panting. I wait for them to come into my room, to do the same to me.

My eyes whip around the space. How can I defend myself? I touch the plate in my pocket, but I know that's not enough. Especially if they have a weapon.

There's commotion outside. I steady myself as best as I can, gripping the plate in both hands. I point it in front of me like a knife. I can barely see through my tears, and my breath feels shallow. I'm on the verge of panic, but I have to keep myself here. I have to be ready.

I have to fight for my life.

29

Now

I think back to earlier tonight.

How Faith didn't show up at the parade. How she came over after. What if she took Lulu for some reason? What if she's had her all along?

My brain can't make sense of things. I recall the woman on the phone, before she disguised her voice. That definitely wasn't Faith . . . was it? Have I been blinded by a villain directly under my nose?

I turn back to the house, Jessie and Lennon waiting inside. This is all such a mess. I don't know what to do about Lennon and Jessie. I don't know if she can get the money or if I need to. I don't know where my daughter is or why that woman wouldn't put her on the phone. Of course, there's only one reason they might not let me talk to Lulu, and the reality is so frightening, my mind can't even go there. I check the time.

Back inside, I tell Jessie I have to see about securing the money. She tells me she'll do the same. I hesitate before I leave. What if Jessie disappears? Takes Lennon and just goes? As I debate my choices, I realize it's a risk I'm willing to take. For extra insurance, I text Joe and ask if he can head to my house. I fill him in on the most basic details, give Jessie my cell number, climb into my truck for what feels like the millionth time tonight, and reverse down my drive.

Faith lives in a proper neighborhood closer to the city center, and my mind spins with every mile eaten. I know Faith. I trust Faith. Yes, she's had a tough time these last few months since the divorce. Her bank account took a massive hit, and she complains about money constantly. *Red flag*, my mind screams.

I ignore that thought and pull up to the sprawling Victorian. As I turn off the ignition, I wonder if she could be the kind of woman to bribe me. If she could have only been pretending to be my friend just to hurt me. To hurt Lulu. Or force my hand for a million dollars. But even as I try on these ridiculous scenarios, I just can't imagine Faith taking anyone's child. She's a *mother*, for God's sake.

Since Tyler's Halloween party is in full swing, I park a little way down the street. It's late enough that there aren't random trick-or-treaters still out and about, but I can hear the thump of the bass from music inside. As I approach, I see the house has been decked out with cobwebs and oversize witches, skeletons, and pumpkins.

Even as I knock on the front door, I know that I'm wasting valuable time. Lulu can't be here. Faith can't be involved. But the photo burns a hole in my pocket. How would anyone get a photo of Lulu from Faith's house? And why? It must be a clue.

When no one answers, I twist the knob. It's open. Letting out a shaky exhale, I step inside. The boys sound like they're having fun in the basement, but I don't see Faith. I consider calling her name but instead hurry up the stairs toward the guest room with those blue starry sheets.

Outside the bedroom door, I pause, feeling foolish. Do I really expect Lulu to be asleep on the other side? I reach for the door just as Faith walks down the hall. When she sees me, she slaps a hand to her chest in surprise.

"Cora? Are you okay? Did you find her?"

Faith is beside me in a few quick steps. She's scrubbed her face free of makeup, but I can still see the inky remnants of mascara smudged beneath her eyes. Her hair is pushed back with a flowery cloth head-band, and she's wearing sweats and a T-shirt. Suddenly, seeing my good friend makes me rethink everything. Faith could never do this. She would never take Lu.

Before I respond, I push into the room anyway. It's simple and clean: a full bed with a light-blue bedspread, a white dresser, a TV, and two matching nightstands. Simple art. I march over to the bed and rip back the covers. The sheets are different.

"Cora? What are you doing? What's going on?"

I whip out my phone and show her the photo from the mystery number. She looks at the photo of Lulu and then back at me. "Is this from them?"

"Yes, it's from them," I say. "Except it's not from tonight. It's from here."

Faith looks like I've slapped her. Her jaw has stopped working, and she grabs my phone and squints at the photo. "What do you mean?"

"The sheets," I say. "They're yours. And she has her stuffed animal, which she dropped at the parade tonight." I grab the phone back. "When did you take this, Faith?"

"I have no earthly idea," she says. "Those sheets haven't been on this bed in ages." She chews on the inside of her cheek as she thinks. Finally, she snaps her fingers. "Wait. I remember. I watched Lu for you. When was that? The beginning of the year, maybe? I sent you a video once she fell asleep. Maybe they grabbed a still shot from that?"

I rack my brain for a memory, but nothing comes up.

She tells me she's going to grab her phone. In the interim, I can't help myself. I search under the bed, in the drawers, in the closet. Hunting for clues. Clues that my daughter might have been here tonight.

Finally, she returns and scrolls endlessly through her texts. After a few minutes, she locates the text exchange between the two of us, back in January. "See?" She asks me to pull up the photo on my phone so we can compare her video to the still shot. Sure enough, they're the same.

"Is this supposed to make me feel better?" I ask. "How would someone get this video unless you were involved?"

123

The look on her face is one I've never seen before, not even when talking about her ex. "I really hope you're not insinuating what I think you are," she says quietly, so quietly I strain to hear.

But I don't back down, not for a second. "What am I supposed to think? How would someone get this photo?" My voice booms over the sudden crescendo of voices from downstairs.

"I have no idea how someone got that," she says. "How did they get into your house? How did they hack your phone? That photo was probably taken from your phone, not mine."

"Why weren't you at the parade tonight, Faith? You said you'd be there."

Again, she appears as though I have physically assaulted her. "I *told* you I was getting ready for this party. How can you think for one second that I would ever harm Lulu? That I would take her? Maybe you should be looking a little closer to home, Cora," she snaps. "Not pointing fingers at your very few friends."

It's a dig at my small, private life, but I let it slide. Faith is always encouraging me to meet more people, to go out, to live my life instead of hiding from it. I'm her plus-one to events. I go to dinner with her. I do my part as her friend. But she can always tell I'd rather be home than out. I'd rather be quiet than talk. I'd rather stay small than take risks.

"Stop it," I say. I know what she's insinuating. I shove my phone back in my pocket and start to retreat toward the landing.

"You know I'm right, Cora," she says as she follows behind me. "It makes sense. You never let them see her. And now your dad's out of prison. What's stopping him from seeing her now?"

I hurry down the stairs and burst out her front door without bothering to apologize for accusing one of my only friends of being involved in something so sinister. I call Joe to update him.

"Bad news," he says when the call connects.

My stomach flips. "What?"

"I found four cameras, three trees."

"You're kidding." I don't understand how someone could have gotten cameras into my trees without me knowing about it. True, I run errands a few days per week, but I have my own security systems in place when I'm not home. None of it makes sense. "Can you check my regular cameras?"

"Already did. They're all out. Whoever did this knows what they're doing, Cora."

"Okay. Thanks for letting me know. Are Jessie and Lennon still there?"

"Yep. They're inside."

"Keep them there. I'll be back soon." I disconnect the call and squeeze the wheel, trying to forget what Faith said.

Because there *are* two people who could definitely take Lulu. Two people who need money. Two people who are so desperate for a connection with Lulu that they might do something stupid like stage this whole thing.

Yet that doesn't ring entirely true either. My parents would never be able to hack my security systems, or leave ransom notes, or take photos of creepy dolls, or convince anyone else to help them. Especially on Halloween, a day that brings up so many hard memories for all of us. Plus, my father has served his time and probably wants to stay off society's radar, much like I do.

No. It can't be them.

Can it?

Before I can think about what I'm doing, I turn left to merge on the highway.

Though I haven't been back to that house in years, I still remember my way home.

30

THEN

I stab the air with my plate, shifting from foot to foot.

I count to twenty, then fifty, then one hundred. When it's clear they aren't coming, I drop my arm and sprint back to the wall, then bang on it. "Evie? Evie! Are you okay? Please let me know you're okay."

I wedge my ear against the wood, but I don't hear anything. No breathing. No movement. No crying. Nothing. A whimper escapes my throat, and I pace in a tight circle, thinking.

I have to get out of here. I have to get *her* out of here. She might need serious medical attention, and I'd never be able to live with myself if I could have done something to help but didn't.

If I am somehow able to escape, I have no idea how long I'll be running or stuck outside. I move back to the heater to try to warm myself and think through scenarios. If I'm able to get outside these walls, I have to be ready for anything. The other guard could be standing just outside. They could attack me the moment I escape. They could torture me or break my bones with hammers, just like Evie. I quiver at the thought.

An injury at this stage would mean the end of everything. I almost laugh at my own absurdity. Here I am, locked in a creepy cabin by two men, listening to them torture the girl next door, and I'm still worried about not getting hurt?

"Focus, Cora." My voice sounds strangled in the dark. What choice do I have but to try to escape? Maybe their guard is down. Maybe they're going to get rid of Evie and come after me next.

Even though I'm in front of the heater, a chill shimmies up and down my spine. After a few more minutes of warming myself, I walk to the bathroom and flip on the shower. I can barely make out my reflection in the dark, but I give myself a small nod. *I can do this.* I have to do this. For myself. For Evie. For any hope of survival.

I crack open the bathroom door and slink out, hopefully undetected by any hidden cameras in the dark, and then slip next to the main door. I strain to make sure I can hear the whoosh of water from the bathroom. My hope is that, if the men *do* have cameras, they'll think I'm in the shower. Then, when they come to deliver my dinner, I can squeeze through the opening of the door, undetected, as one of them bends to put my food tray on the ground. Hopefully he won't even notice I've escaped. That is, if there's no one else waiting outside. I retie my Doc Martens and take a deep breath.

Though it's the riskier plan versus me stabbing someone, I need to play to my strengths. I know how to be light. I know how to be fast. I've been training for it my whole life.

I just hope I can help Evie in time. My heart pounds visibly against my breastbone. That, coupled with the aching cold and the hours-long nap I took before, makes me feel alert. I don't know how long I hover there in the dark, jumping at every sound.

But finally, there are footsteps outside. Before I can change my mind, I take a deep breath. My heart skips and thuds in a succession of rapid beats. The keys jam into the lock.

My fingers twitch. I'm ready to move, but I have to be quiet and careful. There's such a small window for escape when he opens the door. I have to be like a shadow. I have to be invisible.

I have to be quick.

31

Now

The house looks tired.

I kill the headlights and stare into the black windows of our red-brick ranch, the only house my parents have ever owned, even when I paid off their mortgage decades ago and offered to buy them a new one. The landscaping is minimal. Once-vibrant flower beds are riddled with damp autumn leaves and broken stems. Molehills pepper the front lawn in neat little mounds, always a problem, even when I was a child.

The giant magnolia is the one bright spot. Its thick, waxy leaves are a reminder of the life I once lived. I used to snuggle under her trunk and read for hours when I had a day off from the gym.

I always thought my parents would leave this place, maybe upgrade to something nicer once all my success hit. Deep down, I think my father knew that trouble was coming for him and that he needed to save every penny he had. He knew what he'd done, even when I didn't. What a fool I'd been.

I check the time. It's nearing midnight. They'll both be asleep, I'm sure. I exit my truck and walk up to the front stoop. It's like stepping back in time. I search the perimeter for anything unusual, but what am I even looking for? Do I expect to knock on the door and find Lulu eating cereal and watching cartoons?

The image stops me before I step onto the porch. What I wouldn't give for a scenario just like that. For Lulu to simply be with her grandparents, this whole night some cruel, horrible joke. My legs refuse to move, I'm so stupidly hopeful, but finally, I force myself up the concrete steps and ring the doorbell. I expect the floodlights to trip on from the sudden intruder, but nothing. Not much for security, then.

My mother has been asking me to come home for years, and now she's getting her wish. I shift nervously, stuffing my hands into my hoodie pockets to calm my nerves.

As expected, it's a few minutes before the porch light flickers on. I squint from the shocking brightness. The lock is flipped, the chain is unbolted, and then the door moans open. My mother's face peers out into the darkness between the gap—older, rougher, looser. Her once-smooth skin is peppered with wrinkles and sunspots, her jawline melting into her neck. She grips her glasses from a gold chain around her neck and clenches her floral robe closed with her other fist.

"Cora? My God, *Cora*! Is that you?" Her voice wobbles, and as I soak her in, I realize the impact my father's mistakes must have had on her life too. It hasn't tainted only him. Maybe all this time, she just needed a lifeline, some tether to her before-world. She needed her daughter to come home.

"Hi, Mom." I can't believe my voice is calm, but I don't have a lot of time, and I need to know if my daughter has been here. "Can I come in?"

"Has something happened? Where's Lulu?" She searches behind me, as if maybe I've orchestrated this midnight surprise meeting between grandmother and grandchild. I can see the hopefulness even behind the sleepiness and shock. As she searches the black behind me, I notice the creases from her pillow etched into the side of her cheek, like a pocked scar.

"That's why I'm here," I say, moving inside. The house smells like chicken soup and a fresh fire. I can't help myself. I glance around, searching for changes, but I see none. It looks exactly like it did then. Just more worn. Smaller. Less of a home.

Before I can take my next breath or explain the situation, my father appears from down the hall like an apparition. He stands in the darkness, dark-blue robe billowing above the floor vents. He's bald and overweight, and I have a visceral response when I see him.

Once upon a time, this man was my lifeline. I trusted him with my career, my health, my body, my future. And he took them all from me, just like he took them from other girls.

"Hello, sweetheart," he says finally. "I was hoping you'd come."

His voice is more certain than my mother's. Despite this night and what's happening, there's a moment when I realize these people feel like strangers. These two people, who were once my world, reduced to nothing more than toxic memories. It's a horrible realization, like learning Santa Claus isn't real. But I don't have time to mourn anything. I'm here for my daughter. And if they don't have her, maybe they can figure out a way to help.

I motion to the living room. "I need to talk to you both, and I don't have a lot of time."

"I'll put on some coffee," my mom says excitedly, like she's entertaining.

"I'll start a fire," my dad says. "The heat's been acting up."

"I'm just going to run to the bathroom," I say. They don't question me as I disappear down the hall. The moment I turn the corner, I run from room to room, searching every last nook and cranny. At my own bedroom door, I hesitate. Have my parents boxed everything up and changed my childhood room to something else, like an office? I open the door and peer inside, shocked to find it's exactly the same as I left it. A shrine to gymnastics. My whole world reduced to my sole obsession.

The brown carpet, patchwork quilt, and bookshelves full of trinkets are what pull my attention first. My mother knitted that quilt. My dad built those bookshelves. My eyes skim the posters. The brown carpet hides everything. Knowing no one is in here, I check under the bed and in the closet anyway, my heart breaking a little for the sweet, determined girl I used to be. Who I was before and after the kidnapping. Before and after the Olympics. Before and after my father went to prison.

Who I am now.

I bypass my parents, who stop talking when I enter the room, and I search the garage, climb into the attic, and return to the living room, dejected. They both stay quiet. I think they know me well enough to understand I'm here for a very specific reason and it's best to let me speak first.

"Lulu has been taken, and I need to find out who's behind it. I'm wondering if you two can help."

"What?" My mother grips her robe again, her face growing pale.

My father jumps up, sloshing his coffee onto the rug. "What in the world, Cora? Tonight?" He sucks some of the scalding liquid that splashed on his wrist. "How?"

I fan out the cards and clues and take them through it, though I leave out the horrible Polaroids. They follow as best as they can. I ask my father about the settlement, about who didn't get paid. He shakes his head, his cheeks darkening.

"I don't know anything about that, hon. My lawyer handled all of it." His eyes fill with tears, and he pinches the inner corners of his eyes with his left thumb and index finger. "I'm just so sorry for what I put you through," he says now. "All of you." His shoulders shake, and I tamp down the annoyance at this unexpected display of emotion. I don't have time for him to grow a conscience. I just need to know if they can help.

"Look, I've had a lot of time to think about who took me back then," I say, hoping to steer them back to the present moment.

"Do you think it's connected?" my mother asks, aghast.

"Yes," I say. "Can you two think of anyone it could be? Someone who would have something to gain now, after all this time? Someone who needs money?"

My parents are silent, and then my dad looks up at me, his eyes watery. "Cora, did you come here because you thought it could be us?" His voice is so quiet, I barely hear him. Now that I'm here, it's clear they're not involved.

"Yes," I say flatly. "I thought it could be."

"Oh, Cora." My mother's voice drips with disappointment.

I check the time. I have to go. I scribble my cell number down for both of them.

"If you think of anything that could help, please call. I'll let you know when I get her back." My voice sounds more confident than I feel. Seeing my parents again has rocked me to my core.

I don't wait for them to walk me out. I don't hug them goodbye. Instead, I practically run back to my truck, climb into the driver's seat, and gun it back to my cabin.

I'm going to get the money and do whatever these people ask. No more games. No more trying to outsmart anyone.

I just want to bring my daughter home.

32

THEN

The key seems to stick in the lock, but finally the door creaks open, and the moment the man pushes it wide enough to step through, I ease noiselessly behind him, completely unnoticed.

In my mind, it's all so much more dramatic: a fight scene; me, ducking a hammer; a forceful shove; a bloodcurdling scream; something.

Outside, it's colder than I thought. My eyes take a moment to adjust. The moon hides behind the cover of clouds, casting everything in shadow. However, I can see those ten stairs in front of me. I tiptoe as silently as I can up to the top, then crouch out of the way behind a bush.

In the distance, there's a sprawling cabin with a few interior lights on inside. Is that where the men are staying? Now that I'm outside, I can see I've been inside some sort of hunting bunker, not a tiny cabin, as I imagined. There are two identical doors side by side: one for me, one for Evie. I move directly to the right and duck behind a hulking tree, calculating how long it will take the man to drop the tray and exit. Not long.

It's less than thirty seconds, and he's back outside again. After he locks the door, he rips off his ski mask, but I can't make out his features in the dark. This is the bigger man of the two. He stalks, heavy footed, back toward the main cabin. I take all of it in, gleeful that I've managed to outwit him, but without a clear lay of the land or any idea where I am, I'm not sure how victorious I can be.

The temperature is settling into my skin, and I revolt against the cold. I look for a vehicle and see the van in the driveway by the cabin. What are the chances that the keys are in the ignition? Probably none. And even if they were, I don't know how to drive. Maybe Evie does?

Part of me wants to run straight to the cabin, peer in the windows, if only to know who's behind this, but my survival instincts take hold instead.

There's a long gravel driveway from the bunker to the right of the cabin and beyond. Everything else is flanked by trees. My escape is right there. I could just go, run, get as far from here as possible. But then I turn back to the bunker. I can't do any of that without Evie.

Keeping myself low, I scurry over to her door and try the knob. Locked. I bang as softly as I can and whisper, "Evie! It's Cora! Can you hear me?" I press my ear to the door, but again, I hear nothing, which tells me one of two things. Either she's passed out, or she's not there. My heart pounds as I whip back toward the cabin. Could they have moved her? Could they have . . . *killed* her?

Dread takes hold again, threatening to paralyze me, but I don't have time for that. There is a small window for me to get help, and if I don't do it right, Evie and I are doomed.

I crouch as I hurry down the length of the driveway. Surely there's a main road where I can hitch a ride with someone and tell them what's happened to me, what's happened to Evie, and they can call for help.

A small thrill tramples through the nerves. If we get out of this alive, if I escape to get us help, will I become famous? The thought takes hold like a secret obsession, and it begins to grow with every step. Maybe I can be a hero. Maybe I can finally be something else besides a gymnast. I squat low to pass the cabin, and once I'm on the other side, I take off into a full sprint.

My breath heaves from my mouth in thick white clouds. My boots slap the gravel and spray rocks in all directions. A few sting my thighs, but I don't care. Part of me worries I'm too loud, that these strangers will come outside and snatch me back before I've reached the main road. So I run faster. I run like I'm going to perform my hardest vault. I run as if my whole life depends on it—my future, everything I've been working for—lies just beyond those trees.

The end of the driveway seems to drag on forever, but finally I reach it and am faced with a main road and miles of woods in every direction.

If only the moon was out, I could see where the bright side is facing, which signals west. Of course, that tells me nothing, because I have no idea where I am. Plus, it's so cloudy I can make out only the towering outlines of trees.

My teeth chatter, and I hesitate before I take off. What if I find help but don't remember how to get back here? What happens to Evie? I turn back again, drowning in guilt. I can't just leave her here. But I tried her door. Should I have kicked it down? Should I have tried harder?

Time is running out. I can feel it slipping through my fingers like sand. Which way should I go? And what if I freeze to death before I can find both of us help? For once, I wish I had more padding on my bones. Not having much time, I choose to go right. As my muscles shake awake, I can hear and see only my breath, which swirls like fog in front of me.

My feet hurt in my boots, but I keep pushing myself. Once I feel like I'm far enough away and no one is after me, I begin to walk. There's a massive cramp in my side, and my quadriceps feel like jelly. I stop for a moment, hands on my knees, trying to bring my heart rate down to normal. Once I'm steady, I stand back up and turn in a full circle. I haven't seen another house or driveway yet, and the road just seems to wind on and on forever.

I'm trying to keep up with any landmarks, but it's just endless rows of trees. Because of my training schedule, we rarely take any sort of trips to the mountains. My dad isn't very outdoorsy and hasn't taught me much about surviving in the woods, though now I wish I was one of those rural girls who hunted and fished and spent all her time outside.

That type of girl would know what to do. She would know how to survive.

My muscles begin to cramp, and I slow down again, careful not to tax myself too much. The last thing I need is a pulled muscle, out here in the cold. That makes me think of Evie. Her broken ankle and, now, maybe worse. I can't think about what they did to her, that she could be lying in a pool of her own blood or worse, and I made it out without her.

I shake the guilt free, intent on finding help. I blow into my cupped palms and hear the hoot of an owl somewhere in the distance. My breath steams from my open, panting mouth, and everything in me wants to scream for help. I need to get home. I want to be in my own bed. I want all this to become nothing more than a deranged Halloween nightmare.

I walk for what feels like days, curving around a road with endless switchbacks. My toes are numb, and my extremities feel like ice. Where are the cars? Where are any signs of life?

As if on command, from behind, I clock the faint flame of headlights. *Oh, thank God.* I turn and begin hopping up and down, already waving my arms wildly in the air.

"It's almost over," I whisper, my teeth banging sharply together. Everything is stiff and frozen. My legs have gone numb, as if I've been left in an ice bath for too long.

But help is here, finally.

I'm almost free.

33

Now

When I pull up to my house, I bypass the cabin and walk straight to the fallout shelter near the back of the property.

The trees are a comfort as I shuffle through them and come to the hidden trapdoor buried in the earth. Hopefully Joe has dismantled any hidden cameras he found out here, which will keep this spot hidden from view. But at this point, I don't even care.

I brush away the dirt with my boot until I find the padlock. I carefully input my combination, jerk open the hatch, and descend into darkness. It's a safe space for storms and big enough only for a few personal items. I unlock the safe. Piles of cash hide my passport and Lu's, my Olympic gold medals, and a few guns. My eyes track back to the cash. Maybe Jessie can get it from her husband, but am I willing to wait? Or simply hand my money over without any guarantee of getting my child back?

My brain is still trying to decipher every clue. How Lulu was taken at the parade. How my security cameras are out. How someone hacked my phone. How Lennon has been dragged into this, and now Jessie.

I pile half the requested amount into a duffel, then climb the ladder, lock the padlock, and circle around to the front porch. I stash the bag outside.

I search for Joe's car but don't see it and fire off another text. He responds right back.

Got Madeline's address. Going to check it out so we can rule her out.

A tiny swell of gratitude cuts through some of the trepidation. Hopefully soon, we can mark her off the list . . . or not. Inside, Lennon and Jessie are speaking in hushed whispers. Jessie's head snaps up, and she stands and rushes over. "Where have you been?" Her eyes are wild. "Richard can't get the money tonight. I'm sorry. I tried." Isn't this just the scenario I played out in my head?

I study her with new interest. Could she be in on this somehow? Yes, her reactions seem genuine, but what if she's just acting? What if she's a woman willing to put her child at risk to get my cash?

"So now what?" I ask.

She barely skips a beat before responding. "I mean, don't *you* have that kind of money? All those deals and endorsements you got, I just thought . . ." Her voice trails off, confirming my suspicions. The room goes completely silent, as if I've pressed mute on a remote.

"You just thought you'd orchestrate all this to get paid?"

She sputters and looks from me to Lennon and back to me again. *"Me?"* She presses a hand to her chest. Man hands. I remember that about her. Her fingers are wide and short, and she always had calluses hard as rocks. She used to take needles and jam them into the thick skin, opening her palm wide so that we could see how tough she was. "What in the world do I have to do with any of this? My daughter is involved!" Tears fill her eyes again. "She's injured! You did that, not me."

"So is mine," I say quietly. The gun is cold against my waistband, and I know, as I stare into her dark-blue eyes, that if things go wrong tonight, I will have zero hesitations about using it.

From the couch, Lennon licks her chapped lips. In this light, soft-purple pockets bulge beneath her blue eyes. Her nails are brittle.

Her hair looks fried, just like Jessie's used to. She looks as depleted as I feel.

"It's not me, I swear." Her eyes go completely dead. I remember that, too, the way she could pretend to care and then swing the other way. "I have nothing to do with any of this."

"Maybe," I say. "Or maybe you and Madeline want your turn in the spotlight."

Despite the situation, she rolls her eyes. "Cora, believe it or not, I haven't thought about you once since the Olympics. Frankly, I got tired of hearing your name."

"But there were rumors after I moved back, right? So what if you two have been plotting this all along? Waiting for a Halloween story to capture the public's attention? And right before trials?"

"Really, Cora? We've been plotting to take your child for the past four years? Come on. No one is that patient. Or deranged." She sinks onto the couch and massages her temples. "This is all beyond insane."

I waver. If Jessie isn't in on it, then it's either about my father's lawsuit, the money Richard owes Madeline, or both. "Call Madeline. Put it on speaker."

"Why me? I told you, I'm not in on this."

"Then prove it."

She scoffs. "Or what?"

I'm so tired of playing games. I'm so tired of not having the answers. After a moment's hesitation, I remove the gun from my waistband and point it right at Lennon's chest. "Or your daughter is going to the Paralympics instead." I cock the hammer and steady my gaze on Jessie. Lennon whimpers and moves toward the arm of the couch.

Jessie looks outraged, but she says nothing because I'm the one with the gun. We both know I'm not going to shoot Lennon, but even with a gun pointed at her daughter, Jessie hesitates, debating what to do. Perhaps I've used the wrong bait. Grumbling, she taps out Madeline's number on her phone with her short painted nails and stabs the speaker button.

We all wait for the call to connect.

"Why are you calling me so late?"

Madeline's voice explodes into the quiet room. Jessie doesn't say anything at first, so I aim the gun at her head instead.

"I'm here with Cora," Jessie says.

"Cora *Valentine?*" Madeline exclaims after a moment. "Whoa. Tell her I said hey."

I listen for clues in her voice, but there aren't any. I know Joe will find out more, get to the bottom of things. They chat for a second; then Jessie ends the call and pockets her phone, letting out a weary sigh. "Happy now?"

After a moment, my phone buzzes.

Bring the cash to 4322 Chester Lane. 2:00 a.m.

"Does this address mean anything to you?" I rattle it off.

"Not to me," Jessie says, pinching the skin above the bridge of her nose.

"Let me see your phone."

She unlocks it, and I scan through the text chain between her and Madeline. There's the occasional text exchange about the girls, but other than that, nothing much. I thumb through the rest of her phone: photos, contacts, and endless texts. It seems she's a well-connected woman who is also ridiculously lonely. Constant invitations to go out with friends that are mostly ignored or rebuffed. Unanswered texts from her husband. I study their most recent messages, which mention nothing about the money. I check her call log. There's no call to Richard either.

"I need you to step outside with me, Jessie. Lennon, we'll be right back."

Jessie's nostrils flare, but she does as I tell her and stands. Lennon nods, and I'm grateful she doesn't put up a fight. Before I leave, I stop and turn to her. "I'm sorry about the gun," I say, waving it in the air. "I would never hurt you."

"I know," she says, but she doesn't look certain. She looks scared.

Outside, the temperature has dropped at least another ten degrees. "This way," I say, pointing toward the woods.

"I swear to you I have nothing to do with any of this."

"And yet, when you were supposed to be calling your husband, you didn't. Even with your child's life on the line." I poke her in the back with the barrel of the gun to keep her moving deeper into the woods. "And the only reason I can think why someone would do something like that is if their child actually *wasn't* in danger." We crunch over the frozen earth as my words land, but then she stops and turns, hands in the air.

"Okay, you're right. I didn't call Richard, but not because I don't care about my daughter." She looks at the sky and finally back at me. "I can't ask him for that kind of money, Cora. He keeps his funds separate for a reason."

"And you don't think he'd be willing to help if he knew Lennon's life was at stake?"

"No, he wouldn't. Richard is funny about his money. It's going to have to come from somewhere else."

Somewhere like me.

"But I swear I'm telling you the truth. I would never intentionally bring my daughter into some sick, twisted game. Or involve yours, for that matter."

"And yet now it's all on my shoulders to come up with a million dollars for your child and mine. That's pretty convenient, wouldn't you say?" I don't wait for her to respond. Instead, I guide her east on the property, where I have another unseen shelter. This one doesn't have safes or guns. It's for emergencies only. I unlock it with one arm and point toward the tiny metal ladder that descends into nothing more than a black six-by-six fallout shelter.

"Uh-uh, I'm not going down there," she says, as if she has a choice. "I'm claustrophobic."

"You know, for years, people have told me how lucky I am. That the kidnapping led me to stardom, to fame. Because I have money, everything must be great, right? But what no one talks about is what it's *really* like to sit in the dark, practically freezing to death, hour after hour, and wonder exactly when you're going to die. To hear someone else tortured. To wonder when you're going to get tortured too."

"But you didn't die." For the first time, I clock a hint of fear in her voice.

"Lucky me." I gesture to the shelter. "In. *Now.*"

"You can't leave me here, Cora. Please. I could freeze to death."

When I don't back down, she curses under her breath and gathers her skirt around her ankles before she wobbles on her bright-pink heels down each rung of the ladder. She hops off the bottom step and stares up at me. "Please don't do this."

Her pleas remind me of my own back in that bunker. How scared I was. How desperate. With a groan, I hoist the door up from the ground and study her face. Is she guilty or not? I drop the metal door and lock it, then scatter leaves back over the top. I know it will be cold, and the more humane part of me feels hesitant to leave her here without knowing if she's truly involved or not, but the other part—the part that was endlessly bullied and made to feel less than year after year after year—doesn't feel that bad. Because at the end of the day, despite how old I've grown and how far I've come, I'm still some version of the same girl who ached for a gold medal and for her teammates to like her. I'm still the girl in the bunker. I'm still the girl who almost died in the woods.

I stalk toward my other shelter and grab a few extra weapons, stash the bag of money in the bed of my truck, and then head back inside to find Lennon in the exact same spot I left her. I arrange my firearms and strap them to various body parts as Lennon's eyes go wide.

"Are you for real?"

Once I'm done, I look at her. "Can you walk?"

She tests the waters by standing again and carefully twisting left and then right. "I think so."

I eye her as we prepare to leave. "Aren't you going to ask about your mom?"

Lennon stares down at her toes and shakes her head. "I trust you," she finally says before looking back up. "I know you won't hurt her."

There's no way she can know that, really, but I appreciate her trust. "Let's go." I hit the lights, grab the keys, and quickly read a text from Joe that all is clear at Madeline's. I text back that we're on our way to him before we're back on the road. I stab down the window as we pass the shelter and listen for Jessie's screams, but all is quiet.

Still as tough as she used to be, it seems.

For now.

34

THEN

The vehicle slows to a crawl about ten feet out, and before I can make out the driver, I glimpse the shape of the vehicle.

It's a beige van.

I blink rapidly and feel my stomach drop, like I'm flipping in the air and have forgotten how to twist. I shuffle a few steps back into the protection of the trees. It can't be the same beige van, can it?

Fear grips me like a vise. They don't know I'm gone . . . do they? I can't afford to find out. Before I can think about what to do next, I dart into the woods. My legs feel like rubber, but I force them ahead anyway. Branches whip my face until I taste blood. Tiny lashes sting every exposed inch of skin, ripping open my cut lip. I will my legs to work faster, but my muscles are seizing up.

"No, please, no."

Behind me, I hear the slam of a van door and two male voices talking low.

They must have some sort of video surveillance back at the bunker, or maybe they saw me run by their cabin. Regardless, this is make or break. If I don't get away, if I don't escape right now, I'm dead. I just know it. I heard what they did to Evie.

I can only imagine what they'll do to me.

Their footsteps close in behind me, heavy breathing charging at me like something from a horror film. I look for places to hide or trees to climb, but I don't have time to slow down enough to attempt it. A tiny whimper, like an injured animal, works its way up my throat and out into the endless expanse of trees.

I'm going to die, alone in the woods, with two awful men hunting me like prey. I attempt to muster the last bit of fight in me, but I can't. I'm so tired. All at once, I stop running. Every muscle cramps like one big charley horse. I muffle the strangled cries from the shooting pain and slump down at the base of a tree. I'm so cold. So tired. Everything hurts.

Their footsteps grow farther away. Maybe they're going in a different direction. Maybe they're giving up. Suddenly, my fear turns to a weird kind of acceptance. I can't feel my hands or feet. My heart rate is sluggish. Everything is slowing down.

I need to keep moving. I have to. I try to make my body work, try to push myself off the ground to keep running, but my limbs refuse. I flop forward on my belly and attempt to crawl under a heavy pine.

My teeth chatter, but I can't feel anything.

Come on, Cora. You have to fight.

Tears freeze on my cheeks as my brain screams in protest. It takes everything in me to move an inch. My face rests on the ground, my head cranked to the left. Dirt and frost mix with the cuts on my skin. I smell blood and the earth. But still, I feel nothing.

My eyes flutter closed while I fight to keep them open. I can no longer hear the men's footsteps. I can no longer hear anything beyond my own shallow breath.

It's so hard to breathe.

You have to breathe, Cora.

You have to stay alive.

35

Now

Joe's house is dark except for a few warm lamps in the sitting room.

He meets us on the front porch.

"Cora, thank God." He exhales and rakes a hand through his hair.

I know he's usually asleep by now and appreciate his willingness to help me see this through. He eyes Lennon, and when he doesn't see Jessie behind us, he braces me with a stern look. "What did you do?"

"Nothing," I say. "Jessie's fine." He quickly fills me in on Madeline. I tell Lennon to go inside and that I need to talk privately with Joe for a moment. Once she's out of earshot, I tell him what I found out.

"Jessie never called her husband. She didn't even try to get the money." My brain is sifting through worst-case scenarios. The only saving grace is it takes my mind off of what might have happened to Lu, why I haven't seen a real photo of her. I swallow, ignoring the agony pulsing through every vein.

"Okay, so if it's Jessie, then who's helping her? We've ruled out Faith and Madeline," he says, tapping fingers along his scar. "Who else?"

I look at my feet. "I went to see my parents."

"You what?" Joe knows enough about my parents to understand the complexity of that relationship. "Are they involved?"

I shake my head. "No." I think back to the parade. "What about Adele, Dave, or Janina? They were there tonight."

"Does Jessie know them?"

I let out a frustrated sigh. "God, I have no idea."

"I talked to them, Cora. I don't think it's them."

"What else do we have to go on, then?" I say, all sense of control leaving me again. The entire world is opening up, endless and infinite. It could be *anyone*. She could be over state lines by now. She could be gone forever.

"I don't know," he says honestly.

I close my eyes, the weight of tonight settling over me like a lead blanket. "I don't know what I'm doing, Joe." I lean forward on his porch railing. "I don't know where else to look."

"What about Kayla's mom?" Lennon finally offers.

I jump when I realize she's standing in the doorway and not inside, like we asked.

"Who's that?" I ask. I don't remember whose kid she is from Joe's list.

"Laura Hunter."

Laura Hunter. Laura in her mittens on Halloween night. Laura being taunted about her crush on Ryan. Laura and Madeline teasing me about having a crush on Luke. I briefly mentioned Laura to Jessie, but she dismissed her as a possible suspect. "Why would she be involved?"

Lennon glances nervously between us. "Maybe because Kayla is second best on the team? I know Madeline thinks her daughter is second best, but she's not. It's Kayla. It would kind of make sense if her mom wanted Kayla to take my spot." Her voice fades away as I mull over this idea.

"Joe?"

He touches his scar again, a nervous habit he can't seem to quit. "I mean, I don't know enough about the girls on the team or their mothers, but maybe it's something new to go on?" He seems uncertain. I'm not sure he's convinced this is tethered to gymnastics in any way, and I have to think maybe he's right.

"What about Jessie's phone?" Joe asks. "If she and Laura are working together, maybe there's something there?"

I grab Jessie's phone from my pocket but realize it's now locked. "Shit."

"Here." Lennon unlocks the phone and hands it to Joe. "It's her birthday."

He thumbs through the phone and finally stops. "That's interesting." He turns it to show me. "Her name is in here, but there aren't any texts between them. Maybe she erased them?" He scrolls through every other chain in Jessie's phone, some dating back years.

"Or maybe they just weren't close," I say. "If they were, why would this one be wiped clean but no one else's?"

"That's what you do when you don't want anyone to read what you're up to," he confirms.

I think this through. If Laura would do anything for her daughter, would she bribe me? Would she take my child? Would she hurt her? Could she and Jessie have staged this entire night to get me back for making the Olympics? Even as I work it out in my head, it doesn't add up.

"Why would Laura insist Lennon get hurt, though?"

He shrugs. "Maybe she double-crossed her."

I glance at Lennon. "I'm sorry you're hearing all of this. I know this is hard."

Lennon pulls the ends of her sweatshirt sleeves over her hands. "It's okay. I'm not sure this helps, but Laura totally has a thing for Coach Ryan. They're, like, dating or whatever. Kayla told me."

I almost laugh. That crush has spanned thirty years. I guess some things don't change.

Joe looks from her to me and shrugs. "Could be something?"

"If Laura is involved, I don't want to tip her off," I say.

"Which means what?" Joe asks.

"Which means I need leverage." I glance at Lennon. "Do you know where Kayla is tonight?"

"Jesus, Cora. No." Joe slices his palm through the air. "You're not taking another person's child. That's too far."

"In case you haven't noticed, this entire night has gone too far! What other choice do I have?"

Lennon pulls up Instagram on her phone, then cranks it our way. "She's at Drake's party. Drake Amanu. Most popular guy in our class. He has a big Halloween party every year."

"And you didn't want to go?" I ask, surprised.

She shrugs. "Not really."

My heart aches. I know that body language all too well. It means she wasn't invited. The inner child in me feels for her, but the mom part of my brain needs to find Kayla so I can possibly get my daughter back by leveraging Laura's.

"Do you know where he lives?" I check the time. It's late. The party could even be over if they live in a fancy neighborhood like Lennon's.

"Yeah. His parents are out of town too, so . . ."

"Okay, let's go." I turn to leave, but Joe clamps a hot hand on my shoulder. "Cora, look at yourself. You're strapped to the nines. You can't walk into a teenage party with guns. *Jesus.*"

I look down at myself. My weapons are concealed, but he's right. Mostly. It's apparent I've lost all sense of rational thinking tonight, but he can't understand this primal ache inside me because he doesn't have kids of his own to protect. "I don't see another play here. They've already hurt her, Joe. I need something to wave over their head. Something to make them think twice before doing anything else."

He motions for me to unarm myself, and I do, except for my handgun.

"Let me follow you at least."

I nod, not wanting to argue. I tell him about the drop spot and that we'll bring Kayla just in case. As I'm jamming my key into the ignition, my breath halts in my lungs. Taped to my steering wheel is another Polaroid, turned backward so I can't see it. There's something on the edge of it. Red.

Blood.

Lulu's blood?

"Joe!" I scream.

He jogs up to my window, and I pluck the Polaroid free, avoiding the bloodstain. Lennon is deathly silent. I close my eyes, open them, and flip around the photo. I scream when I see it. The same doll, missing its eye, its left hand, and now its left foot.

There's no note. I begin to scream, banging my palms against the steering wheel until they sting. I fly out of the car, sucking in air. What sick fuck would ever torture a little girl like this?

"Cora, Cora. Just breathe. Breathe." He tries to follow me around but limps behind until I stand still and fold into him, just as I did earlier tonight.

"They can't do this, Joe. She's going to die. My little girl is going to die." I beat against his chest with hard, ineffective fists. The logical part of my brain understands that if they have, in fact, harmed Lulu, then amputation probably means death. She could be dead already from a loss of blood. Shock starts to set in, bit by bit, until Joe pulls back, squats down to eye level, and looks me deeply in the eye.

"They want you to fall apart," he says now, clearing the emotion from his voice. "They want you to give up. But you can't. You have to fight for Lulu, Cora. Okay? We're going to get her back."

His platitudes do little to calm me. This has all gone so wrong. Tonight was never supposed to turn into this. "I can't live without her, Joe. I can't." I know I keep saying the same things over and over, but I mean it. My entire life has led me to being Lulu's mother, and I cannot have that ripped away because of my past.

I need more time.

Tears flow freely again. Lulu has been tortured. Just like Evie was tortured.

My eyes fly open. Evie. Could there be a connection here? Someone sending the same type of message decades apart? I claw my way up Joe's arm and look into his eyes. "There was a girl," I say now. "Back when I was kidnapped. The same type of thing happened to her. Maybe it's connected?"

Joe shakes his head, clearly not understanding. I never talk about what happened to me then. Certainly not tonight. "We'll get to the bottom of this, Cora, but we have to stay focused. We're running out of time. If you want to get Kayla, we need to do it now, okay? Do you need me to drive?"

That slaps me awake. Kayla. Laura. The money. The drop-off. The limited time. I take a few steps back, once again embarrassed by my swing of emotions. One minute, I can keep it together. The next, I'm undone.

"I can drive," I say.

"Okay. I'm right behind you." He squeezes my arm and climbs into his car.

Once we're on the road, he trails at a safe distance. Lennon helps navigate toward the party. Something soft croons over the speakers, and warm air blasts from the vents and calms a bit of my anguish and adrenaline. I flex and release my hands around the steering wheel. All this time, I've tried to protect myself from experiencing terror just like this. I thought if I hid deep enough, ran fast enough, and made myself small enough, I'd be safe. It seems no matter what I do, unfathomable situations find me.

And now they've found my daughter. They've found Lennon.

In the passenger seat, Lennon sighs, and her breath fogs the window. She draws little shapes in it the way Lulu does.

Dear God, *Lulu.*

Jessie's phone buzzes, and I whip it out and read the text carefully, expecting a clue. It's not. It's from her husband, Richard.

Going to sleep at Lance's tonight, it says.

That's it. No *I love you* or questions about her night.

151

Lennon has stopped talking, and I realize we've arrived. Suddenly, it's like the sound has been violently cranked back up. There are expensive cars parked all over the lawn and packed bumper to bumper against the curb. As in Lennon's neighborhood, this house sits on ample land, so there aren't neighbors to call and complain about the noise. The bass of the music adds to the excitement from kids in costumes who get free rein without adult supervision.

I glance at Lennon, still in her leotard with her sweatsuit over it. "I'd ask if you want to stay in the car, but I need you in there." I motion toward the door. "We'll make it quick. Get in, get out, okay?"

She gnaws on her bottom lip until tiny droplets of blood sprout up on the thin, torn skin. She sucks the blood, running her tongue against the tender flesh. "Okay." She shrinks inside her sweatsuit and tugs the sleeves over the ends of her hands again.

We exit the car. Once again, the shock of the cold slaps me fully awake. I can't believe I'm doing this, raiding a party to snatch yet another kid who's not mine, but at this point, nothing is off-limits.

I stuff my hands into my jeans and let Lennon walk in front of me. I can tell her back still hurts, but she's good at hiding it.

I expect kids to tell her hello, but she moves through the throng of young, energetic bodies completely unnoticed. Never mind that she's an Olympic hopeful and will probably garner more success than most of these kids. They don't notice her at all.

Inside, the house is sprawling. The floors are marble, and there's a massive spiral staircase immediately off the entrance to the right. A crystal chandelier sparks fractured light over the costumed bodies, almost like a disco ball. It's dark and packed, and it smells of teens, sweat, pot, and sloshed alcohol. Couples dance, dry hump, and make out in every available corner, and Lennon's mouth drops into a soft little O of surprise. I wonder if this is the first real party she's been to. I create some distance between us so she can acclimate.

"See her?" I finally yell over the loud music.

She scans left and right, still working her bottom lip between her teeth. "No." She gestures toward the stairs and shrugs. "Should we go up?"

"Lead the way!" I shout.

I never got to go to many parties when I was her age. That Halloween night at the haunted house was the closest thing to a big teenage crowd I'd been a part of with the whole team, and I hate how what I thought would be my one special night turned out so horribly. After, I assumed the world would forget what happened to me, would forget my name, but when I became an Olympian, all bets were off. Then the invitations came from every direction, but I still didn't trust the world, didn't trust anyone, really. Except my parents. And then I learned that I couldn't trust them either.

At the top of the stairs, the hallway splits left and right, with at least eight doors. "How many bedrooms are in this place?"

Lennon shrugs again, offering a sigh much too heavy for a child her age. We start knocking and peeking inside, issuing apologies and moving on. Finally, in one of the bedrooms at the end, there's a girl sitting on a windowsill, vaping. She's blowing vapor out into the open and is dressed like a fairy.

"Kayla." Lennon's voice is sharp and dull, which tells me everything about their rivalry I need to know.

She turns and offers a vicious smile. "Who invited *you*?"

Lennon shifts uncertainly, and I quickly step in. "You need to come with us," I say. "Your mother had an accident."

Lennon flicks her eyes toward me but knows well enough by now to play along.

"It's really bad," Lennon adds. "My mom is with her now. They sent me to grab you and take you to the hospital."

I'm impressed with Lennon's improv. Immediately, Kayla's bravado slips, and when she stands, I can see one of her hands is shaking. "Is she okay?"

"No" is all Lennon says. She turns and walks back out the way she came. I make sure Kayla follows by bringing up the rear, weaving back through the house and down the stairs.

When we're outside, she eyes my truck before getting in.

"I'm Lennon's aunt, by the way," I say. "In from out of town. I was with her tonight when we got the news."

I can see all the questions she's not asking, but Lennon issues a stern look. "Are you coming?"

"Yeah." She fits into the back beside Lennon, and they keep a safe distance between them.

I check the time. Almost 2:00 a.m. Almost time to face these monsters, whoever they are. Almost time to bring Lulu home.

36

THEN

I startle awake.

My body is no longer freezing, and when my eyes adjust, I realize I'm back in the bunker.

"No, no, no." I scramble upright and scrub my eyes with my fists. They feel gritty and dry. How did I get back here?

The men. The woods. There's a heavier blanket on top of me, and the heater is directed toward my feet. Quickly, I scan myself to make sure I haven't been tortured or maimed. Slowly, I pull my knees into my chest and begin to rock back and forth. I was *free*. I was outside. What happened? The last thing I remember is falling asleep on the ground. Did they capture me . . . or save me?

My brain spins, tossing aside scenarios left and right. If they wanted me dead, I feel like I would be. If they wanted to torture me, they would have done it already, right? If they wanted me to freeze to death, then why give me a blanket and heater? Obviously it seems they want me alive for some purpose . . . but who are *they*, and how long am I supposed to stay here, biding my time?

When I feel oriented, I scoot closer to the wall and call out Evie's name. "Evie? Evie, can you hear me?"

I wait for what feels like forever, but there's nothing. No signs of life. No breath. No screams. No idle conversation. Is she really gone? Could they have killed her? Somehow, that thought alone scares me more than the others. If they've killed her, then that means I'm next. And I was so close to being free, so close to getting help.

Outside, the sun begins its slow descent. My stomach growls, and everything aches. My thoughts swing back to my parents. They must be going out of their minds. But the police are looking for me, I remind myself. That small bit of comfort immediately dissolves as easily as it came. We are in the middle of nowhere. There are zero leads. And no one has come for me yet.

I try to remind myself that if I got out once, I could do it again, but where would I even go? I felt like I was running for days and got nowhere. And to survive in these temperatures, I'd have to have different clothes. The reality that I almost froze to death is not lost on me. And if those men hadn't found me and brought me here, then I would be dead. A giggle works its way up my throat as I think about the irony of it all.

My kidnappers inadvertently saved me.

Inadvertently: unintentionally; without meaning to.

I go over various words in my head, reciting their definitions. I keep my mind off of gymnastics, off of Evie, off of torture, off of what will happen if I miss trials. A moan begs to come loose at the back of my throat, but I swallow it.

I will get out in time. I have to.

As I'm lost in thought, there are keys in the lock. I gasp and hike the blanket back over myself as some sort of flimsy protection.

The door barely cracks open, and the thinner man steps in, then slams it behind him. Footsteps thud confidently toward the center of the room. I can see only the whites of his eyes behind his black ski mask. He drops the tray on the ground. An orange rolls off it, as does the bottle of water. He retreats the way he came, keeping his eyes on mine.

So they know how I escaped.

"Wait." My voice is hoarse, and I don't expect him to actually stay, but he hesitates, his gaze glued to mine.

"What happened to Evie?" I ask. "Is she . . ." I can't bring myself to say the word *dead*. "I need to go home," I continue. "Please." I know I sound pathetic, but maybe if he senses I'm a real person and not just a job, he'll let me go.

He closes his eyes briefly, opens them, and shakes his head, as if there's a sad truth about to descend into this ominous space. As if he knows something I don't. Wordless, he steps back outside and locks the door behind him.

I sit against the wall, unmoving, until the sun fully rises. I need a new plan of escape, a better idea. As I assess each corner of this tiny bunker, I know I'm going to have to hurt someone in order to get out. To find the keys to their van and figure out how to drive. Or get into the main cabin and find a phone.

All this seems impossible, but it gives me something to cling to.

Because if I don't believe I can truly get out of here, then what's the point? I think about being sprawled on the forest floor again, begging for my body to move . . . a body that just wouldn't cooperate. I shiver and retrain my brain on the task at hand, making a list in my head like I do for assignments:

Hurt whoever I have to.

Get out of here.

Find my way home.

I have to do it for Evie, for my parents, for myself.

Time is up.

37

Now

The drive is awkwardly silent, even though these girls know each other and train together most days of the week.

It's clear from their silence they aren't friends.

"The hospital's back there," Kayla says now. There's a tinge of hysteria to her voice. Her fairy wings clog most of the back seat.

I weigh my options and decide to tell her the truth. "We're not going to the hospital," I reveal. I glance at her in the rearview so she can see my face when I deliver the news. "I think your mother kidnapped my four-year-old daughter and is trying to extort me for a million dollars. She's luring me to some abandoned warehouse, so we're bringing leverage. Namely you." I readjust the mirror.

"What?" she shrieks. "That's, like, *totally* insane." I can see her glassy eyes, stoned from whatever she was vaping. "My mother wouldn't do that," she insists.

"She might," Lennon adds. "That's Cora Valentine."

"*What?*" In true teenage fashion, Kayla seems to forget the imminent danger and is fixated on an Olympian sitting in the car. An Olympian whose poster is hanging in her gym. "My mom has told me all about you! You went to the Olympics. Oh my God." She smears her tears away and scoots up to grip the passenger seat headrest.

It always shocks me that certain people want to know only about the Olympics and others want to know what it was like to be kidnapped. It's rarely both.

"That was a long time ago."

"Still, that's so fire," she says, finally slumping back in her seat. "But my mother wouldn't do what you're saying. She just wouldn't. She's a *mom*."

I'd like to think a mother wouldn't do this, but I have to be sure. "Has she mentioned me at all?" I ask. "Said anything recently?"

Kayla's quiet as she contemplates the question. "I mean, no? But if I'm not at school, I'm at the gym. We don't really talk about other stuff."

Isn't that the truth. If my father hadn't been the USA team doctor, I would have never seen him. But he was always busy too. There was rarely time for just the two of us, and now, with everything that's come out about him, maybe that's a good thing. Regardless, it's a lonely world, being an athlete at an elite level. Especially back then.

"So what's going to happen now?" Kayla asks.

"Not sure," I say. "Someone told us to meet at this address. You know anything about that?" I share the address, and she shakes her head.

The car descends back into silence, and before I can think of more questions, we arrive. "You've *got* to be kidding me." The address hadn't registered when the text came. The parking lot is large and bare, but this building is as familiar to me as that bunker. It's Smorgasbord, the infamous haunted house. After that Halloween, it got closed down permanently due to what happened to Jessie, and as far as I know, nothing else was ever opened in its spot.

"What?" the girls ask.

"This is the place." I motion to it. "The haunted house I was taken from. The place where your mom got injured."

"No way," Lennon breathes.

Kayla takes out her phone to record.

I search for Joe but don't see him yet.

"So what's the plan?" Lennon asks from the back.

"Good question," I say. Joe finally pulls in front of us, his headlights blinding. "Stay in the car." I grab the bag of money from the bed of the truck, hoist it over my shoulder, and walk to his window.

He keeps his engine running and stabs the window down. "What's the plan?"

"I was hoping you'd tell me," I say.

He rummages in his pocket and produces a pair of handcuffs. "Cuff yourself to Kayla."

"What?"

"Just do it. You want leverage, so use it." He drops them into my hand and motions toward my truck. "I'll take Lennon, make sure she's safe. I called in a favor from an old friend. Backup. He'll be here if anything goes sideways. You good?"

I steel myself for what's to come, packing away the emotion of this night, the kidnapping, the blood, the Polaroids, *Lulu*. This could be another dead end, nothing but a wild-goose chase, but I feel I'm getting closer to finding my daughter. To bringing her home. "I'm good. See you in a sec."

I walk back to the car. "Lennon, you're there." I motion to Joe's car. "Kayla, you're coming with me."

After they exit and split up, we pad across the empty parking lot. Kayla, hardly dressed for this weather, shivers beneath her thin costume. It reminds me of my own scant clothing when I went to that haunted house as a teen. If only I'd known what I was in for.

I think about making small talk, but I don't have the energy. I pause as we near the entrance and swallow the panic, my heart a wicked hammer swinging violently in my chest. It's like stepping back in time, being here, watching a version of myself who was so nervous but excited for the night ahead. Inching her way toward the door. Wanting to run back to the safety of her home.

Much like then, questions swell inside me now—why I'm here, why all this is happening. The possibilities braid together in my mind. If this is all some crazy stunt to catapult Kayla into the limelight, I can't see how it will all work out the way Laura wants it to.

I gauge the front again, take a breath, and tug on the door. It's locked. I try again. After taking a few steps back, I glance around.

"This way." We walk along the side of the building until I glimpse the door I slipped from that fateful Halloween night to wait for my parents. It's almost as if I can see it happening in real time, that beige van careening toward me, the men spilling out of the back to take me. The hood. The screams. The vanishing.

"Are you okay?" Kayla severs the moment, and I remember the handcuffs. I ask to see her wrist and slap the cuffs around hers and mine, making sure I can still get to my gun.

"What the hell?" she screams, pulling away from me. The metal bites into both of our wrists.

"Leverage," I say, lifting our banded wrists up high. I motion toward the back. "Walk."

I warn her to stay quiet so I can keep my eyes and ears primed. At this point, I don't trust anyone or anything, and I have to be ready for any sort of surprise.

As we approach the back of the building, I see a blue van but nothing else.

"Holy shit," Kayla whispers. The edge of her purple lipstick has bled below her lip line. "That's Coach's van." I can tell from her disbelief that she knows nothing about this. "Why would he be here?"

I think about the Ryan I used to know. That cocky grin at the haunted house the night I was taken. His breath on my neck, his hot hands around my waist. Was he involved back then too? Is that what this is all about? He and Laura planned my kidnapping then and want me to remember now? I strain to see if Lulu is anywhere and can only assume she's in the van.

Blue van. Rear entrance. Don't see anyone yet, I type to Joe.

"You ready?" I ask Kayla.

She looks as uncertain as I feel, but I muster any sense of bravado I have and march toward the van. Other than the vehicle, the parking lot is empty.

I pull my gun, motion for Kayla to stay quiet, and tiptoe toward the van. First, I peer into the windows, even though they're tinted. I try the doors next, but they're locked. Moving to the rear, I try again. Also locked.

"Cover your ears," I tell Kayla before I fire a shot at the lock. The sharp pop rips through the barren parking lot. I move forward, take a breath, and yank open the rear van door. Inside, the interior is worn and smells like the inside of a gym bag. In the middle of the van sits the same creepy baby doll from the Polaroids. Dismantled. Missing an eye, a hand, and a foot.

Beneath it is another bloodred card. Glancing behind me to make sure we're not going to get shoved into the van, I half drag Kayla toward the doll and flip over the card.

HEAD INSIDE
FIND THE DOOR WITH THE NEXT CLUE
LEAVE THE MONEY

My mouth goes dry. Where are Joe and Lennon? Where's the guy he brought in for backup?

"I'm not going in there," Kayla insists.

I search the perimeter for cameras. Are Laura and Ryan watching right now?

"We have to," I say to her now, sounding more confident than I feel. I would rather eat glass than walk back into this place. My palms are sweating. My heart is racing. It's like I'm fourteen all over again.

I lead her toward the door, the bag of cash heavy on my shoulder. No way I'm leaving the cash. In my head, I count to three and tug the door open.

Nothing but darkness awaits.

38

THEN

The days pass in a blur.

Evie is gone or dead—that I'm certain of. The men are careful now. They don't even step inside the room. Instead, they simply shove in my food tray in the middle of the night, when I can't see anything. They bring all three meals at once. With each hour moving closer to trials, I'm feeling desperate. How could I have escaped, only to sit here and wait?

I try on different scenarios, wondering what these men want with me. They wanted Evie for something, and now she's gone. They must want something from me too. There must be some merit to keeping me alive, unharmed. Once that reason goes away, I'll become expendable. I shiver as I think about the sound of the hammer breaking Evie's bones. It makes me think of Jessie. What happened at Smorgasbord already feels like a lifetime ago.

Over the last few days, my mind has started to swerve into some deep, dark places. I've imagined how they will kill me at least a million times. What my last words will be. How I will want to be remembered. And because gymnastics is my whole life, this has given me a slightly new perspective.

I've not gone to a normal school since the fifth grade, instead spending most of my time training and the rest with various tutors.

I've never attended a school dance or been on a field trip. I've not walked down a hall with a pack of my friends and gossiped or shoved books into my locker, hurrying to get to the next class. I've seen these things on TV and longed for them like a missing limb. These seem like tiny, nothing moments, but right now, they *matter* to me. They give me something to live for.

While I've spent literally all my time building toward this one shiny thing, I realize now how far-fetched my dream really is. Because how many gymnasts really make the Olympic team? How many girls get everything they want in this sport?

If I do get out of here, I want to do more, take more risks, and have more fun. I don't want to be so serious all the time. I want to get in some trouble, shake things up. I want to kiss a boy. I want to fall in love.

I think of Luke again. I know he's several years older, but could he ever like someone like me? Would I *want* him to? My stomach aches, and I grip it, knowing I need to eat. The food is awful, and the guilt from just sitting here, doing nothing, is the real killer. I haven't been this sedentary in years, and my body doesn't know how to respond. Rest isn't something I know how to do. I'm not built to sit still. I'm built to flip.

Outside, I hear several doors slam and the rev of an engine. I sit all the way up and grip my head as I see stars. My head feels fuzzy. I'm dizzy all the time.

I pull myself up, then steady myself until the vertigo passes. I move closer to the main door, straining to hear. Is that the van? Are they leaving? In all this time, I haven't heard the van even once. Sure enough, I can hear the spray of gravel and then tires grinding down the driveway. After a few moments, it's completely silent. I stare back down at my tray. They left me three meals last night. Does this mean they're my *last* three meals? Are they leaving for good? Are they going to let me die in here? Or will they be back?

Oh God.

Maybe they're not going to torture me. They're going to *starve* me. I'm going to die from lack of food and water.

Even though I know it's useless, I move to the door and begin to bang on it, screaming until my throat is raw. No one comes. Is this how Evie felt? Did she *know*, in her bones, that the end was near?

The stark reality that they are gone and I am here all alone takes my feet from under me, and I slump against the door. At least I can take a shower now, knowing they are probably gone. But I don't have the strength.

I stay like that, slumped against the door, until my parched throat forces me to grab one of the bottles of water. I take a long sip and assess the tray. It's barely morning, and the food is hard to make out. It's been some version of the same thing the entire time. All processed food. All barely edible.

"I'm never getting out of here." My voice sounds strange to my own ears, but the sentence rings true. I'm never getting out. I'm never going home.

They've left me here to die.

39

Now

The warehouse is damp and cold.

It's too quiet. Our footsteps echo over the wet concrete as we shuffle farther into the space. If Lulu is somewhere in here, I can't imagine the psychological damage this might inflict. The fears it might create. Up ahead, there's music playing. As I get closer, I realize it's the theme song from the movie *Halloween*.

"Are you serious?" Kayla hisses. "I don't *do* haunted houses." I can feel her trembling beside me, but I tell her to stay quiet and follow my lead.

I glance up toward the ceiling and spot a few cameras. Is this part of the plan? Bring me back to an infamous haunted house and capture it on video? And now I'll look like the crazy one, handcuffed to an innocent girl.

My heart rate intensifies, just as it did back then. My knee throbs, and in an instant, I remember Jessie's knee getting destroyed by that psychopath, Brian. I remember everything that came after. Evie. The hammer. Almost freezing to death in the woods. Waiting to die in that cabin. Starving slowly, one day at a time.

Snapshots of my past stalk me with every footstep. Why am I here? What am I going to find? I lurch to the right as something bangs down the hall. I pull my gun and point it into the dark, unseen places. Into the shadows, where anyone could be lurking.

As I move deeper into the damp black of the warehouse, I try to figure out why—and how—Laura could orchestrate something like this. She was always a follower, never a leader, always doing everything Jessie said.

I stop in my tracks as that thought unspools into something bigger.

"What? Did you hear something?" Kayla asks, gripping my arm with fake nails. She butts up against me, some of her glitter rubbing off on me.

Jessie insisted she had nothing to do with tonight. But what if she really is the one at the helm? Regardless, I have to find Lulu first. If she's here, I'm not leaving without her.

The *Halloween* theme music intensifies as I approach another long corridor. "Lulu?" I call tentatively. Overhead lights flicker on and off, a strobe effect. Doors line either side, just like they did back then. Will people be waiting on the other side to scare us?

I'm a rational, logical person. Always have been. I like facts and numbers, words and their meanings. I prefer hard work, keeping busy, and to never be too still with my thoughts. I've always been great at puzzles, but this one I can't piece together.

I swallow, take a breath, and kick open the first door to the right. Kayla screams. The strobe effect lingers. There's nothing inside but a metal box in the center of the room. After checking behind us to make sure we're not going to get trapped, I run over with her, pick it up, and then take it back to the safety of the hallway. I set the bag of money on the floor and examine the latch before flipping it open. Inside is another red card, thankfully without a Polaroid or blood.

THIS IS WHERE IT ALL STARTED
SADLY, YOUR DAUGHTER ISN'T HERE
BUT THE TRUTH IS . . .
IT'S TIME FOR YOU TO REMEMBER

I read and reread the card, not understanding. It's time for me to remember? Remember *what*? I've spent years trying to get to the bottom of what happened that night. To find Evie. To uncover the truth so I could move on. I snatch the card and the bag of money and barrel through the rest of the warehouse with Kayla, pushing my way through scary props and sounds. Why did I step foot in here? What did I expect to find?

I squint into the darkness and read the card again. What is the truth, and where could it be hiding? Is it here?

We continue back and forth through the warehouse until Kayla's teeth are chattering, ducking past things that would have once made me cower in fear. Once I'm sure Lulu isn't here, I sprint back toward the doors I came through, my knee catching as it often does, scarred from my botched ACL surgery.

When we burst through the doors, the lot is just as we left it, except there's no van. I blink into the biting cold and spin in a circle, not understanding what is happening. Did Joe find them? Take them to the local precinct? Where did they disappear to?

I retrieve my phone with numb fingers and stab clumsily at the keys to text Joe.

Where are you?

The message fails. I glance around, wondering if I'm in a dead zone. "Joe?" I call his name now, suddenly worried. I try my text messages again and then pull out Jessie's phone to see if it has service.

And that's when I see it. A text from Laura to her, sent just minutes ago.

She has the cash. Where are you?

Before I can make sense of what I should do next, something sharp cracks the back of my skull. My world turns blindingly white and then fades to nothing.

40

THEN

Trials have come and gone, according to my count of how many days I've been here.

I'm out of food and water, though I've been drinking straight from the tap in the bathroom. My lips are still parched, however, and I feel like someone has clawed at my skin and picked all the sore wounds on my flesh until I'm nothing but a scab.

Over a decade of my life trashed in the span of a few days.

I think of all the girls in Boston who most likely placed: the girls I know and the girls I've met at competitions or at camps. Shannon Miller, Dominique Dawes, Dominique Moceanu, maybe Kerri Strug or even Amy Chow. I think of Jaycie Phelps and Amanda Borden, two girls who were super friendly to me at the last meet. I hope they all do well.

I tap my head lightly against the wall behind me, thinking how much of a difference a week can make. My muscles are so weak from inactivity and lack of food that I don't have much of an appetite. Everything feels pointless if I'm not getting out of here. The men haven't been back. I've been out of food for almost two days.

I don't know what the point is in all this. If they weren't here to hurt me, then why did they hurt Evie? If they brought me back only to starve me . . . what was the plan in the first place? Why didn't they just leave me in the woods? None of it makes sense.

Despite knowing I'm going to die, alone and hungry, I still can't help thinking ahead. If I don't think ahead, I will focus on what's going to happen: how my organs will shut down, how I will literally die from lack of food, how I will go to sleep and never wake up. Once, with our tutor, we read about a group of people who got into a plane crash and froze to death. We studied the way their organs shut off one by one. I remember thinking what a horrible way that would be to die, though now I know there are worse things. When I was out in the woods, it had mostly felt peaceful, like I just needed to rest.

I tap my head harder against the wall. A dull throb pulses behind my eyes. Out of all my teammates, I wonder who made the team. Even if they didn't make it, they can set their sights on the 2000 Olympics. What a cruel sport: training your mind and body for a decade so it's ready *now*. But the moment has passed. The opportunity is gone.

Outside, something shrill pierces the air. I stop my pity party and scramble to stand, but my legs buckle, and tiny silver spots explode in front of my eyes. I push through the dizziness. What was that? My heart thuds, heavier and slower than normal. It sounds like a siren. A police siren?

I strain to make sure I didn't just imagine it, and sure enough, the distinctive whine of a police siren gets louder and closer. My survival instinct—something I thought I had lost—kicks into gear, and I begin to scream. I bang on the door as hard as I can.

The sirens break off, and I muster the last bit of strength I have left to scream at the top of my lungs. Outside, car doors slam one after the next, and I ratchet up my voice until my throat burns. Voices escalate outside. Footsteps descend toward the main door, and then a male officer announces himself.

"Please!" I scream, banging against the door. "Please help me! I've been here for a week. Please get me out!"

"Stand back!"

I move back, and then something splinters the door as easily as if it were made of paper. I blink at the sunlight streaming in from outside, lifting my hand up to block the brightness. Several armed officers rush inside, charging into the bathroom, searching the premises, and then shouting "Clear!" one after another, like dominoes falling on a board.

The main officer lowers his weapon. "Cora Valentine?"

Tears spring to my eyes at hearing my own name. I am real. I am alive. I am saved. This simple act of nodding yes, that I *am* Cora Valentine, makes me lose it all at once. I haven't cried in the last few days because, mostly, I've been enraged. Enraged that everything I've worked for has gone to shit. Enraged that I'm stuck here while someone else takes my place. Enraged that I escaped but didn't make it to freedom. Enraged that I hadn't been found. Enraged that I couldn't save Evie. Now it all gushes out in an ugly, hoarse sob. The officer doesn't even flinch as he talks into a walkie.

"We got her. Alert the parents." He takes a big breath and empties it into the freezing room.

Someone drapes a heated silver blanket around my shoulders, and I snuggle into it, even though the material is scratchy and rough against my dirty skin. "How did you find me?" I ask. My throat aches, and I'm desperate for something hot to drink.

"Someone left an anonymous tip. Said they saw movement out here. Asked us to come inspect."

I shake my head. "I've been trapped here for a week. I escaped days ago and ran into the woods, but they found me and brought me back. Then they just left me here." My voice fades. My brain must not be working right. Who called in a tip? Who saw me here? There's no one around for miles. "There was a girl," I say. "Next door. Evie . . . they hurt her." My voice fades as the officer alerts someone that there is a possible second victim. "I think she might be dead."

"Okay, Cora. We'll look into it. Let's just get you home safely."

My legs refuse to work as they guide me up the steps. I stop at the top and turn back toward the second door. Someone has already broken inside where Evie was kept, and curiosity gets the best of me. I limp my way over and step inside the small space, which is almost identical to mine. I search for blood or a body, but the place looks untouched.

"She was here." I turn around to the officer. "We talked to each other through the wall."

"We'll find her." He gently guides me away from the scene of the crime toward a police cruiser. I point to the cabin. The van is gone. "That's where the men were staying. They were driving a beige van."

The main officer, Ronald Bishop, jots those details down. "Did you see who took you?"

I shake my head. "Two men, one bigger, one skinny. They wore ski masks."

"The cabin has been searched. It's vacant," another officer confirms now. "Doesn't look like anyone's been there in years."

I remember the warm lights from the inside and the van parked in the drive. "But I *saw* them." I hesitate. Did I, though? Did I ever actually see them inside? No, I didn't. I just saw the lights when I ran by. Why didn't I look inside to be sure?

"Where are my parents?" The daylight is blinding. My eyes stream with tears from the strength of the sun.

"They're going to meet us at the police station. You've become quite the local superstar, young lady."

I let the words float right over me. Superstar or not, I've missed my shot at the Olympics. I'm so grateful they found me, of course, but what happens now? What am I supposed to do with the rest of my life? All those plans I made—doing other things, having more fun—seem impossible.

I step into the back of the police cruiser, which is thankfully warm. I shiver beneath the blanket and wait for someone to drive me to see my parents. At least they found me. At least I'm safe.

At least I finally get to go home.

41

Now

My head throbs, and my eyes slide around in their sockets before I peel them open.

Bright fluorescent lights make me wince. My hands are bound behind me, and I'm propped up against the vault. I'm at Woodward's again. The handcuffs are gone. And so is Kayla.

My throat is dry, and my body aches from having my shoulders wrenched behind me at such a severe angle. I can already feel my gun is no longer in my waistband. A patch of hair at the back of my head feels damp where I got hit. As I take inventory of myself, I scan the room.

"Lulu!" I scream as loud as I can muster. "Lulu!"

I'm met only with the tinny echo of my own voice.

"Seems you're a bit light," a voice suddenly says. After a moment, Laura appears. She is still mousy, her thin blond hair scraped back in a loose ponytail. She's holding my bag of cash in her hand and shakes it once impatiently. "This isn't a million."

I don't say anything as I finger the rope at my wrists and start to twist back and forth to see if I can loosen them. After I was taken the first time, I learned everything I could about escaping from precarious situations.

"You must not love your daughter as much as you pretend to."

"Where's Joe?"

"If you mean that *oaf* who was with you, you both have grossly underestimated who you're dealing with," she spits. "Him and his dumb friend. They're gone." She drops the bag and takes a few steps toward me.

I refrain from asking what *gone* means. "Where are the girls?"

She ignores my question and crouches down to stare at me, her head cocked to the side. "Look at this. The infamous Cora Valentine, bound next to the very apparatus that ended her career. How's that for poetic?"

My skin begins to tingle as she moves closer. Her eyes look dead, cold.

"Why are you doing this?"

She smiles, revealing two rows of artificially white teeth. "Because it takes a hell of a lot to be noticed in today's world, Cora. Short attention spans. You know how it is." She flicks her wrist in the air as if we're having a casual conversation. "And I want Kayla to have the best opportunities possible. *The* best training. *The* best coaching. *The* best facilities. The best of *everything*. Period."

"And my money is going to help you do that?"

She laughs and then pretends to frown. "Tonight is going to help us do that. Cora Valentine, Olympian, survivor, had a nervous breakdown on the anniversary of her own kidnapping. She went nuts, injured a gymnast, kidnapped another." She pauses and offers me that toothy grin again. "Good improv by the way, bringing Kayla into all this, because now I have video footage of the two of you in the haunted house where all this started. Makes for a pretty good story, yeah?"

"You left out the part where you took my child."

"Eh, that part will get edited out."

Has Laura always been this crazy? What must have happened for her to plan something as maniacal as this? I think of how to stall for time, but I have to know where Lu is first. "I have to hand it to you," I say now, appealing to her ego. "I always thought Jessie was the mastermind of the group."

Her blue eyes flash. "Jessie could never come up with something like this."

Hadn't Jessie said the same thing about her? "But you can?" I'm hoping she'll reveal whose idea this was and give me any clue as to where she could have taken Lu.

"What's that saying?" She cocks her head. "Two heads are better than one?"

"So what? This is payback for me making it to the Olympics when you two didn't?"

She shrugs. "This is payback for you stealing all the limelight. There wasn't any left for us. It was always Cora, Cora, Cora. Well, now it will be Kayla, Kayla, Kayla. Has a better ring to it, don't you think?"

"And what? You get my money and just let me go? We pretend none of this happened?"

"Oh, Cora, sweetie," she says, clucking her tongue. "You're not getting out of anything." She digs something from her coat pocket and brandishes it with that evil smile. A switchblade. I work feverishly at my wrists, trying to be subtle so she can't see me. She plays with the blade, bringing it dangerously close to my face.

"You know, I've spent all these years thinking I was the only one who thought you got unfair treatment. You got all the fame and attention after your kidnapping, and you didn't even get that banged up when you were taken. *Then* you qualified after trials were already over, without the pressures of normal competition. And you ultimately won gold and got everything that none of us did. Even though we all trained just as hard. Even though we all deserved it just as much as you." She swallows. "My whole life, it's like I've been in your shadow. Even now. Even here." She waves the blade toward my poster on the wall. "No matter how good Kayla is, she'll never have her own story. Not unless it's bigger and better than *yours*."

I don't know what to say to that. In some ways, I guess that's what it looks like—that I received preferential treatment, which gave me an unfair advantage to qualify. But I worked harder than almost anyone else on that team, and I didn't deserve to have my shot taken away. I know I can't reason with her; there's no point.

"Where's my daughter, Laura?"

"You know, you haven't trained that one very well." She tuts and wags the blade back and forth near my heart. "Shouldn't a kid like that know better than to just wander off with anyone? Snatching her was like taking candy from a baby," she whispers now. "Or giving candy to a baby."

"Lulu would never walk away with a stranger." One of my hands is nearly free.

"Who said it was a stranger?" Laura gives me a villainous smile, just as I rear back and headbutt her. Because I've never actually done this and have only practiced it in self-defense class, the blow is crushing and does little to help my already throbbing head. But the blade is out of her hand, and she is unconscious for the moment. I mount her anyway, pinning her arms beside her with my thighs while awkwardly leaning down to retrieve the blade with my mouth. I drop it beside me, twist around to grab it, and attempt to saw through the rest of the ropes.

After a few moments, with my thighs on fire and my injured head pulsing along with my heart, the ropes break free. I jump up and run to the front desk to look for something to gag her with. I grab a T-shirt and a roll of duct tape. I stuff the T-shirt in her mouth and roll the duct tape around and around her head. My vision is blurry as I grab the ropes. I need to tie her up. I need to secure her. But I also need to know what she did with Lulu.

"Cora, thank God!" Joe rushes in through the front door, panting, blood dripping from a similar wound on his head. He looks from me to Laura, then back to me again.

"I'm so sorry. I got here as fast as I could. I got knocked out."

"Help me tie her up," I say.

Without question, he moves to help. I fill him in on what Laura revealed.

"What happened?" I ask as Joe works the rope expertly around her wrists.

"When you went in, we were hiding out. Some guy—their coach, I guess—pulled a gun on me and Lennon. I wrestled it out of his hand." He motions to his head. "Eventually. But then he took off running. I had my friend take Lennon to safety. I went after him, but it's like he just vanished. When I got back, I went inside the haunted house to get you, but you weren't there either. Then I got knocked out by something. When I came to, I drove to every place I could think of. This was my last stop." He grins, almost proud of himself for figuring it out.

"Where's Kayla?"

He motions to Laura. "I'm assuming she stashed her somewhere safe. And Lennon is at my friend's cabin. He's a good guy. He'll keep her safe."

I nod. We count to three and then drag Laura to the bars as though moving mats, not a body.

"Did she tell you where Lu is?" he asks hopefully.

"No, she didn't. But, Joe, I know who's helping her."

"So do I."

I stand and place a hand on my woozy head after we secure Laura to the bars. "Are you thinking what I'm thinking?"

"It has to be Jessie," he says, confirming the suspicions I've had all along. "She knows where Lulu is."

42

THEN

I memorize everything on the drive to the station.

I want to know exactly where I was kept. The sun hurts my eyes, and I blink rapidly, tears streaming down my face. I marvel at the dappled leaves of the trees. I marvel at the two officers' voices as they chat casually up front. I marvel at their radio, which squawks calls and updates every few minutes. I marvel at my cold hands in my lap. My fingers look like they've been gnawed on by a rat, bloody and inflamed. I must look like a total mess, with all those cuts from the branches and my still-swollen lip.

Though I cleaned myself with a washcloth and soap, I can still smell myself and cannot wait for a change of clothes and a hot shower. My stomach flips as I realize I get to see my parents soon. I get to go home. I'm still Cora Valentine, the gymnast, only now I have a crazy story to tell. Something happened to me beyond gymnastics. I am a survivor. I escaped a kidnapping.

But what happened to Evie?

Even as I replay the last week of my life, it seems like it might have happened to someone else. Not only did it happen, but I am mostly unharmed. Mostly intact.

The realization that the trials are still over and that I will have to wait another four years to compete pushes in again. Despite how happy I am to be driving in a police cruiser back to my side of the woods, the reality still hurts. I was kept away from my dreams. Someone took it from me, and I want to know who. One day, I will make them pay.

I grip my hands into fists and can feel my breath grow shallow in my chest.

One of the officers says something, but I'm not paying attention. I'm too focused on what was taken from me, what I was robbed of.

"Do you have any idea who did this?" My voice is still raspy. It hurts to talk.

"That's what we're hoping you can help us with, Cora," Officer Bishop says, turning around in his seat. "We'll get to the bottom of it."

I nod, training my eyes back out the window. So far, it seems we've just been driving in a straight line south for an hour. "Where are we?"

"We're about ninety minutes south of Atlanta now," the other officer says. "No one lives out where you were kept. Nothing but forest."

"Then who called in the tip? A guy or girl?"

"It was a guy," Officer Bishop says. "Unknown number."

Was it one of the men who took me? I shake my head as if answering my own question. How would *that* make any sense?

"It's quite the story, young lady," the other officer says. I haven't seen his name tag. "You're going to be a hero."

"I'm not a hero," I say. My voice sounds strange and flat to my ears. I might be a survivor, but I'm not a hero. And I just want to find who did this so all this makes some kind of sense.

My body is still cold despite the heat and blankets. I close my eyes for a moment, suddenly more exhausted than I've ever been in my whole life. But I can't go to sleep. I have to know where we are, to see if there are any clues I can take from these surroundings. So far, it all seems random. Though I know none of this is random. Someone was behind this. Someone planned it.

"We'll be there in about half an hour, Cora," Officer Bishop says. "Why don't you just rest your eyes? We'll let you know when we arrive."

I almost snort. If they think I trust them enough to drift off to sleep, then they have no idea what I've just been through. I wonder if I'll ever sleep soundly again.

The men turn back to their conversation, laughing and joking as if they are old friends. Will I ever laugh again? Will I ever feel normal again?

I pull the blanket higher onto my shoulders and resume my gaze outside. The trees whip by, one after another, bringing me closer to my parents.

Closer to home.

43

Now

"How'd you figure it out?" I ask now.

Before we left the gym, Joe got me a bag of ice for my head. I adjust it from the front to the back, until my entire head feels numb.

"I started doing a little digging," he explains now, speeding back toward my property. "When the lawsuit hit with your dad, there were only two girls from the team who testified, but the records were kept sealed, of course, to protect the victims' privacy."

I remember. I'd been desperate to know who flung those accusations at my father.

"I got the records."

"Let me guess," I supply. "Laura and Jessie."

"Ding, ding, ding. *Not* Madeline, like Jessie said. But get this: I also looked up both their financials, and let me tell you." Joe whistles. "They're a mess. They've both gone into debt with tutors and coaching and travel for the girls."

I know Laura is single, but I thought Jessie had money. "What about Jessie's husband?"

"They basically live separate lives. They signed a prenup, and since he's not Lennon's real father, he doesn't pay for *any* of her training."

Well, at least she was telling the truth about that. I nod, some of this starting to make a little more sense. "So they were both in a financial bind and saw an opportunity to get paid from a lawsuit against my father." Even saying it out loud makes me sick. "Then they burn through that money and decide to stage a kidnapping to come after me?" It sounds even more ridiculous out loud.

"Well, the timing is pretty spot on. Trials are around the corner. They want the spotlight on their kids."

I scoff. "And they really just thought they could pull all this off?"

"Well, it appears their plan has gone off the rails a bit. It seems Laura could have double-crossed Jessie," he says. "Lennon has the best shot to make trials, and Laura knows it. So she went rogue when she told you to injure Lennon. There's no way Jessie would have gone along with that."

"And tonight at the haunted house was nothing more than a publicity stunt," I confirm. "Jessie was going to say her daughter was kidnapped on Halloween, just like I was all those years ago. That she was held for ransom. That I was involved. And then Laura would leak footage of me at that haunted house handcuffed to Kayla . . . like I'd lost my mind."

"And what a sensational story right before trials," he supplies.

Chills stud my skin as the timing of all this sinks in. "They'd be center stage, so their daughters get more attention." I massage my sore temple. "But what if their plan backfires?"

He snorts. "Cora, somehow I don't think you're dealing with the most intelligent criminals here."

"But they still have Lu," I say as Joe swings a right on my main road. "They hurt her. They hacked my security system; they took her right from under my nose. And now that I know it's them, do you really think they're going to just give her back to me? That they're just going to take my money, let me walk, and trust I won't go to the cops?"

"In all honesty, I don't think they expected you to figure it out at all, which is why things have gone south. Laura panicked when you stashed

Jessie and brought Kayla in her place. I think it caused her to make some big mistakes. But don't worry," he continues, clearly seeing the worry on my face. "I've already contacted Officer Bishop and the rest of the department. Now that we know Laura and Jessie are behind this, they'll find Lu, okay? Once I drop you, I'll have Bishop send officers to the gym to take Laura into custody and question her. And they'll send people to Jessie's house too. We'll see what we can get out of her before then, but it might be best to hand this over to the cops now," he says.

I agree. It's what we should have done to start with. "Jesus, Joe." I close my eyes as we bump over the long gravel road leading to my cabin. "So what's the play while we wait for the cops?"

He taps his fingers on the steering wheel. "That's what we need to figure out. And fast." He stops at the edge of my driveway. "What do you want to do about Jessie?"

I stare into his eyes, this man who has become my friend, my lifeline. "I think I should keep playing along, see if I can get anything out of her before the cops arrive."

"Agreed."

We talk strategy. We decide to tell Jessie that Laura is dead and see where that leads us. If Jessie thinks Laura is out of the picture, maybe she'll want to keep all the money for herself. He hands me one of his guns, which I secure in my waistband. He tosses me the duffel of half my cash.

"Lure her with this. I'm going to be waiting at the cabin. I'll hide the car so she doesn't get spooked. Hopefully the cops will be here soon."

"Copy that." I hesitate with my hand on the door, the duffel in hand. "Joe, if all this goes south . . ."

"It won't. I won't let anything happen to you or Lu. We're going to bring her home. Together. I promise."

I nod as I get out of the car and watch his taillights fade away. The bag of ice has made my head cold, and with the frigid temperatures and my ramped-up nerves, I begin to tremble. I start to jog toward the fallout shelter, hoping that Jessie hasn't somehow frozen to death before I can find out where Lulu is.

It's all coming full circle: me confronting my old team captain on Halloween. Except this time, it's not me calling her out for being cruel; it's me calling her out for being a kidnapper.

I sprint through the woods, the duffel heavy on my shoulder. Only Jessie stands between me and my daughter now, and this time, I'm not walking away until she tells me everything.

I'll do whatever it takes to uncover the truth.

44

Then

My parents storm the police cruiser before it's even come to a complete stop.

My mother wails as she gathers me in her arms, and my father cries openly, something I've never seen him do. They take turns gripping every inch of me, whispering loving words into my dirty hair, and I squeeze them back with as much strength as I can muster and finally go limp in their arms.

I'm safe.

"We just don't understand how this happened," my mother says, wiping her eyes. "Oh, sweetheart, what did they do to your face?"

"They hurt you?" my father asks, examining my cuts. "I'll kill them."

They toggle back and forth like this, vacillating between questions and statements. A menacing headache hits me right between the eyes. I'm too weak to talk, though the officers are motioning us inside. What happens now? Statements? A national manhunt? A trial?

I don't want any of that. I just want this to be over. I want to go back to my normal life. Already, the thought of walking back into the gym to face everyone elicits fear, agony, and ultimately defeat. I will have to wait another *four years*. Another four years of routines and growing and training and competing and trying to prevent injuries. Can I do it? Can my body do it?

My knees buckle, and my parents each clutch an elbow.

"Oh, baby. Let's get you inside. We'll get you home just as soon as we can, okay?" My father loops a steadying arm around my waist. "You're so thin, sweetie."

Reporters line both sides of the walkway. People with homemade posters wave their kind words at me. Flashbulbs, microphones, and simultaneous questions fly at me from every direction. My parents act as a physical barrier as we move inside the precinct.

I slump against a wall, beyond exhausted, and ask the single question I've been dreading for days. "What happened at trials?"

My mother adjusts her glasses and looks at me, a strand of her curly hair coiled in the hinge. "What?"

My father looks at his shoes. "No one from the team qualified, hon. I'm so sorry."

Sorrow burrows a hole straight through my heart. That could have been me. That *should* have been me. "What about Jessie?"

"She's done," my father continues. "Doctors already did a surgery, but . . ." He shakes his head. "She won't ever compete again."

Why did we have to go to that stupid haunted house? If only we hadn't gone, everything would be fine. Everything would have worked out. None of this would be happening.

A police officer guides us back to a room, but I don't want to be questioned. I didn't see who took me. I don't know who did this. I just want to take a hot shower, go to bed, and pretend none of this ever happened.

I'm guided to a chair. My parents stand back, hovering near me. A telephone sits on the desk, and the fluorescent lights hurt my eyes. Noticing, my mother walks over and flips them off.

"Thanks, Mom."

Her whole face lights up, as if I've just given her the highest compliment. Someone enters the room, a detective, by the looks of him. Noticing it's dark, he flips on the switch, but my mother interrupts.

"Her eyes are sensitive," she says. "Can you please turn it back off?"
He does as he's told and then slaps a file on the desk.

"So, Cora. You've had quite the adventure, I see." His thick mustache hides his lips. His eyes look as tired as I feel, and his belly strains against a wrinkled work shirt. There's a ketchup stain near his tie.

My jaw clicks. "It wasn't an adventure," I say. "I was kidnapped."

He looks stricken and quickly self-corrects by clearing his throat. "Of course, of course." Before he can start his line of pointless questioning, I speak up.

"You have to find the other girl I was with."

My parents look at me, stunned. "There was someone else down there with you?" my mother asks. "Stan? Did they tell you this?" She glares at the detective. "Why didn't you tell us this?"

"She was kept in the room beside mine," I clarify. "Her name was Evie. They . . . they tortured her with a hammer. She was injured, and then she just disappeared." A tear trickles down my cheek. "I think they killed her."

The detective should be jotting down notes, but he doesn't. Instead, he adjusts his belt. "About that, Cora." He clears his throat. "We've put out a BOLO for another missing girl, first name Evie. There are no missing person reports, nothing at all."

"So?" I say. "She could have been an adult, or maybe she wasn't from here. She said she was a cheerleader."

It's so silent in the room, I can hear the ticking of the clock. Why isn't anyone saying anything?

"We'll look into that, Cora. We will, but first, we're going to focus on you, okay?" The phone rings before he can continue. "I'm sorry. Excuse me for a second." He answers it, and I close my eyes. I've never felt so exhausted in my life. I could sleep for a year. Already thinking about a shower, brushing my teeth, a warm meal, and my stuffed animals makes me feel marginally better. Something to look forward to when so much has been stolen.

"Oh?" The detective perks up. "How about you tell her?" Suddenly, he extends the receiver toward me. "Béla Károlyi on the line for you." One eyebrow raises as he says it.

In a flash, my father's hand is on my shoulder, fingers dancing with curiosity. After a moment, we look at each other.

"Take it," my father whispers. He claps me on the shoulder this time, then squeezes it.

"Hello?" There's a bit of static on the other end before I hear Béla's infamous voice.

"Cora, my dear, we are so thankful you are safe." His thick accent fills my entire heart.

I don't know what to say, so I say nothing.

"We know you could not help missing trials, so we come to you for tryouts, yes? You get do-over," he says. "We judge you just like other girls. You want to make team, yes?"

My heart is beating so rapidly, I fear he can hear it. "Yes!" I exclaim, practically jumping up and doing a flip on the spot. "More than anything," I add.

He chuckles, a deep, low rasp. "We give you one week; then you try out, yes? You be ready. Show us what you've got, superstar. Okay, bye-bye." The dial tone rings in my ear before I register what he's said. I have one week to make my dreams come true? I get a second shot? I can still make it?

I hand the receiver back to the detective in a daze. I stare up at my father, the man who has been with me my entire career.

"They're letting me try out," I say in utter disbelief. "In one week. Here. At home. I've still got a shot, Dad." I bite my sore lip in an attempt to keep from crying.

He crushes me in a hug before I can finish, and we jump up and down in a circle. All the energy rushes back to my body, and I'm beside myself. From agony to joy. From hopelessness to promise. From lost to saved. Just like that.

"I have to be ready." A week isn't a lot of time. I need rest; then I have to get back to training. My routines are already a flurry in my head as I deconstruct them.

"Cora." The detective interrupts my happy moment, piercing my protective bubble of training preparation. "We need you to answer some questions first."

I'll do whatever they say if it means I can get out of here sooner. Suddenly, I am obedient Cora, good-student Cora, the Cora who still has her shot.

"Okay," I say. I sit up straight, cross my hands over each other, and focus. "I'll answer whatever I can."

45

Now

I jog through the woods until I'm at the fallout shelter door.

I steel myself to keep the charade alive, even though it's going to take everything in me not to force the confession out of her. After flinging open the door, I peer inside.

"Jessie? Come on up."

"Cora?" Her teeth are chattering as her pale face springs into view. "Oh, thank God." She's barely able to move as she climbs stiffly up the rungs. "Did you find your daughter?"

I almost shove her back to the bottom of the shelter. "No," I say. I grab her arm, which is like ice. "Let's get you inside."

Every few steps, I have to slow down so she can keep up in her high heels. Once we're inside, I drop the heavy duffel, grab Jessie a blanket, stoke the fire, and heat up some water for tea. Joe must be somewhere, but he's staying out of sight. Smart. Just knowing he's nearby makes me feel like I can handle this. I can force the truth from Jessie. Find my daughter. End this once and for all.

She takes in the bump on my head. "Jesus, what happened to you?"

"Well, let's see," I say, handing her the hot tea. "We figured out Laura orchestrated everything. She lured me back to Smorgasbord."

"What?" Jessie looks genuinely shocked as she takes a sip of tea. "Why?"

"Doesn't matter. What does matter is that she knocked me unconscious and tied me up, but I got away."

"So where is she?"

I take a sip of my own tea, hoping the hot liquid can thaw me out. "Dead."

Life seems to pour back into Jessie's limbs as she jumps up. The blanket falls to a puddle at her feet. "She's *dead*? Where's Lennon?" She glances around, as if just now realizing her daughter isn't here.

"She's fine."

"Where is she, Cora?"

"Like I said, she's fine," I say now. "But with Laura gone, I have no idea how to get my daughter back."

I watch her like a hawk, waiting for any signs or tells. I also keep my ears alert for sirens, not wanting them to come too early and spook her. Bringing us back to the task at hand, I kick the bag of money at my feet. "At least she didn't get this."

"I just can't understand how or why she would do all this," she says, the perfect picture of innocence. "Hurting Lennon. Taking your daughter. Bringing me into this. How could we have been on a gymnastics team with a *psychopath* all that time and not even know it?"

"Amazing how that works, isn't it?" I'm impressed by her acting ability.

"I need to get to Lennon. I need to be with her."

Suddenly my need to know the truth outweighs playing this the "right" way, and I cave. "Sure, Jessie. But I'm going to need you to tell me where Lulu is first."

She freezes and looks at me, her small eyes unblinking. "How am I supposed to know?" She presses a hand to her chest again, just as she did earlier. Her fingers are ugly and purple from the staunch cold. "I knew Laura, but I had no idea she was capable of anything like this. I swear."

"Jessie, do you have any idea what I've been through tonight?" I can feel my patience slip away completely. "I have been on a wild-goose chase around this town. I have been knocked out, tied up, bribed, and lied to. And I'm done." My voice is much too calm for the riot happening inside. "I need you to cut the act and tell me where she is."

"Cut *what* act? I swear to you, Cora, I have nothing to do with this. I've said that all along."

Something bangs from the back, and I exhale. Joe is here, and hopefully Officer Bishop will be next.

Jessie continues. "Look, I don't know *what* is going on, but I need to get to my daughter." She moves toward the door, but I grab her phone from my pocket and throw it at her.

"You got a new text."

She stares at her phone. "So?"

"Read it."

She unlocks her phone and shakes her head as she reads Laura's text out loud, then looks up at me. "What is this? I swear I have no idea what she's talking about."

"You can just wait to tell that to the cops," I say, gesturing for her to sit back down on the sofa. She sighs and plops back down, crossing her arms.

Maybe I can't get the truth out of her, but hopefully Officer Bishop can.

Then this will all be over.

46

THEN

I steady my breath and chalk my hands.

For trials, I'm starting with bars. Though I'm shaky with nerves, the fact that I get to compete at my home gym, on my own turf, with familiar faces all around, calms me. My body feels nowhere near normal, but I am as ready as I can possibly be.

Once I got home, I was shocked to see I'd lost nearly seven pounds in that short week away. My dad said it would be an advantage. I don't feel as physically strong, but because I'm lighter, I've been getting more air on vault and floor, which is where I'll finish today.

I clap my hands, and a puff of chalk clouds my face. I hold my breath so I don't sneeze. While I adjust my grips and wait for the judges to raise their hands, which is my official signal to begin, I scan the small crowd that is permitted to attend. There are reporters; some outside spectators; the Károlyis, of course; my coach; my parents; and the girls from my team.

They have all been seminice to me since I returned, even Jessie, who is scheduled for her second surgery in two weeks. Her kneecap is completely shattered. She will never tumble again. I feel awful for her, but I can't think about that now.

I know it doesn't all come down to today. The Olympic team is chosen cumulatively, as gymnasts are judged and assessed across the most recent competitive season. I've had solid showings across the board, but for me, it feels like it's all about today. I have Béla's and Márta's full and undivided attention. This is what I dreamed about while I was stuck in that bunker. It's what I hoped and prayed for. And now it's here. My second chance.

The judges raise their hands, and I raise mine back, then take a cleansing breath as I mount the bars. I pop off the springboard and am over the low bar in a hollow body position, gliding into my first kip on high bar. I cast into a perfect handstand, then complete two giants before my full pirouette. Then, it's my first release move. It's not as high as I'd like, but I sail over the bar in a wide straddle, then pop back to the low bar. I complete my salto and then am back at the high bar to prepare for my dismount. I have three giants and then a double back dismount. I make sure I gain enough momentum and then fly off the high bar. I know I'm going to stick the landing before I'm even on the mat.

I do. I raise my arms overhead, chest thrust proudly, before jogging off to hug my coach and high-five the girls. That was possibly the best bar routine I've ever done. I await my score, gnawing on my bottom lip, which has finally healed.

When I see it, I jump up and down, then hug my coach again. It's a 9.85, my personal best on bars.

One down, I tell myself. Beam is next. I clear my mind before I mount the beam. Normally, there are other routines going on during this part of the competition, but I feel all eyes on me. Today, I won't cave to the pressure. I won't hide behind the spotlight. Instead, I embrace it.

As I mount the beam and begin my routine, I channel every bit of confidence and artistry I have. I make perfect turns, high leaps, and flip as if I'm on floor. I don't wobble or shake, and by the time I'm lining up my back handsprings for my dismount, I've already seen myself nail the landing. I make the tiniest of hops, but I'm happy with the overall performance and rush off to await my score. The beam judges are notoriously tough, so I get only a 9.75, but I know my best two events are next.

It's floor first, then vault. I grab a drink of water and get a pep talk from my coach. We both know I've got this in the bag. Floor is the one place I feel most at home, and as I take the floor, I cannot wait to show everyone what I've got.

When the music starts, I channel everything from the last few weeks: my hopes and fears, the journey to get here, and almost having it all taken away. I tumble higher than I've ever tumbled, but it's like I have superglue on the bottom of my feet. I stick every landing, I execute every move, and when I finish, there is a collective roar from the crowd.

I hurry off the floor, dazed, and await the score.

"It's a ten!" my dad screams before I even see it, and there it is: the first perfect 10 of my competitive life. My eyes well with appreciative tears as my coach crushes me in yet another hug. I am doing it. Just one more event. One more event, which is my favorite, and I might have made it after all.

I try to compartmentalize what I've done so far, because it really does all come down to this. Two vaults, which span maybe twenty seconds of my life. This is my make-or-break moment. Every competition, every practice, every hour, every drop of sweat, every tear. None of it matters if I can't execute these two vaults to perfection.

"Okay, Cora," my coach says, lowering herself to eye level. "Let's go with the easier vault, okay? You've already proved yourself today. No need to push harder than you need to. Let's take this home safely." She taps me on the bottom, and I move off to the runway. I have two prepared vaults, one easier, one harder, but I can opt for the lower level of difficulty for both. It will lower my score, but at this point, it shouldn't matter much. I need to protect myself. I need to be safe.

I brace myself at the end of the runway and wait for the judge's go-ahead. When I get it, I raise my own hand; clap my hands, which are covered in chalk; and take off like a bat out of hell. Because I'm lighter,

I am running faster than I ever have. I hit the springboard perfectly and perform the easier vault, sticking the landing.

My coach gives me a thumbs-up. It's a 9.80. Not bad. I'm supposed to do the exact same vault but with a full-twisting layout at the end. I wait, and when signaled, I take off running again. Before I can change my mind, I perform the harder vault. I flip onto the horse and spring off with enough twists to land blindly, stick the landing, and thrust my arms high.

I stand there, stunned for a moment, and then trot back to the start. My coach gives me a surprised look but crushes me in a hug.

"Someone came to play," she says, kissing my head.

We wait with bated breath for the score, and I jump up and down when I see it's a 9.9.

Somehow I have had the best meet of my life, despite not having trained, losing weight, and being kidnapped. It's a ridiculous thought, and I burst into nervous laughter as my team surrounds me. The girls congratulate me, but I can see it behind their eyes: They are jealous. They are not happy for me. Maybe they never have been.

I pull on my warm-ups and drink my water, knowing I will have interviews and then have to wait for the committee to make the final decision. I remind myself that I've waited this long. I've done everything I can. What's a few more months?

As I ready myself for the postcompetition interviews, Béla and Márta bound up to me and embrace me in a hug.

"That was some of the best gymnastics I have ever seen," Márta says. Her eyes are kind behind her thick glasses. She never gives compliments unless they're deserved, and I can only nod, I'm so moved by her words.

"We have already made decision," Béla says, clapping a large hand on my back. "You are in. You've made Olympic team. Celebrate, okay? And then you show up to Atlanta just like that. We will make announcement now." He snaps and points to a news camera operator, who comes over. I am yanked to stand between Béla and Márta, but my brain is spinning.

I made the Olympic team. *I did it.* After everything, I'm in.

I think I black out during the interview. I don't even remember what I say in response to all the questions. After a few more interviews, the crowd thins. My coach talks animatedly to my parents. Our gym is going to be represented after all. I've done what I always set out to do. The relief is an anchor. *I* did it. No one else.

"Way to go out there."

I turn to find Luke standing against the small row of bleachers we roll out for local competitions. He's wearing a hoodie and looks even cuter than normal. What would he say if he knew I'd thought about him in that bunker? That he'd crossed my mind more than once?

"Thanks," I say, moving a step closer. "I just can't believe it."

He offers me a shy smile. "I can. You really earned it, Cora. Congrats." He moves to leave, but I stop him with a hand on his arm.

He turns, surprised, and I can feel my heartbeat whooshing through my ears. "I never got to thank you," I say. "For that night at the haunted house."

"What do you mean?"

"For calming me down. For helping me out of that mess. I guess I should have let you take me out of there, huh?" I try to make a joke, but it falls flat.

"But then all of this wouldn't have happened, right?" he asks. "Everything happens for a reason, Cora," he says. "Maybe this is yours." He offers his hand in a wave and leaves me standing there. Could he be right? Could the kidnapping have been a *good* thing?

My body certainly seems to think so. I've never performed like that in the history of competitive gymnastics. I just hope I can keep it up for the actual Games.

I've never wanted anything more.

47

Now

"I need to go to the bathroom."

I motion for Jessie to go, knowing there's no exit from that part of the house. Once she's locked the door, I peer out back and find Joe sitting on the back porch.

"Can you see where the cops are?"

He nods and dials Bishop's phone. "Bishop," he says. "We're at Valentine's. How far out are you?" He nods before hanging up. "They've detained Laura and are headed here next."

I exhale. "Did he get her to talk?"

"Didn't say." He drums his good foot on the porch stairs. "This is all so out of hand, Cora. I'm so sorry."

"It's not your fault," I say, meaning it.

He gestures inside. "Should you have your eyes off her?"

"Good point." I head back inside just as Jessie emerges. I point to the couch, and she rolls her eyes again.

"This is all a huge misunderstanding," she says. "I'm as much a victim in this as you are."

I let out a sharp laugh. "Oh really, Jessie? You're as much a victim as I am? The last I recall, your daughter is safe and sound, unlike mine."

"I've never even *seen* your daughter before, Cora. I don't know why you won't believe me."

"Enough!" I shout with enough force to make my throat ache. "Enough with the lies!"

"They're not lies," she fires back.

My burner phone buzzes. It's Joe. Annoyed he won't just come in, I step outside, one eye trained on Jessie.

He meets me at the door. "Bishop's got a lead on Lu," he whispers now.

I grip his arm. "Where?"

He hesitates and glances inside at the couch. "Her house."

The rage lands like a slap. How can she just sit there and lie to my face? How can she pretend she's not responsible for all this? It takes everything in me not to rip her to shreds. "Then let's go."

He gestures to her. "Should we bring her or put her back in the shelter?"

I vacillate. She needs to be arrested, but what if she finds a way to escape? "If we take her, she needs to be restrained."

He nods. "I'll take care of it. Let's go."

Before I can calculate what he's doing, he walks up to Jessie and strikes her precisely on the head with the butt of his gun. She slumps forward, unconscious immediately.

"Joe!" It's the most aggressive thing I've ever seen him do, and it reminds me he had a whole life of police work before we met.

He gestures to her and puts his gun back on his hip. "The blow was precise. She'll be fine. Grab some rope so we can carry her to the trunk."

I do as I'm told. Once she's restrained, I hoist her legs while he scoops from under her arms. As we lift her, a few items tumble from her pockets, and my eyes snag on one of them.

"Oh my God." I drop her legs, which causes Joe to stumble backward and almost lose his balance.

"Cora," he groans. "What are you doing?" He lowers her carefully to the earth.

I drop to my knees. On the ground, next to her keys, is the worry doll I lost the night I was taken. I inspect it to see if it's the same one. It is. But it couldn't be. I turn it over in my hands in utter disbelief. Why is this here? And how would Jessie have it? I'm speechless. All I can do is hold the little doll in the palm of my hand, offering it up to him like a long-lost fossil. "How does she have this?"

He squints down at me. "I don't even know what that is."

"It's my worry doll. I had it with me the night I was kidnapped, but I lost it. If she has it, then that means . . ." No. I can't even fathom what that means.

"We'll work all this out at the precinct, okay? Let's get her in the trunk before she wakes up."

Once she's inside, I hop in the passenger side of his car and fasten my seat belt, then turn the doll over and over in my hand. How could she have been involved back then? Were her and Laura in on it from the beginning? What if the whole team knew?

"We'll get to the bottom of all this," Joe says now, reversing expertly down my drive.

We're both quiet as we head toward Jessie's house, me for the second time tonight. We pull onto the main stretch of road and drive for ten minutes. Joe's street is up to the left.

Suddenly, Jessie starts kicking and screaming from the trunk.

"Should I just keep driving?" he yells over the absolute fit Jessie is throwing from the back.

"Your house is up ahead. Can you grab some duct tape?" The last thing I want to do is take a pit stop before we finally get to my daughter. Lulu could have been in Jessie's house this whole time, and I didn't even know. I'd never even thought to check the rest of the house.

"Yeah. I'll be two seconds." He speeds into his driveway, leaves the car running, and heads inside. Jessie's screams intensify my throbbing head. I search for my ice pack. I must have dropped it on the floor. The last thing I want is for it to drench his floorboards, though does that really matter? I reach under the seat and find it, then open the door to empty out the ice and shove the rag in his glove compartment. With damp fingers, I clutch the worry doll again, glancing at Joe's cabin. I know I shouldn't, but I can't help myself.

I walk around to the driver's side, pop the trunk, and stare down at a startled Jessie. I pinch the worry doll in my fingers.

"Where did you get this?" My voice is hysterical, but I don't care. No one knew I had this worry doll. Only the kidnappers. I always thought it fell out in the van the night I was taken. "Tell me!"

She screams and starts to cry, shaking her head. "I don't even know what that is! Let me go! Please!" She bucks her body, but I don't believe anything she says. She's not innocent. She never was.

"Cora!" Joe's harsh bark brings me back to myself. "Help me."

He tosses me a roll of duct tape, and once Jessie sees it and Joe, she begins to scream again until I secure the duct tape around her mouth.

"This doesn't feel right," he says, hesitating with his palm on the trunk as we slam it closed.

"No shit," I say, motioning for him to start the car. "Let's go."

48

In the days after trials, I search for Evie.

I hunt for her like a missing child. I go to the library. I bring her up in interviews. I ask everyone I know and piece together what little information I have. I research all the nearby schools with cheerleading departments. No one has heard of her.

The cops are no help. No parents reported a child missing within the area, so she must not be local, they've said. I want to beg them to reconsider. She was real. She was somebody's child. Her parents deserve to know what happened.

I thought I wanted to be back home, but now, when I'm in my room at night, surrounded by all my stuffed animals, all I can think about is Evie. Evie's screams. Evie's bones being bashed with a hammer. Evie going silent. Evie disappearing for good.

It seems I've forgotten how to sleep, how to concentrate, how to act normal. If I thought I was ostracized before, now the girls treat me like a ghost. They look right through me. They don't ask questions. I'd like to think no one knows what to say, but it seems most of them are jealous I qualified.

It's like I cheated, because I got a second chance.

My parents take me to therapy twice a week, even though I don't really have time. It's awkward, and I don't know what to say. Mostly, I want to talk about Evie. My therapist thinks maybe Evie wasn't real—that I created her, like an imaginary friend, to keep me safe in there. I want to tell her that she's wrong. She was real.

But when she gives her assessment to the police, they seem relieved. Now they don't have to hunt for someone else. They can focus on me. They can focus on finding my kidnappers. Even with what I've told them, the leads have run cold.

They can't seem to find any beige vans, or traces of DNA, or whatever it is the cops use. I feel like a spectacle everywhere I go. There are clumps of reporters who wait outside our house and the gym. As the Olympics draw near, people want to know more about the kidnapping. They want to know more about *me*.

After my last practice before the Olympics, I decide to walk home. My dad is tied up with the coach, and I've found a private path through a walking trail that leads straight to our neighborhood. The reporters haven't discovered it yet. I've thought twice about walking alone, even in the daytime. What if I get snatched again?

Has that ever happened? A girl being kidnapped twice?

As I pull on my street clothes and start down the path, I realize that I'm not as scared as I used to be. Because I did survive. My dreams are coming true. So why don't I feel more excited? Why don't I feel relieved?

I'm so lost in thought, I don't even hear someone say my name. I jump as I turn. It's Luke. I smile before I can catch myself and tuck a strand of hair behind my ear. "Hey," I say.

He motions around me, his eyes wide and concerned. "Cora, do you really think it's smart to be walking by yourself after what happened?"

Some of my excitement at seeing him slips. He sounds like a concerned older brother, not someone who might be interested in me.

"I'm fine," I say, my voice sharper than I intended. I turn and resume walking, but he jogs to catch up.

"Hey, I didn't mean it like that. I just . . ." He runs a hand through his hair, and his green eyes catch the light. "I want you to be careful."

I stop, clenching my jaw, a rage I didn't even know existed festering and building like pressure in a balloon. "You know what?" I say, gripping my backpack straps tightly. "I've been careful my entire life. I've gotten good grades. I've been a good athlete. I've done everything right," I say. "And you know what that's gotten me?" He doesn't respond, so I continue. "It's gotten me no friends." I tick the items off on my fingers. "It's gotten me nearly killed. It's gotten my teammates to hate me even more, because I made it and they didn't. It's gotten me to where I can barely eat or sleep or see anything other than what almost happened to me, and I just don't know how to escape it. I don't know if I'm ever going to feel like myself again." Tears spill over my cheeks, and then I'm crying in great heaving sobs. I'm too overcome with emotion to be embarrassed. It all spills out in an ugly rush. I smear away the tears and continue. "When I was taken, I made all these promises. That if I got out, I would focus on more than just gymnastics. Maybe I could finally find a boyfriend. Maybe I could finally be kissed." My cheeks warm at the confession. "But here I am, training like always, about to represent my country. I'm scared shitless, and I don't feel excited *at all*. Instead, all I feel is dread."

The words ooze from me at last, and I feel empty, wrung out. I suck in a shaky breath, and I fully expect Luke to run away as fast as he can. Instead, he takes a step forward, nearly holding his breath. He extends a hand, and I watch his beautiful brown fingers reach toward my cheek to tuck an errant strand of hair behind my ear. He doesn't say anything, but it's all over his face. I see it, maybe for the first time. He *understands* me. He gets exactly what I just said.

Before I can apologize or make some sort of joke, he bends down, and at first, I think he's just going to whisper something comforting in my ear. But then I see his eyes are closing, and so are mine, and there's this delicious moment when there's nothing between us, and then there's *everything*. When his lips touch mine, it's the most sensational thing I've ever felt.

Luke's mouth is warm and gentle, and I find myself parting my lips to search his tongue with mine. We've never kissed each other before, but it's the most natural thing in the world. It is electric, as if this one kiss is shocking me back to life. I drop my arms from my straps and lean all the way into him, snaking my fingers around his neck.

His hands caress my face, my neck, and the outline of my chest and then tug on my hips. I gently bite his lip, and he moans. Then we break apart, panting.

I touch my swollen lips. I've never felt more alive in my whole life.

"Now you can say you've been kissed, Cora Valentine." His chest heaves, and his eyes are doing things to me that I didn't know existed. "Can I walk you the rest of the way home?"

He offers his hand. I take it. My fingers thread through his, and I decide right then and there that everything that has happened to me up until that point has been worth it for this single moment.

It might be the very best moment of my life.

A moment I'll never forget.

49

Now

As we near Jessie's house, Joe's phone buzzes.

He answers, one hand on the wheel. "You're kidding," he says after a few minutes. He slides a wary glance at me. "So now what?" He mutters a few one-word responses before hanging up. "Lulu's not there. They've searched every square inch."

"So where are we supposed to go now? The precinct?"

"He's already en route to you. Wants to search your property."

"Why would he want to search my property?" Joe is quiet for so long, I'm afraid he didn't hear me until I figure out what he's not saying. "They think *I* did something to Lu?"

"Cora." Joe makes a swift U-turn and heads back to my cabin. "It's just how cops think. It's the anniversary of when you were taken. Maybe he thinks you've done something just like Laura wanted them to think. They always look at the parents in cases like these."

I smack my hand on the dashboard. "I would never hurt Lulu!" My voice shakes with genuine emotion. "He should know that. He knows what I've been through."

"I know, I know." Joe squeezes my knee, but it brings little comfort.

"So what? I'm just supposed to sit there while they drag the woods for her? No. No way." I gesture to the trunk, which has finally grown quiet. "Jessie and Laura are behind this. They're wasting valuable time at my house. We have proof that they did it. They need to go back to where the parade was. They need to start there."

"Cora, calm down. They have officers there too. They've put out an alert. They'll find her. They *will*. Searching your house is just procedure. It's part of the reason I didn't want to call them in the first place."

"I just can't believe this is happening." My eyes sting with tears again. Did Lulu go with them because Jessie and Laura lied and said they were my friends?

I clench the worry doll in my hand. I used to bring this everywhere with me. I was almost superstitious about it. I'd lost several over the years, but not this one. This one was my favorite. Once I get Lu back, I'm giving it to her. I want her to have it. Without warning, a sob surges up my throat. Once I start to cry, I can't stop.

Joe gently guides the car to the curb and shoves it into park. He waits for me to calm myself. I turn away, embarrassed. "I'm sorry," I say as I wipe away my tears. "Now is not the time to fall apart."

"It's okay." There are tears in his eyes too. "I get it." He grabs my hand and strokes the back of it with his thumb. "It's all going to be okay, Cora. I just know it."

I nod, sniff, and tell him to go. He pulls the car safely back on the road and parks in front of my cabin. I don't want this to turn into a crime scene. I don't want officers in the woods. It's the wrong place. It's a waste of valuable time.

We exit, but I stall by the car. "Should we bring her in?"

He scratches the back of his head and gestures to me. "That's your call."

I weigh my options. On one hand, keeping her quiet seems easier. On the other hand, I don't want Bishop to point fingers at me any more than he already might tonight. "Let's bring her inside."

Joe hesitates for a moment, then nods and pops the trunk. Jessie's eyes are wild as she looks between the two of us, and she starts screaming and writhing again the moment we get her out of the trunk and lead her into the house.

I'm sweating despite the cold temperature. I feel wrung out from crying. I haven't cried like that in years. When we get inside, we drop her onto the couch.

"Bathroom," Joe says.

As I stare at Jessie, who is screaming behind the duct tape, I try to work all this out. How she and Laura could have orchestrated my kidnapping back then, because they were just kids, like me. Plus, Jessie got injured that night. None of it computes.

She is going nuts trying to say something. Curiosity gets the best of me as I rip off her duct tape, which makes her flinch.

"Cora, Jesus Christ, you need to let me go right now," she pleads. "I swear I didn't do this."

"Jessie, stop playing games. It's over. Officer Bishop is on his way."

Jessie is crying now and wriggling to get free. I place the duct tape back over her mouth. What did I expect? That she'd suddenly confess?

Before Joe emerges from the bathroom, there's a sharp knock on the door. "Finally."

I rush to answer it, but it's not Bishop on the other side.

50

"Cora, thank God you're home. I was worried." Faith pushes into the room.

I check the time and shake my head. "Why are you here?"

"I've been texting you nonstop, but you didn't respond." When she sees Jessie bound on my couch, she freezes. "What the hell did I just walk into?"

I have no good answers. She shouldn't be here. Things feel messy enough without her temper. And I know I accused her of taking Lu, but we can mend that later. Now is not the time.

"I need you to go home. The police are going to be here any minute."

"So you did go to the police?" She presses her hands in a mock prayer beneath her chin. "Thank God."

Joe lopes back into the main room, wiping his hands on his jeans. He lifts his hand in a wave when he sees Faith. "Hey, Faith."

"Joe." Faith has a soft spot for Joe and loves that he's been good to me these past few years, especially when I've needed it the most. "So the police are coming. Does that mean they found her?"

My eyes fill with tears again, and I quickly shake my head. "No, they haven't. Not yet." I gesture to Jessie. "But she knows where she is. And Laura Hunter, another former teammate."

She grips my arm. "Tell me this is a joke."

Rea Frey

"It's not," Joe says, walking to my kitchen. He fills the coffeepot with water and shakes grounds into the filter, then opens my cabinet to pull down three mugs.

It's too much to unpack. Again, I check the time. "Joe, where are they?"

"I don't know. They should be here any second." He pulls out his phone again to check.

Jessie has grown incredibly still on the couch as she takes everything in.

His phone buzzes. "That's my buddy. I need to take it because . . ." He drifts off and gestures to Jessie. Right. Lennon. I completely forgot about her. He disappears out the back, and Jessie once again begins making noise.

"Good lord, what's going on with her?" Faith asks.

Finally, I rip off the duct tape. "Jessie, just stop. Please."

"Listen to me." Mascara carves twin tracks down her cheeks. "We need to get out of here right now."

I laugh. "*We're* not going anywhere. You are."

"Dammit, Cora. I swear I didn't do this. Think about it. I've been with you all night. If Laura is working with someone, it's not me. Someone has access to my phone. Or someone has convinced her to *pretend* it's me. But it's not."

I look at her, annoyed. "Then who else could it be?"

"Literally anybody!"

"Everything all right?" Joe reenters the room and looks from Jessie to me and back again.

"Fine." I shove the piece of duct tape back onto her mouth and hop up to pace the living room. "Every second we wait, I feel like Lulu is slipping further away."

"I know, but Bishop will be here. He'll find her." Joe swallows. I stare into his face, my eyes tracking to that terrible scar. It's what most people see when they look at him. Will this be what people see when they look at Lulu too? A missing eye, a missing hand, a missing foot? I move into the kitchen and slump against my island.

210

"Hey, Cora. Come on. Let's sit down." Joe guides me onto a bar-stool as Faith eyes both of us from the door. I can feel her nerves from here, which does nothing to help mine. After I'm settled, he places both hands on my shoulders, leans down, and stares right into my eyes.

"Hey, hey. Breathe, okay? Just breathe. It's all right. Look at me. Breathe with me."

Something sparks in the back of my mind, a memory seared into my brain, even after all this time. My skin erupts into chills as I back out of his grip. "What did you just say?" All at once, my head clears, and Jessie's words come barreling back to me. *Maybe it's someone else.*

His eyes look cloudy and bloodshot as he stands back up. "Just trying to help you breathe," he says. But it's too late. He knows what he said.

My mouth has gone painfully dry. I root around for the right words, finally spit them out. "There's only one person who's ever said those words to me," I say, my brain spinning. "Those *exact* words." And, of course, I memorized them back then because I was so scared standing in that haunted house, all alone, panicking and wanting to go home. But Luke had come to my rescue. He'd placed his hands on my shoulders, gotten down to my level, and told me to breathe. Just like Joe.

"Oh yeah?" Joe asks, avoiding my gaze. "And who would that be?"

"Jakayla's brother," I say. "Luke. From the gym."

From the couch, Jessie screams behind her duct tape in recognition, but I keep my eyes trained on Joe.

The name is like an explosion behind his eyes, a remembrance, a recollection. And just like that, I can see it. Behind the different hair, colored contacts, facial surgeries, and the beard covering that horrific scar, he might be the same boy who was always so nice to me. The boy who saved me that night at the haunted house. The boy I was starting to have feelings for. The boy I kissed.

I shake my head now, but everything warps. My world, tilting. My heart, breaking. My breath, stopping. Like time expands and contracts at once and everything is hovering sideways without gravity. My heart climbs into my throat. Could Joe really be *Luke*?

I wait for him to tell me I'm wrong or that he has no idea who Luke is. But he doesn't. He just stands there, shifting from foot to foot, waiting for me to piece something together that I can't possibly comprehend.

I try to work it out in my head. I've spent *years* with Joe. And I would recognize Luke. Wouldn't I? I remember those green eyes and that kind smile. His lips on mine. His tenderness. After Jakayla died, Luke had simply disappeared. It had been just like Evie, like they were both just figments of my imagination. I never heard from him again, even though I looked for him for years.

And when I met Joe, there was something warm about him, something familiar, even. With a sickening feeling, I wonder if that's because he is the same boy who stood up for me that night all those years ago. The boy kind enough to give me my first kiss on a lonely walk home.

Slowly, pieces of the night start to shift into place. I replay the scenes in my head. Joe helping me search for Lu at the Halloween parade. Joe walking me to my truck. Joe finding the red card. Joe giving me the burner phone. Joe inspecting my security equipment. Joe bursting into the gym to "save" me. Joe checking Jessie's phone. Joe knocking Jessie out. Joe calling the police. Joe insisting this is all going to work out.

"Can I see your phone?" I ask. "I just want to talk to Officer Bishop. See where he is."

Joe sucks on his bottom lip, glancing back and forth between all three of us. "He'll be here."

I want to believe him. I want to believe that this is my friend Joe. Not Luke. That I have it all wrong. Joe can't be the boy from my past.

"Okay, then I'll call him," I say. I reach for my phone, and in an instant, Joe's face transforms from uncertain to remorseful.

"Cora, put the phone down."

My breath literally halts in my chest as I consider the truth. I feel dizzy and hyperfocused all at once. "Why, Luke?" My hand shakes as I lower the phone.

Jessie gasps behind her duct tape again from the couch, and so does Faith. Finally, he speaks.

"I really wish you hadn't called me that."

The silence blossoms between the four of us. All the questions from tonight swarm at my feet like overactive bees. I'm not sure where to start. "Did you even call the cops?"

"You already know the answer to that," he says quietly.

Before I can think about the ramifications of what this really means, I pull the gun on Joe. Faith winces as I aim the barrel right at his chest.

"You're not going to shoot me, Cora. Put the gun down. Let me explain."

I keep the gun steady. "Not going to happen."

He rakes a hand through his hair. "Go ahead. Pull the trigger. It's not loaded."

"What?" Carefully, keeping my eyes on him, I examine the chamber. Empty. That's when I realize: Joe gave me this gun. I didn't even think to check if it was loaded. Finally, I lower it, too shocked to feel afraid.

"This isn't what it looks like." He lumbers over and removes the gun from my limp fingers. I'm at a loss for what to say. Joe *cannot* be involved in any of this. It doesn't make sense. Joe is my friend! He's been my friend for years. He loves Lu. Lu loves him.

"Where is she?" I ask, trying to keep my voice in check.

"She's safe," he says, stalking back and forth behind the couch. "And as long as you do what I say, she'll stay that way." He motions to the couch. I sit. Faith sits too. Though I don't believe anything he says, I have to cling to that. Otherwise, I'm done for.

"Start at the beginning," I demand. "You owe me that, at least."

Something sparks behind his fake brown eyes, but he nods. "I can do that."

51

Jessie shifts nervously between me and Faith, still tied up.

"Let's start with how you're even involved in this," I say. "Or why."

"Laura is my ex-wife."

I'm sure I misheard him. "Laura, as in my old teammate Laura? The one I just knocked unconscious and you helped me tie up?"

He nods, as if simply confirming a time or date. "Yes."

"But how is that possible?" I sputter.

He sighs. "It was brief. We dated when we were kids, then reconnected in Atlanta several years back."

I shake my head, not understanding. "You dated back then? But she used to make fun of you."

"I know," he says. "But we were just kids. She was different behind closed doors."

"So what? You fell in love, you got divorced, and the two of you decided to take my daughter?"

His eyes look as pained as I've ever seen them, and I stare at my lap to keep my emotions in check. "No." He shakes his head. "She left after my motorcycle accident. That part's true. But she left for a different reason. She knew . . ." He swallows and looks me in the eye. "She knew I was still in love with you."

Faith sucks in a sharp breath, as does Jessie.

"What do you mean *still*?"

"Cora, come on. I've always been crazy about you. When we were kids and now. It's why I kissed you that day."

I shake my head. "But you left. You disappeared."

"I was really messed up after my sister died," he explains. "I disappeared from everyone and everything. When I moved back here, Laura and I reconnected. But it was never going to work. Then, she came to me with this crazy idea to get Kayla into the spotlight right before trials. What I told you tonight is true. She needs the money. She could sell the cabin, of course, but she wanted to do something worse. Something to hurt you."

"Because by hurting me, she's hurting you," I supply.

"Right." He nods. "I tried to stop her, tell her it was a ridiculous plan and she'd never get away with it, but . . . she has something over me, so I had to go along with it. I didn't want to. Believe me. But I convinced her to let me handle Lulu, at least. I would never let anything happen to her, Cora."

"I don't believe anything you say," I spit back now. The fact that my closest friend has known where my daughter is this entire night is unforgivable. The acting. The suggestions. All the fake, misguided help. And I bought it all. "But why change your name? Why not just tell me who you were?"

"I don't know. I wanted a fresh start. I didn't want to be Luke anymore." He opens his mouth to say more but then thinks better of it and shrugs. "And I wanted to be the hero. I wanted to bring Lu home tonight. I wanted you to finally look at me as more than just a friend."

Jessie and Faith swing their gazes to him, and I do the same.

"This isn't some deranged rom-com," I spit back.

"I know. Trust me, I know." He hangs his head. "I just thought if you could maybe see me in a different light, then . . ." He motions to his leg. "But look at me. I thought, at the very least, if I could be the one to bring Lu back to you, the one you . . ." His voice fades.

"The one I what?" My chest heaves.

"The one you could maybe love someday, then we could all be a family."

This confession is so juvenile and unexpected, I'm literally at a loss for words. Finally, I find my voice. "Where is she?"

"I don't want to hurt anyone," he says instead.

"Where *is* she?" I ask again. I think about all those Polaroids, the missing eye, the wrist, the leg. Did *he* do that? Are he and Laura both completely insane? Jessie is practically jumping out of her skin on the couch, and I rip the duct tape free.

"Is Lennon really safe?" she blurts out. "Oh God." She shifts uncomfortably. It was so easy to believe she was the villain, when the villain was under my nose this whole damn time.

I think about the worry doll I found, the texts on Jessie's phone. Joe planted them. He put that worry doll in Jessie's pocket when I was getting something to tie her up with. He orchestrated all this. One giant setup. One big lie.

"Oh my God." I sit up straighter. "It was you." The truth lands like a lightning strike. After all this time, all the years of wondering and torment, the truth slides instantly into place. "The night at the haunted house," I say. "*You* took me. Is that what Laura has on you? She knows the truth, and that's why you went along with this whole thing?" It has to be. He wouldn't take Lulu for anything else.

Jessie and Faith gasp again and look up at Joe.

He's chewing on his lip again, as if debating telling me the truth. But that look says it all.

"I don't understand," I say. "I thought you *liked* me. I thought we understood each other. I—"

"I never meant for it to happen that way. At first, it was just a prank. A joke. But I needed Jakayla to have a chance to make the Olympic team."

I jump up, enraged. "You what?" It's what I'd always assumed—that someone was trying to destroy my chances—but *Luke* of all people? "You *kidnapped* me to give your sister a shot?"

He sighs and rubs an aggravated hand vigorously over his face. "I know how it sounds, but I was really messed up back then."

"Back then?" Jessie mumbles under her breath, eyebrows raised.

Joe throws her a look, and she quiets instantly.

"I was so angry." His voice trembles. "My parents died, and Jakayla and I had to live with our aunt. But what no one knew was my aunt blew through the inheritance my parents left us. She was a drunk. Used it all. I had to work three jobs just to make ends meet, but I couldn't afford all the training and the travel. I was barely hanging on, and if Jakayla made it to the Olympics, then maybe . . ." His voice fades. "Anyway, it was our one shot. Our one chance to turn things around."

"So you had already arranged it?" I exclaim now, not understanding. "How?"

Joe begins picking at his jeans, over and over again. "I watched all of you for years," he says softly. "I knew everything about each of you. Your strengths and weaknesses. Your habits. And Laura would tell me things." He shrugs. "I was the one who told her to invite you to the haunted house."

Holy shit. It *had* been Laura to invite me. I'd forgotten that. "So she knew?"

He shakes his head. "No, of course not. But I had everything arranged. Jessie's knee. The van. Lou leading you to that side door. All of it."

Jessie's head whips his way so fast, her neck cracks. "*What* did you just say?"

Silence descends between us again as more puzzle pieces click into place.

"You're the man in the mask," I say.

He falters for a moment but finally swallows and continues. "I switched with the guy who worked there. I needed to make sure Jessie wouldn't make the team either. And she was always so mean to all of you, I just—I just snapped."

"You monster!" she shrieks now, lunging at him with her torso. With her arms and legs tied, she doesn't get far, but I don't blame her.

He swallows guiltily. "I really thought Jakayla would make the team at trials, and when she didn't, I called in the tip so they could find you, Cora. I vowed to never do anything like that ever again. And then Jakayla died, and I was so lost. I moved away, changed my name, became a cop, and got my life together. But then Laura came into the picture again." He swallows. "After we broke up and she got into financial trouble, she reached out and said she'd tell you everything about who I was back then unless I helped her tonight. I'm so sorry. I never meant to hurt Lu."

The blows keep coming, one after the next. I need to keep him talking, need to figure out a way to call Officer Bishop for real and get all of us safely out of here.

"You didn't have to do all this, Joe," I say to him now. "I liked you then, and I trusted you now. You were my friend."

To my surprise, Joe's eyes fill with tears. In those eyes, I see who he was back then—a sad, angry boy who'd lost his parents and had to become a fill-in dad for Jakayla, before he lost her too—and I see who he has become now due to his bully of an ex-wife and all the bad decisions he's made along the way. All the lies he's told. All the sordid secrets he's kept. That can ruin a person.

"You can still do the right thing," I insist. "All you have to do is tell me where she is."

For a moment, I think he is going to cave, but then he offers me a regretful smile. "You know I can't do that," he says.

The words barely leave his mouth before I fly across the couch and use the knife edge of my hand to chop him in the throat. When he reaches for his neck, I move behind him, locking him in a rear naked choke. I squeeze harder than I ever have in training. This isn't sparring; this is real. Joe is bigger and stronger than I am, but with my daughter's life on the line, I will die before I let him win. He struggles and swats at my arms, but the choke is sunk in. With my legs hooked around his torso, I extend back until my bad knee pops. I ignore the screaming pain. There's nothing he can do, no way to get out of it. Finally, he goes limp in my arms, and I release him, looking for something to tie him up with.

"Faith, grab a knife and some rope. Garage. Top shelf."

She's up in a heartbeat, then banging around the garage.

"Holy shit," Jessie breathes from the couch. "I can't believe it's Luke."

Once Faith has the supplies, we secure his hands to his ankles behind his back while I shuffle through the mounds of lies he told me. I ate up every single one. All this time, I thought he was *helping* me. I thought he was on my side. What an idiot I've been. When I'm sure he's secure, I stab Officer Bishop's number into my phone with shaking hands.

"Ronald!" I scream. In so many words, I explain what's happened tonight and tell him to hightail it to my house. I explain about Laura and that Joe has Lu and maybe Lennon and Kayla too.

Once we cut Jessie free, she frantically tries to reach Lennon but isn't having luck.

"Guns, I need guns," I say.

Jessie stands on shaky legs and stares down at Joe. "I can't believe he did that to me." Her eyes are wide. "He ruined my life."

My brain is all mixed up. I think back to the men in the van. He must have been the tall, lanky one. That's why I knew his smell. He would wear patchouli oil. How did I not put all this together over the years? How did I not recognize that boy from thirty years ago posing as my best friend?

Rather than kill myself with questions, I swing back to the mission at hand: Find Lulu. Bring her home safely.

Joe moans from the ground, and Jessie, Faith, and I flinch. I need a gun. And I need one now. I unloaded most of my weapons at Joe's house. I have a shotgun, but that won't do.

"Jessie, go out to Joe's car, and see if there's a gun strapped to the visor or under the seat."

She stands there for a moment, stunned, but I clap and bring her back to the present moment. "Jessie, now!"

She races out the door, and I crouch down beside Joe, staring deeply into those fake-colored eyes. "You're going to spend the rest of your life behind bars," I say. "Were you really a cop?"

He sighs and closes his eyes. "Yes, Cora. Not everything was a lie."

That should bring me some sort of solace, but it doesn't. Why didn't I ever think to look into him? I simply took everything he told me at face value. Was I *that* desperate for male companionship that I overlooked everything I'd learned to watch out for in the first place?

"Just tell me one thing. Did you ever care about Lu? Was it all fake?"

"I love Lulu like a daughter." Tears leak down his face. "I know you don't believe me, but it's true."

Jessie bangs through the door, a pistol awkwardly clenched in her hands.

"Give it to me," I demand, standing to retrieve it.

Instead, she aims the gun at Joe, fingers shaking.

"Jessie, give me the gun. You cannot shoot him. We need him to find the girls."

Faith scoots back against the wall. Jessie's fingers shake on the trigger as she clasps both hands around the gun. Her face is a mess, fresh tears streaking down her face. Her makeup is mostly wiped clean, her hair disheveled. She looks wild, unhinged. Unsteadily, she moves closer, inch by inch, until she's standing almost directly over him. I don't want to make any sudden movements, but she cannot kill him. As much as it pains me to admit, we need him alive.

"You *ruined* my life," she whispers now. "You took everything I worked so hard for. Everything."

In the distance, I can hear the police sirens, and I exhale an audible breath. "Jessie, the police are almost here, okay? Put down the gun." I extend my hand slowly toward her. I'm inches away. I can almost grab it.

Her finger is still on the trigger as she contemplates what to do. "I'm sorry, Cora," she says. Her eyes find mine, then slide back to Joe. Finally, she lets out a massive scream and fires a shot that hits him right beneath the heart. The pop is violent, and the kickback rears her into the arm of the couch. Immediately, she drops the gun.

"Oh God!" She covers her mouth with her hands while I grab a throw blanket from the couch to staunch the bleeding. With both hands, I press down over the dime-size wound, blood gushing into the cream throw.

Joe's eyes flutter closed, and he begins to cough.

"Tell me where she is, Joe. Please. You have to tell me where she is." I press harder, and he moans. "You're not this person. You can still do the right thing. Please."

He coughs again, a line of blood trickling from the corner of his mouth.

"Joe. Stay with me, okay? Please. You have to stay with me."

A few seconds later, Officer Bishop bursts inside, his white shock of hair askew at this late hour. His uniform is misbuttoned, but his eyes are wild with possibility as he takes in the scene before him.

"I need an ambulance!" I scream to him now. I realize we still have Laura—that even if Joe dies, we can still hopefully find Lu. Unless he never told her where she is, and that's why she could never supply a photo. Because she didn't know. Were the Polaroids all fake? I turn back to Joe as officers pile in around us. "Please tell me where she is. Where's Lulu, Joe? Tell me!"

Joe reaches one hand toward my face, and I resist the urge to flinch. He needs to think I'm on his side. He needs to believe I still care. "I've always loved you, Cora Valentine. More than you'll ever know. I would never hurt you or Lu. You have to believe me."

With that, he takes a shaky breath, closes his eyes, and grows still.

"No, no, no!" I let out every ounce of frustration from this night in a bloodcurdling scream. I start to administer CPR, not even knowing if it will keep him alive. But I can't let him go. I can't let him die.

Faith and Jessie watch me in silence. I keep at it until the paramedics roll inside my house and Officer Bishop pulls me off Joe. I sit back on my heels, hands drenched in blood. He has to live. He has to.

As the paramedics strap him to a gurney and wheel him outside, I find Jessie rocking back and forth on the couch, head in her hands. Faith is white as a ghost.

"We still have Laura," I whisper now, to no one. I close my eyes. The cops can force the truth out of her. She can still lead us to Lu.

52

Once Joe is taken to the hospital, they haul Jessie in for questioning.

I gauge Officer Bishop's face as reality sets in. Officers who detained Laura have reported back that she swears Joe never told her where he hid Lulu. She was just the face of the operation, while he was the brains.

Every worry I've ever had about being a parent is coming true. Without Joe, I might not get my daughter back. I might never see my precious little girl again. And all that is on me.

"We'll find her, Cora," Bishop says now, as if reading my mind. "We've secured the area. Stay here until we take you in."

I collapse on my couch. My knee throbs as sensation spills back into it after putting Joe in a rear naked choke. This whole night is like some horrible Halloween movie, and I can't understand how Joe agreed to go along with something like this.

As Bishop's men comb the woods, a new flood of terror sets in: What if Joe lied to me and they recover Lulu's body? How will I manage to go on?

Faith sits beside me but says nothing. Her presence is a comfort. All Joe's confessions run through my head. He was the man in the mask. The man who took me. Laura's husband. The mastermind behind tonight.

But none of that matters now. The only thing that matters is where Joe took my daughter. I glance around. Certainly not here. I think of all the places he's ever mentioned, all his frequent haunts. Nothing is private. Nothing is off grid enough to stash a little girl.

Not like he stashed me all those years ago.

A lingering thought tunnels its way through my aching heart. If Joe isn't with her, and Laura's with the police, then who is with Lulu?

I sit straight up as the realization lands. "I might know where she is," I say, the first semblance of hope swirling in my chest. Before I have a moment to reconsider, I swipe Joe's keys and am out the door in a flash. Faith follows closely behind and climbs into the car, no questions asked.

On my way out of town, I shoot an urgent voice note to Officer Bishop with the coordinates of the bunker. It's deep in the woods, with no official street address, but I don't need GPS. This place I know like the back of my hand. After I was rescued, I memorized everything I could about the place.

"Where are we going, Cora?"

It's the first time Faith's spoken, and I can tell by the look on her face that she is in shock from everything she's seen tonight.

"The place I was held," I say. I never talk about the kidnapping with her. Anything she knows she's read about or heard about, but going back to the scene of the crime feels more significant than I can name. Because now I *know*. It was Luke who took me that night. Luke who arranged this whole thing. Luke who tried to sabotage my career. Luke who changed his name just so I wouldn't know it was him. Everything I've come to know about Joe is an illusion . . . nothing more than make-believe.

No one could ever figure out who was behind my kidnapping back then. And now, knowing the truth, I understand why. Who would suspect a teenager could pull all that off? Part of me doesn't know if Joe is a true psychopath or just severely wounded. Either way, it's no longer my concern.

After an hour, I take a right down the road I used to escape all those years ago. I slow right around the clump of woods where I nearly froze to death before Luke and his friend brought me back to the cabin. As I press harder on the gas, my heart begins to pound. When they made a movie about my kidnapping, they filmed at the actual bunker. There was no mention of Evie. By that point, the property went for sale in a bidding war. Honestly, I'm surprised someone hasn't made it into an Airbnb and capitalized off of its sordid history.

But my current theory banks on the fact that Joe might have bought it. Why wouldn't he? Preserving his legacy, keeping it away from everyone and everything. The perfect hiding spot to finish out his master plan. Or Laura's.

While I drive, I dissect everything Joe confessed, some of it still not gelling in my head. Laura and Joe dated when we were kids. They got married. She found out his secret and created a sinister plan to thrust Kayla into the spotlight and get my money at the same time. All of it so carefully constructed. All of it such a lie.

I almost miss the hidden driveway, I'm so lost in thought. I swing a left and inch down the now-paved drive. The cabin looks exactly the same, and for a moment, I'm shuttled back in time. I slow to a crawl as my breath catches in my throat.

"Cora? Are you okay?"

I nod and keep inching toward the bunker. Except the bunker is no longer a bunker. Instead, it's a modern tiny home with its own deck, firepit, and Adirondack chairs. Still, just the sight of it almost paralyzes me. This is the scene of the crime—the place where I thought I would die. The place where I met Evie. The place where I thought all my dreams would be stolen forever.

I kill the headlights and practically explode out of the car. Faith follows. Everything in me wants to scream for Lulu, but I don't want to alert anyone I'm here. Even as I approach, I can tell no one is here. All my hopes plummet to the depths of my stomach as I try the door of the tiny home. Locked.

I grab a bobby pin from my hair, jimmy the lock open after a few attempts, and step inside. My world shifts as flashbacks hit me like stray bullets. The mattress against the wall. That tiny heater. The crappy bathroom. Evie's screams from next door. Instead, this place is clean and minimal. I examine every inch of it to be sure no one is here.

"So this is where you were kept," Faith says now, softly. She takes her time examining the room and turns to me, shaking her head. "That must have been so terrifying, Cora."

It's what everyone says, especially after they see the movie. It's easy to read a book or watch a movie and think you know the terror that lurks when you're kept in an unfamiliar place, alone. But no one knows. No one knows how it feels.

"Let's check out the main cabin."

I exhale when I leave that tiny space, knowing I will never set foot here again. Crunching over gravel, I remember making my escape and sprinting toward the woods, toward what I thought would be my freedom. Instead, I almost froze to death and was brought back to this place. Is that why Luke saved me? To keep me alive? What about Evie? Why didn't I ask him when I had the chance?

The main cabin is dark. I peer inside the windows, but there are no cars or other signs of life. I call Officer Bishop, defeated, and tell him she's not here. But where else could she be? The cops didn't turn up anything at the gym or at my house. Laura has been zero help, and now that they've finished combing the woods at my house, they're heading to Joe's.

"I'll head back to you," I tell him now.

Faith and I climb back into the car, and I cast one last look at the tiny home before we race back toward Joe's.

Time is running out to find Lulu. I can feel it in my bones. But she has to be somewhere.

"We have to find her," I whisper now, over and over again.

"We will, Cora. We will." Faith's voice shakes, and I can hear the terror there.

Lulu has to come home. She can't disappear like Evie.

53

Officer Bishop is waiting outside Joe's when we arrive, his men deep into the acreage with dogs and flashlights.

"I'm still sending officers out to the bunker," he explains when I exit the car. "Make sure you didn't miss anything." He scratches his head, which makes his hair shoot in several directions. "This is really complicated, kid."

I fill him in on everything Joe revealed, including the past.

He places a hand on my arm. "We're going to find the girls. I promise."

Right. The girls, plural. Because it's not just Lulu; it's Lennon and maybe Kayla too. God, I will never forgive myself if anything happens to them.

We step inside. The interior has been tossed. I assess the now-messy living room, dining room, and kitchen. It's small, so there aren't many places one could hide.

"Can I take a look around?" I ask. "I know it's already been searched, but . . ."

But maybe they missed something. Maybe there's a clue. We divide and conquer, covering all the square footage in just ten minutes flat. There's no attic, no exterior shed. Only an attached garage.

"He must have kept her close, though," I say, breaking the silence between us. "He was with me at the parade, which means someone else must have taken her." Why hadn't that thought dawned on me before?

I rotate in a circle. "She has to be somewhere near here. It's the only thing that makes sense."

Officer Bishop stares at the fireplace and the giant rug underneath the modern sectional that's been flipped back on the corner. "Help me with this, will you?"

He motions to the couch. We shove it out of the way and peel back the thick, plush cream carpet.

"Search for notches in the wood," he says, toeing the smooth floors with his boot. "Maybe a trapdoor we missed? We looked, but let's look again."

Faith hangs in the periphery, and though I want to tell her to go home, I know she won't. I drop to my knees and inspect the wood, but there's nothing. I knock on the floors, listening for any changes. Finally, I sit back on my heels. I stare at the blood still staining my hands. Joe's blood. Luke's blood. Feeling dejected, I swing my gaze over to the dining room table, which also has a thick Persian rug beneath it. Officer Bishop sees me eyeing it and gestures for me to follow. We push the table out of the way and remove the carpet, and there it is: a lever to a hatch.

Our eyes lock.

"Stand back." Officer Bishop pulls his gun, leans down to open the hatch, and waits.

Everything in me wants to shove him aside, race down the thin metal ladder, and see if Lulu is there. There's no sound from below, but Bishop signals for me to stay here, though we both know that's definitely not happening. He descends the ladder, and I follow, even without a weapon. It takes my eyes a moment to acclimate to what I'm seeing. There's a long hallway, which is freezing, with a door to the right. How is this here?

"Stay behind me," he whispers.

I do as I'm told, and we rush down the hall. When we come to a metal door with a tiny window in the top, Officer Bishop peers inside and immediately talks into his walkie.

I practically crawl on top of him to see what's inside, but it's not Lu. It's Kayla and Lennon, sitting on the floor, huddled together. Officer Bishop taps on the window, but they don't seem to hear.

"Soundproof?" I ask.

"Must be," he responds.

Before we can figure out how to pry open the door, a man steps out from the other end of the hallway, a burrito in hand. The lighting is dim. As I take in his squat stature, I wonder if this was the same man from that night thirty years ago. Joe's accomplice. Luke's friend.

When he sees us, he drops his burrito and reaches for his gun, but Officer Bishop is too fast and fires off a single shot right to the leg. The man crumples like a leaf and falls forward, still alive.

I try the door, but it's locked.

"See if he's got the keys," I say.

Once Bishop cuffs him and retrieves his weapon, he throws the keys to me. I find the right one after a few failed attempts and pry the door open. Both girls startle. When they see me, they erupt into relieved screams and run toward me.

"Oh my God, we were, like, kidnapped!" Kayla says now. Her cheeks are puffy from crying, but I can also clock the excitement there. Everything Laura wanted out of tonight is coming to fruition. There will be a huge news story, and her daughter will be at the center, along with Lennon. And Jessie. And me. Lennon says nothing, just puts her arms around me in a tight hug. I kiss the top of her head and squat down to her level.

"Are you girls physically hurt?"

They both shake their heads.

"Did you see a little girl anywhere down here?"

They both shake their heads again. Officer Bishop calls on his walkie again for assistance, and soon, more officers are climbing downstairs. Once the girls are taken up, Bishop and I fan out. He walks toward the left, and I branch off to the right.

I'm reminded of Smorgasbord, with those long hallways and endless rows of doors. While there are no monsters lurking down here, I'm
more fearful now than I've ever been. As I'm circling back to the ladder,
I spot an almost invisible lock on the wall to the left. When I move
closer to examine it, I realize there's a door that blends into the smooth
metal wall. But it's there. A hidden compartment.

"Bishop!" I scream. He finds me in an instant. I squat down to
inspect the lock. "Still got those keys?"

He hands me the ring, and I try a few with shaking hands before I
once again find the right one. It slides into place, and I turn it, preparing myself for the worst.

When I open the door, I spot Lulu lying prone on a small bed.

"Holy Mary, mother of Joseph," Officer Bishop says as he crosses
the threshold and takes in what's on the walls.

I can't look at anything but Lu. I rush to her small cot in the corner.
There's a TV blaring cartoons across from her. I roll her over, horrified
at what I might find. The Polaroids flash through my mind one after
the next. No eye, no hand, no foot. Instead of a cold, lifeless corpse, my
baby is warm, breathing, and wholly intact. Those photos were nothing
but a cruel game played by an old teammate. I pan the space, and that's
when I see it: a bottle of NyQuil. They drugged her.

"Oh, thank God. You're okay, you're okay." I gather her in my arms
and secure her sweet face against my chest. I breathe in the heady scent
of her skin and kiss every inch of her head.

"Lulu. Lu, baby, can you hear me?" I shake her gently.

She's too groggy to respond, but she sighs and snuggles deeper
into my arms. It's only then that I can take in what Officer Bishop was
commenting about.

Every inch of wall space is clogged with photos of me from all
stages of life. Candids from the gym, photos from team competitions,
newspaper articles, stills of me being kept in the bunker all those years
ago, close-ups of my face, my author photo, and then more recent shots

of me and Lu in our home, when I thought we were alone and no one was watching.

I clutch Lulu tighter and step deeper into the shrine of Joe's twisted mind. He's been watching me for years, and I'd never sensed it, which is the scariest truth of all. He's the one who helped with my security system, so he knew how to wreck it. He's the one who hacked my phone. He infiltrated his way into my life, and I let him.

He's the mastermind behind tonight.

And underneath it all, I didn't recognize that boy I used to know. Instead, I trusted Joe, the ex-cop I let myself confide in. I chose to let him get close after a lifetime of keeping people at a distance.

That's when the truth really hits: Joe never wanted to hurt me. He wanted to *hoard* me. For years, he's been keeping an eye on me literally and figuratively.

I gather Lulu in my arms, desperate to get her out of here. I know there will be endless questions and police procedure, and it will be quite some time before I can take her home. But she's safe for now, and that's all that matters.

When we are back upstairs, under the harsh interior lights, with the police and the girls chatting a mile a minute and Faith crying and hugging Lulu, only then does Officer Bishop take a steadying breath.

"I told you we'd find her." Despite how cold it is with the front and back doors flung open, sweat pools at his temples. The lines of his face tell the story of a full, well-lived life.

I reach out and grip his soft hand. "Thank you, Ronald," I say. "For saving me then and for helping me now. You're my hero."

He blushes slightly and squeezes my hand back. "Well, let's not do it again," he jokes. Then he's off, calling for another ambulance to have the girls checked out, and I move over to the couch, cradling Lulu in my arms. I have never been so relieved in all my life. Not even when I was rescued thirty years ago, dirty and confused, from that bunker. No matter what else has happened tonight, Lu is safe. She is here. I can take her home.

As I'm lost in thought, Lulu's eyes flutter open. "Mama?" she asks, ramming her fists sleepily into her eyes.

"Yes, baby." The tears leak down my cheeks faster than I can flick them away. How I missed that sweet voice.

"What happened?" she asks now.

"You took a really long nap," I explain. "But we're going to go home soon."

As if just waking from a very strange dream, Lulu takes in all the police officers and bustling bodies around her. "Who are all these people, Mama?" She glances at my hands. "And why are your hands red?"

"It's all for Halloween," I say. "Just a game."

"Did you win?" she asks, yawning.

"I did," I say, kissing the top of her head. "I won the game."

54

"Lu, are you almost ready?"

"Almost, Mama!"

I can hear her thumping around in her bedroom upstairs, getting her costume on. She insisted on dressing herself for Halloween this year, and if I've learned anything, it's that when Lulu says she wants to do something on her own, it's simply best to let her.

Downstairs, Faith is gathering candy to handle all the trick-or-treaters from both our houses while I take Lulu around the neighborhood.

After everything that happened last year, I sold the cabin and moved next door to Faith. Lulu now has friends' houses she can walk to, and despite everything that's happened and all the mayhem and trauma, I realized I do want Lulu to have a normal childhood. Friends. School. A full life.

"Where's my little Pop-Tart?" My father exits my kitchen, dressed like a piece of bacon. My mother emerges beside him, homemade treats in hand, in her egg costume. Despite having already seen them tonight, I laugh again and shake my head. I don't remember them ever dressing up when I was a kid, as my dad was always so busy with work.

But once I got Lu back, I reached out to explain what happened back then and who took me. They needed closure as much as I did. And after some family counseling and hard conversations, I made the tough decision to let them back in. To let them near Lulu. It's clear they are beyond grateful for the second chance.

My dad sips hot cocoa from my Valentine's mug, my new gym's logo plastered on the ceramic in red. He insisted on ordering them in bulk and tells everyone he can about his daughter's gym.

A lot can change in a year. Since helping Lennon with her routines last Halloween, I decided I wanted to try my hand at coaching. Woodward's offered me a coaching job, which I politely declined. I used some of my cash to start my own training facility instead. Many of the girls left Woodward's to come with me. And though Lennon didn't qualify for the Olympics, we're hopeful she'll make the next go-around.

Lennon laughs from my living room as Tyler tickles her and pulls her down onto the couch. I roll my eyes as Faith makes a light-handed comment about the two of them behaving themselves. It thrills me to see how Lennon is opening herself up to experiences beyond gymnastics . . . namely Faith's son.

While Jessie and I aren't friends, exactly, what we went through bonded us in unexplainable ways. Now, we want the best for her daughter, and I find that coaching Lennon is one of the most fulfilling things I've ever done. Lulu has even started taking a tumbling class, but much to my relief, she doesn't seem all that interested.

The doorbell rings, and as I wait for Lu, I grab the bowl of candy from Faith and insist on answering since I won't be here tonight to see all the adorable trick-or-treaters.

When I yank it open, instead of a trick-or-treater, it's Joe.

Or Luke.

My breath catches in my throat just from the sight of him. He clocks the shock on my face and takes an uncertain step back. I place the bowl of candy back inside and move tentatively onto the porch, keeping him away from the door. Away from my life.

Because the bullet went clean through and didn't hit his heart, he didn't suffer any major damage. Once he was released from the hospital, he was charged with accessory to kidnapping, though Laura got the brunt of the charges. Smart Joe kept a paper trail of her plan and bribery. He got sentenced to three years but has served only a year since there was no malicious intent, and I'm assuming, if he's standing on my doorstep, he got released for good behavior. Though I could have added the original kidnapping charges to his bid to ensure he went away for good, I didn't.

He was just a kid who'd suffered enough, and I want to be done with that part of my life. I refused to press charges, much to everyone's dismay. And thankfully, since he didn't die, Jessie didn't serve time.

My blood runs cold as I assess him. He's clean shaven, so his scar is on full display. He's cut his hair short and is no longer wearing contacts. And that's when I see the boy I used to know. No more disguises. No more hiding.

"I know I shouldn't be here." He shuffles nervously from foot to foot.

"No, you shouldn't," I confirm.

He drags a hand over his face, still the same old Joe. "I don't even know where to begin, Cora."

I wait for him to spit out whatever he has to say so I can retreat back inside and slam the door in his face. Get on with my life. Put this all behind me for good.

"I've been getting to the bottom of things," he continues. "And I know words are futile, trust me, but I just want to say I'm sorry. I never meant for any of this to happen. I never meant to hurt you all those years ago. And I never meant to betray you last year . . . especially with Lu." His voice breaks on her name, and I want to slap those two letters from his mouth.

I don't owe him anything, but I offer a quick nod. Because I do know. Over the past year, I've had a lot of time to think too. And although I can never forgive what he did, I understand that what he's saying is true. He never wanted to physically harm me. Or Lulu. But it was all wrong and misguided, nonetheless, even if he thought he was doing everything for a good reason. Even if he felt he had no other choice but to do what he had to in order to keep his secret safe. "Is that all?"

He swallows and glances at his toes. "Yeah." After a beat, he glances up. "Well, no. I know you saw the room Lulu was in, all those photos . . ." He takes a beat. "I know what it looks like, what *I* look like, but it wasn't some childish obsession. It was real." He swallows and finally looks right into my eyes. The vibrant green makes me remember that day on the path when he kissed me, when I thought the whole world was at my fingertips and we might become something more than just friends.

"I really did care about you, Cora. I really was your friend."

I let out a frustrated sigh. I hate that I feel an ounce of sympathy for this man. Because even if Joe wasn't real, he *was* my friend. He was also my monster and my savior, my confidant and my villain. And if I've learned anything, it's that people aren't all or nothing. They're both. They're *everything*.

All of us are dark and light.

"And there's one more thing you should know." He seems to fumble with what to say next and then finally blurts it out. "It's about Evie."

My head snaps up, my heart in my throat. After all this time, she's still the one mystery I cannot solve.

He opens his mouth, closes it. "There's no easy way to say this, but . . ."

Time stalls while I wait for him to tell me the truth about something that has haunted me my entire adult life.

"Well, there was no Evie."

I blink at him, not understanding.

"I mean there was a girl. I don't want you to think you imagined her. You didn't." He scrapes a hand over his face, closes his eyes, and then opens them. "It was Laura." His startling eyes drift down to his boots.

Laura? No. I shake my head. Laura couldn't be Evie. I would have recognized her voice. I would have known my own teammate. I filter back through our conversations through that wall. How terrified she was. Her vulnerability. Her encouragement. Her screams. No one could be that much of an actress.

236

I study Joe in the silence, wondering if he's lying again. And I think that's what hurts the most—that while we shared a friendship, and time, and our homes, and our lives, and our hurts, and our pain, I could still never tell when he was lying to me.

"She knew what I had planned that night," he continues. His gaze lifts to mine again. "She knew about everything and wanted to flex her acting skills and play along. I said no, but she said she'd rat me out if I didn't. So she came up with this whole idea to act like she was being tortured to keep you in line. She thought it would be more dramatic and help pass the time."

His words are daggers. What a fool they both made me out to be.

"But then she crossed a line with my friend, and I made her leave. Her parents were wondering where she kept disappearing to, anyway. But I just wanted you to know . . . she didn't die. She wasn't tortured. She just left."

Betrayal lands once again, clunky but familiar, in my chest. Just when I'm moving on, just when I think I'm finally coming to terms with everything, I'm thrust right back there. I'm stuck in that bunker, my ear pressed to the wall. Except there was no one on the other side. No Evie. Not really. We weren't confiding in each other. We weren't keeping each other alive. She was mocking the whole situation, nothing more than delivering a performance, while I thought she had been hurt, tortured, murdered, even. She was nothing more than a figment, a ghost. A cruel girl's trick. A part to play.

"I've spent my entire life thinking that some poor girl's parents are out there mourning the loss of their missing child," I say, my voice quaking with rage. "Do you know what that does to a person? What that did to me?"

"I know, Cora. Trust me. It was awful. It got so out of hand, and I always wanted to come clean. But Laura held it all over my head, and when the case went cold, well, we thought we'd gotten away with it. And then you came out on top. You were okay."

"I was *never* okay!" I scream now. "Never!" Spit flies from my mouth, and I step forward and shove him hard in the chest. He's caught off balance and stumbles back, ramming into the porch railing.

He doesn't say anything, just lets me take it out on him.

"You played with my emotions." I poke him directly in the chest, right near his bullet wound. "You flirted with me, you comforted me, you kissed me, you kidnapped me, you stalked me, you lied to me, you helped me, you hurt me, you loved me, you tricked me, again and again." My voice is hoarse as I list out all the ways he fucked with my life, twisted it, changed it, ruined it.

"I know." Tears slip down his cheeks, but his eyes never leave mine. "I know."

Then and now tangle together. Luke in that haunted house, crouching down to help me breathe. Joe last Halloween, holding me as I cried about my daughter. Luke, kissing me on the walk home. Joe, confessing he was in love with me while stashing my daughter in an underground lair. Both versions, playing with my heart. Both versions, building these elaborate sets that were never real. I was never *really* kidnapped, never in any actual danger. Neither was Lulu. And I've spent my entire life in fear, running scared, overcompensating, hiding, apologizing for my life instead of just living it. All because of him.

Before I can stop her, Lulu bursts onto the front porch in this year's homemade costume. "Uncle Joe!" She practically flings herself into his arms, and I reach to stop her, but it's too late. Joe smears his tears away, drops down to his good knee, and envelops her, fresh emotion springing to his eyes.

"Hi, sweetheart," he says, sniffing. He pulls back. "Well, well, well. Let me look at you."

I take a moment to gather myself, trying to process this new information.

"Can you guess what I am?" she says, practically jumping out of her skin.

"Hmm." He closes one eye as he assesses her. "A rabbit?"

"No!"

"The Easter Bunny?"

"No! I'm Bun-Bun!" She holds up her tattered stuffed animal, which is still her favorite. "Mama made my costume."

He swallows and looks up at me, still down on one knee. "That doesn't surprise me. You have the best mom in the whole wide world."

That sentiment hits me right in the heart, but I cut it free and pull her back against me. "Joe was just leaving, sweetie."

"Aw, he can't come trick-or-treating with us?"

I almost laugh, the request is so absurd. "No, he can't," I say, pulling her safely into the doorway. "He has to go."

Joe looks at me, pure understanding between us. This is it. There will be no more conversations, no more visits, no more confessions, no more games. He has come to say what he needed to say, offering the last piece of the puzzle. He lifts his hand in a wave and offers that lopsided smile. "Happy Halloween, Cora."

The words are chilling. There is nothing happy about this night, nothing good about Halloween. With that, he carefully treads down the stairs and disappears from sight.

"You ready to go, Mama?" Lulu grips my hand, and I squeeze her small fingers in mine. Though I haven't vilified Joe in front of her, she asks about him often. After a lot of therapy, it's clear the only thing she remembers from last Halloween is Joe's friend, whom she'd apparently met numerous times in town when I was unaware, luring her with candy to go watch movies in Uncle Joe's strange, secret room, staying up much too late, and then falling asleep. There are a multitude of ways that could have gone south, could have scarred her for life. But luckily, it didn't. She's still the same old trusting Lu, friends with everyone she meets.

I grip Bun-Bun in my hand as Lu loops her basket over her free hand, and we wave goodbye to Faith, whose eyebrows are practically buried in her hairline after witnessing that exchange. My parents stand behind her, whispering their concerns, and slip on their shoes to come trick-or-treating with us. I roll my eyes and tell Faith I'll fill her in when we return. My parents join us on the porch. Neighborhood kids are already stomping through yards and spilling into the street, parents struggling to keep up.

"Which way should we go, Mama?" Lulu asks, adjusting her floppy ears.

I attempt to bring myself back to the present moment: Lu's tiny hand in mine. Her adorable costume. Our safe neighborhood. The fact that this Halloween will be different. That the nightmare is over because I finally know the truth. I think of last year, how afraid I was to let Lulu out of my sight, how I've lived decades paranoid and uncertain. Well, not anymore.

That Cora is dead.

I take a deep breath, release it, and untangle her fingers from mine. I know, to the depths of my soul, that it's time to give Lu some space. To let her explore without fear as her constant companion. Without my worry creeping behind her like an actual living thing.

I motion toward the rows of decorated yards and sense her excitement. "Whichever way you want, sweet pea."

She swings her bucket and squeals. She's ready to go, to ring doorbells and gather candy. My parents smile at her as she takes a giant step toward our neighbor's yard.

I let her lead the way.

A NOTE TO READERS

The 1996 Olympics were an exciting time.

I remember watching with bated breath as gymnast Kerri Strug completed her first vault, during which she underrotated and, as a result, injured her ankle. After hobbling back to the end of the runway, she performed her second vault anyway, landing on one foot and hopping up and down in pain. That one vault, that one decision to *push through*, clenched gold for the Americans. After, riddled with pain, she was carted off with a severely injured ankle. But she had brought her team—and country—to gold after a serious dry streak for American gymnasts. I remember watching every single one of the Magnificent Seven's routines and wishing I was one of them.

By 1996, I had been doing gymnastics competitively for twelve years. There was a brief stint in my earlier years when a scout came to offer me a chance to train more seriously, but it would have meant uprooting my family's lives and moving somewhere else.

My dreams flew out the window faster than I could catch them, but I clung tightly to the hope that somehow, I could still be an elite athlete. I competed in gymnastics for years, and after I aged out, it was on to dance, then competitive boxing. (After boxing alerted me to a dangerous brain mass, which led to brain surgery at age nineteen, I finally laid to rest my competitive spirit through sports and found new interests, like yoga, ecstatic dance, hiking, and board games. Seriously, don't play a board game with me, because I will win and then gloat about it.)

Though I never made it to an Olympic level through sports, I did use some of my own experience as a competitive gymnast for this novel. However, in order for the "timing" to work with the Halloween premise, I have made the Olympic trials in winter instead of summer. (So if you are a stickler for the facts, just go with me here on this fictitious journey.)

And instead of the Magnificent Seven, as those infamous gymnasts were once called, I have made this fictitious team the Magnificent Eight. While I allude to some of the real gymnasts from the '96 Olympics, everything in this book is fiction, and any and all errors about the sport, timing, or athletic protocols are mine and mine alone.

I would also like to bring light to what happened to so many gymnasts involved in the horrific Larry Nassar sexual assault case. It saddens me that in a sport so many young women love, they were unsafe, especially during that time. My heart goes out to every gymnast and athlete who has ever been abused or taken advantage of by a coach, doctor, or trusted professional.

Here's to healing . . . and to celebrating a sport I still love, despite its many flaws.

ACKNOWLEDGMENTS

This book was born from my love of three things: gymnastics, the '90s, and Halloween.

While this novel was written fast and furiously, publishing is always a team effort. Thank you to my rock star literary agent, Rachel Beck, for facilitating every single deal over these last eight books. Thank you to my amazing editorial team, Jessica Tribble Wells and Angela James, who really helped ratchet up the suspense and fix my many glaring plot holes. Thank you to my amazing copyeditor, Mindi Machart; my production manager, Miranda Gardner; the entire production team; and everyone at Thomas & Mercer and Amazon Publishing, from sales and marketing, to cover design, to audio production, to the people behind Brilliance Publishing, and beyond. This is truly a machine unlike any other, and my publishing experience here has been top notch every step of the way.

Thank you to my film-and-TV team at IPG, who are trying so hard to make my movie and TV dreams come true! Thank you to the audiobook narrator, who spends such considerate time with my book. Thank you to Tonya Cornish and your amazing group of thriller lovers. Thank you to every author who blurbed this book. Thank you to the book clubs, bloggers, bookstagrammers, libraries, and bookstores who read, share, and use word of mouth as the most powerful tool.

Thank you to my husband, Alex, who helped me figure out who the villain was when I wasn't sure. Thank you to my amazing daughter, who loves to throw out ideas and edit my printed pages. Thank you to *you*, dear reader, for spending time with my story.

Being a creative is unlike anything else. It's hard. It's uncertain. It's messy. It's cool. It requires a lot of time, energy, and the ability to surrender and trust that your book will find its way in the world. I always joke that being an author can feel a bit like being part of a popularity contest. You see what everyone else is doing and achieving and can often compare yourself to them. There are also no guarantees, and while you can be the cool kid one day, you can be an outcast the next. With all that being said, I've learned that this journey is mine, and it doesn't have to look like anyone else's. That is the real work. That is the real gift.

I'm grateful for the ride, for the lessons, and for all the people I've met along the way.

ABOUT THE AUTHOR

Photo © 2023 Kate Gallaher

Rea Frey is the #1 bestselling author of several suspense, women's fiction, and nonfiction books. Known as a Book Doula, she helps other authors birth their books into the world. To learn more, visit her at www.reafrey.com.